DIAMONDS AND COLE

ALSO BY MICHEAL MAXWELL

THE COLE SAGE MYSTERIES

Diamonds and Cole
Cellar Full of Cole
Helix of Cole
Cole Dust

Three Nails
The Time Pedaler (with Tally Scully)

DIAMONDS AND COLE

A Cole Sage Mystery

MICHEAL MAXWELL

Formatting by Robert Swartwood

DIAMONDS AND COLE

ONE

Cole flicked a pickle onto the grass just across the sidewalk. He slapped the bun in his hands back together and took a bite. *Just not the same as they used to be,* he thought. Hamburgers had been his favorite food as a child, now he rarely ate them. Sometimes he wondered, *What is the use?* He bought the burger only because he needed comfort food. He really wanted mashed potatoes and gravy-dark, thick, heavily peppered gravy. He had no idea where to get gravy like he wanted anymore, so he settled for the burger. On the way to the park, it seemed like just the thing. It wasn't. Now he just felt like giving up.

She liked pickles. All these years later, he still remembered that. Frowning deeply, he gazed down at the sidewalk. She hated olives, though. They used to order pizza, a large combo, and she would pick off all the olives. He asked her once, why don't we just order it without the olives? She said she didn't want to be any bother. A faint smile crossed his lips. He dropped the unfinished burger into the bag. As he crossed the park, he dropped the bag into a rusted out garbage can and gave a half-hearted grin.

What do you suppose she's doing today? Cole wondered. He drifted toward the edge of the park and slid deeper into memory. Who is that singer she liked? Kenny somebody. It'd been longer than he thought. A tall, thin, gay couple, skated past him hand-in-hand. Rankin, Kenny Rankin, that's his name. Kind of jazzy style, really messed up the Beatle songs, especially Blackbird. He remembered how he borrowed a Rankin album, on her insistence, and how it warped in the trunk of the car. He knew he wouldn't like it; in fact, it never even made it into the house. His stomach tightened with the guilt of never replacing it. Oh, how he longed to hear Kenny Rankin sing Blackbird.

He reached in his pocket for his car keys.

"Wash your windows?"

"No thanks," Cole said without looking up.

Turning at the sound of guttural muttering, Cole was inches from one of the myriad of homeless people that had invaded the park in the last year. The dirty figure sneered and seemed to grow taller and more erect from the refusal. The thin frame, shoulders pulled back, and chest thrown out, suddenly became the taller of the two men now facing each other on the sidewalk. His pants were held up by a thick piece of rope knotted twice in the front. The extra rope was tucked into his front pockets. A set of ribs showed from under the green army blanket slung over his right shoulder and tied chest-high with a second piece of rope.

"Wash your windows!" The request had become a demand.

"No. I don't want my windows washed."

"What? You think you're better than me? I got rights."

"Rights?"

"I can earn a living same as you. Suits don't rule everything. I got rights."

"Me too. Get out of my way. I said I don't want my window washed."

"There is gonna be a revolution, and you're gonna die!"

"That's it! Get the hell out of my way." Cole said, getting into his car.

"Rise up! Rise up!" the window washer screamed. "The revolution starts here. The revolution starts now!" His screams seemed to ricochet off the buildings. Suddenly, there was a small crowd of people watching. The army blanket now waved over the window washer's head, like a battle flag, rallying an army of revolutionaries, who had yet to show up.

The skeletal form of the window washer in the rear view mirror seemed a pale translucent blue in the crisp April air. As the engine turned over, a half-empty, plastic spray bottle, bounced off the back window.

"I don't need this," Cole muttered, putting the car in reverse.

The window washer began pounding on the roof above the passenger-side window. "You can run, but you can't hide!" he screamed.

"Oh, please," Cole groaned as the car inched back. The pounding on the roof of the car sounded like a huge kettledrum. Turning, he saw the emaciated derelict at his window, fumbling with the rope that held up his ragged Ben Davis khakis. The oversized trousers dropped to the ground, and the window washer grabbed his penis and shook it towards the window.

"We know who you are! We will hunt you down! You will pay!" The window was suddenly awash in yellow-brown fluid.

"I don't need this. Not today." Cole dropped the car into drive and accelerated away from the curb.

In the rearview mirror, the thin bluish figure stood in the middle of the street, khakis around his ankles and fists raised in the air screaming, "Rise up! Rise up! Up, up, up, up!"

Merging into the after-lunch traffic, Cole shifted his weight, settled into the well-worn seat, and laughed. The laugh wasn't because he was amused. It was the only thing he could do. To his amazement, he started to cry. Real tears ran down his cheeks, and blurred his vision; real tears mixed with the sound of sobbing laughter.

He tossed his sunglasses onto the stack of newspapers on the seat next to him, and wiped his eyes with the back of his hand. He never felt so lonely, and he was used to being alone. This was different, though; it was a deep aching sort of my-mother-just-died-and-nobody-knows-my-name freefall into alone.

A doctor would probably diagnose depression, and give him some happy pills. It was depression all right, but not the kind the doctor would see. Cole knew the cause, he knew the cure, but it was about twenty years too late for that. Lately, he had just been down. Maybe it was the onslaught of middle age; maybe it was not having someone or something he felt he belonged to. He used to love his job. Now, it *was* a job. The fire was gone, the focus, the purpose, or whatever you wanted to call it.

Cole had too many memories. Places he had been, people he'd known, things he'd seen. But they all came back around to her. She was the greatest thing in his life, and the worst. He lost her. Why she started haunting his thoughts was a mystery.

For the last two years, she'd been on his mind. He told himself he should find her, talk to her. He knew it wouldn't do any good. It had been over twenty years since he had seen her.

In the years since they parted, he had done all the things in life he set out to do except marry her. All the awards, all the acclaim, seemed so important at the time. He kept a feverish pace for years. It had been a time of turmoil and change in the world, and he'd been there. Politics, war, and scandal; he'd written about it all. Racism, hunger, ethnic cleansing; he'd stared it in the face. Pol Pot, Muammar al-Gaddafi, Slobodan Milosevic, Bill Clinton, and both George Bushes had looked him in the eye and told their version of the truth. His name was well known, and in most cases respected, or had been.

Then it all began to fall apart, or he did. He didn't have the usual excuses. It wasn't liquor or drugs, it wasn't women: It was woman. The one that got away. Maybe she was just an excuse. He slowed down, got tired, gave up. Whatever you wanted to call it, nothing had much meaning anymore. All is vanity, he'd thought time and again. All the words he'd written, all the miles he'd flown didn't lay a foundation for what was to come: a life without her.

Now, after a career spent at The New York Times, The Wall Street Journal, and Time Magazine he was back where he started: The Chicago Sentinel. Not as an editor, like one would expect, as a reward for such a distinguished career, but as a staff writer. No longer finding the news, or digging for the truth behind the headlines, now he was assigned a story. Every Friday he collected a check for writing the kind of shallow drivel any first-year rookie could probably improve upon.

Two nights ago, Cole had cried watching old footage of Richard Nixon's resignation speech on TV. He cried like Old Yeller just died, didn't stop for nearly an hour. Nixon knew how he felt. Nixon had been alone. He never liked Nixon, but he knew what he was feeling, and when Nixon's voice cracked, so had Cole Sage.

TWO

Opening the front door of *The Sentinel* building felt to Cole like he was pushing it through sand. He really didn't want to go in. He could think of a thousand reasons to go in. 'Have to' reasons but no 'want to' reasons. He used to fly through the doors on the run, heart pounding, adrenaline pumping. He used to be the hot-shit reporter with the scoop of the day. Now, he was doing well if he met the deadline for the stories the night editor assigned him.

Mick Brennan tried to throw Cole a bone now and again, but Brennan was tired and burned out. When Cole first came to the paper, Brennan became his mentor. "Got a ways to go, kid," he used to say. Brennan showed Cole that he hadn't really learned anything in college, and untaught him the bad habits he picked up there. Write, write, and rewrite. Brennan used up boxes of red copy proof pencils, and turned Cole into a first-class newspaperman.

Cole would have done anything to show Mick he could do it his way: the best way. But he never got it quite good enough. Never a compliment, always a kick in the teeth. That was Brennan's style.

Cole had introduced her to Mick Brennan after spinning tales of the great newspaperman, and how much he meant to him.

"Too good for you, Cole," was all Brennan said as he walked away.

Cole could still see the hurt in her eyes as they walked back to the elevator. Something broke that day. A bond, an unspoken, gentleman's understanding, between the new kid and the old lion, the hero and the eager-to-please sidekick. It was gone. Not long after that, Cole was gone too. That was the first time he quit *The Sentinel.*

Cole had been 22 and Mick 42. Somehow, it was now twenty-odd-years later.

"What's the problem? You wanna move it?" a harsh voice jabbed from behind.

A brown shirt delivery man, heavy boxes to his chin, stood glaring at Cole. Attitudes seemed to be growing out of the sidewalk. When did service providers become the aggressors in the war on civility? It would have been easy to have shot back a smart rebuke to his societal underling, but why bother? The world Cole now lived in was beyond dueling with taunt-calved, community college dropouts, in tight brown shorts. He pushed the door open, then let it swing back to hit the boxes. As the slurs and curses flew at his back, Cole went through the door marked ID Badges Required beyond This Point.

"Afternoon, Cole."

"Greetings, Queen Jean."

Cole barely glanced at the black woman behind the front desk. How life changes things. Years before, as a new staff reporter, he had bribed a kid guarding the front door of a burned-out apartment building $20 to get as far as the third floor, in hopes of getting an interview with Tashira, the firebrand orator of the Black Women's Urban Army. The Army hated men, hated whites, and really hated white men, but up he went, and banged on the door like the landlord after late rent. An hour later, he left with a notepad full of quotes, and a recipe for sweet potato pie. That was a different world. Ideals, high hopes, and a heartfelt belief in something, that drove people to actually try to change the world. After five kids, 50 added pounds, and three men who took what they wanted and left with the first bump in the road, Tashira once again become Olajean Baker. The radical daughter of the single hotel maid mother, who raised her to fight back, just celebrated her 10th year of sobriety, and being the front desk receptionist at *The Sentinel.* A job she had thanks to Cole Sage. When the revolutionary fire had gone out in her, Cole still remembered the heart that burned white-hot for what should have been.

"Brennan's been asking for you. Something about a dead kid or somethin'. I really didn't get much out of it."

Cole gave her that silent smile that was now all-too-familiar, and slipped through the swinging door at the counter.

Olajean seemed content. *Why am I so miserable?* Cole thought. Maybe it was turning 45. He always believed he would die in some adventurous blaze of glory. He got shot at in the Philippines, saw a car bomb go off in front of his hotel in Tel Aviv, and received enough death threats to wallpaper *The Sentinel* building. But here he was. When had he given up? Twenty-five years in the news business and he was at the bottom. No, lower than the bottom. He started at the bottom, and he was even lower now.

No one looked up as he made his way through the maze of cubicles. Mini flowerpots, kitty posters, and pictures of little leaguers, soccer stars, Brad Pitt, and big-eyed cartoon children blurred past him as he made his way to his corner of the world. Coffee cups, stacks of paper, and an old "Coming Soon to the Bijou" flyer decorated his carpeted "office."

Cole made a half-hearted attempt at straightening his tie. He exhaled deeply as he stared at the numbers on the phone. Punching in 784, he waited.

"Brennan."

"What's up?"

"What, I don't warrant an in-person audience?"

"Thought it..." Cole paused, not having an answer. "I thought I'd save time. Something about a dead kid?"

"Dead kitten. Seems a dozen people tried to get this cat out of a tree until some guy used a swimming pool net on a long aluminum pole. Looks like it touched a power line about the time it snagged the cat. Fried the kitty and shocked the shit out of the guy holding the pole. Anyway, follow it up, would ya? Natoma and 125th."

"That's it?"

"Yep, need filler. Nothing really happening today." Brennan hung up.

A dead cat. Cole just stared, phone to his ear, dial tone humming. The movement of a copy clerk caught his eye. He knew he had to cover the story. That was the ache. Why didn't he quit? The resounding echo was always, *To do what?*

Cole left his coat draped on the back of his swivel chair, and stood looking over the tops of the cubical walls; a sea of gray carpeted boxes, filled with people doing God-knows-what. At the far-end of the room stood three people deep in conversation. Next to them was the water cooler. Cole was not below eavesdropping. He made his way back to the trio.

"It's stealing from the city plain and simple," groaned an Asian man in a Georgetown sweatshirt.

"Prove it, Lionel. How are you going to prove it? Facts, remember?" challenged a tall acne-scarred man Cole knew as Katz. Cole didn't like him. Katz always sounded like he read too many Superman comics, and never realized that Jimmy Olson wasn't the hero.

Erica Sloan, whose bad haircut and wardrobe matched her writing style, chimed in. "Contractors can apply for low-cost city loans as long as they are either renovating existing buildings in low-income areas or building new low-income housing. It has been this way for years. What's the big deal?" Cole helped train her when she first came on the paper. She was smart and knew it, still finding news, just like he taught her.

Cole filled a cup with cold filtered water. *No news here,* he thought as he turned to go back to his desk.

"Hi Mr. Sage, workin' on anything big?" Katz beamed when he caught sight of Cole.

"He really is Jimmy Olson," Cole muttered.

"Carl."

"What?"

"My name is Carl, not Jimmy."

"Of course it is, sorry," returned Cole.

Carl Katz, now why isn't he working on this story? Just

think of the headline possibilities combined with his byline. Cole actually chuckled to himself.

Clouds rolled in from the east. No chance of rain, but enough to cast a gray shadow on the day. Cole enjoyed the cool breeze on his face. His tie flapped in the wind as he walked to the car. Long ago he gave up tightening his ties. His uniform was pretty much the same year after year: Levis, an oxford cloth, button-down collar shirt, and a Harris Tweed sports coat, with oval leather patches on the elbows. He owned three tweed sports coats. Gray for important meetings, interviews, or the rare occasion he was trying to impress someone. Dark brown for those, more and more frequent, dark days, when he didn't feel like leaving his apartment. And camel-colored, his personal favorite, for the times he really needed to feel like his old self. Today he wore the dark brown.

Natoma Street was in the old part of the city, canopied with handsome old trees that lined streets, always keeping it cool and shady in summer. Cole always loved how the huge, old, ash trees loomed over the street, growing together and forming a massive green arch. Small houses set deep on the lots looked like little gingerbread houses. Ivy climbed and covered the chimneys. The lawns were all edged and mowed. Cole always wished he could have lived in a neighborhood just like the Montclare District.

As he turned up Natoma, a Community Service Officer flagged him down. "Sorry, sir, road's closed."

Cole showed the officer his press credentials and asked, "All this for a dead cat?"

"A bit more serious than that. Seems the old lady who

owned the cat has taken the guy who killed it hostage. Says she's got a shotgun. Nobody can get to her."

"Where can I park?"

The officer pointed to the left side of the street behind an ambulance. "I guess that would be okay."

"Hey, who's in charge?" Cole yelled as he pulled away.

"Harris. Lieutenant Harris."

The small street was crammed with fire engines, ambulances, six police cruisers, and three or four navy blue, unmarked, Crown Victorias doing their best to look inconspicuous. The picture-perfect landscapes were strung with yellow police tape and patrolmen. Neighbors from all over the district were pressing against the barricades, and chatting about how nothing like this ever happened here before. Cole approached a bored-looking patrolman who was leaning against the back of a black-and-white, smoking.

"Sage, with *The Sentinel*. What is going on? I heard some guy shocked a cat to death trying to get it out of a tree. What happened?"

"The lady who owned the cat came out with an old double-barrel shotgun while the paramedics were giving the guy who killed it the once-over. Started shouting about how he murdered her baby and how he had always hated her and this was his revenge. Seems she snapped."

"Where's Harris?"

"He's at the yellow house with the hostage negotiator. Seems the old gal won't answer the phone." The patrolman motioned his thumb over his shoulder, indicating the direction of the house.

"Thanks."

Cole made his way up the street with no regard for

the barriers or tape. He always found that acting like you belong somewhere got you a lot further than asking questions.

In college, Cole heard Arlo Guthrie talking on the radio about a little-known verse of "This Land Is Your Land." Arlo told the story of a time when his father, Woody, had been interviewed on the radio. The announcer asked about writing "This Land is Your Land," and the usual bunch of shallow interview-type questions.

Woody had always told Arlo that this one special verse belonged to him and only he knew it. Woody would always sing it to Arlo when he felt down, or got in trouble at school. To Arlo's shock, Woody sang it on the air! He felt hurt and betrayed, but then overjoyed when Woody told the whole wide world that "that last verse belongs to my son, Arlo." As Cole walked along dodging barricades, and ducking under police tape, he hummed "This Land" and sang that special verse in his head: *As I went walking I saw a sign there, And on the sign it said "No Trespassing." But on the other side, it didn't say nothin'. That side was made for you and me.* Now that verse belonged to both Cole *and* Arlo.

"Hey, Sage," Harris said without expression, when Cole finally reached the house. "Lookin' for blood?"

"No, actually a dead cat."

"We're a little beyond that now."

"What's the story on the old lady?"

"Isn't any, really. Never had so much as a parking ticket. Just freaked when the guy killed her cat." Harris motioned to the young man standing next to him. "Cole, this is Trevor Varney, negotiations specialist. Trev, this is Cole Sage of *The Sentinel*."

"How's it goin'?" Varney smiled.

"Any day above ground is a good day, I guess." Cole replied.

Harris chuckled and turned to Varney. "Cole's the eternal pessimist. He doesn't even believe there's a glass, if you know what I mean."

"Don't believe everything you read," Cole smiled.

"Especially in *The Sentinel*," Harris teased.

"Yeah, especially that."

"So, Mr. Varney, what happens if she won't pick up the phone?" Cole asked.

"I'm just getting ready to approach the front of the house. Tom, I think it would be a good idea if we backed everybody up. Just enough to be out of direct sight of the front windows."

"It's your show," Harris said calmly. Turning to a veteran officer on the tape line, Harris waved his arm at the growing crowd. "Okay, Sergeant, I want everybody back. Move the barriers to about that second house. Yeah, the green one." He nodded, confirming the sergeant's indication of a green two-story Tudor.

"How old is this woman? Is there a history with the hostage?"

Cole had been the best of friends with Harris for going on twenty years now. Still, he felt like he sounded as if he were conducting an interview.

"According to the hostage's wife, Mrs. Lemoore, her husband and Mrs. Clark have never got along. Clark's cat used the Lemoore's' front flowerbed for a litter box. It's been a bone of contention for a long time. Mrs. Lemoore said her husband just got caught up in all the excitement of the cat in the tree and offered their pool net. The other neighbors love the guy. He's like the neighborhood fix-it man and barbeque king," Harris added as he watched the officers move the crowd and first set of barricades back. "Hey, watch the bushes! I don't want the city getting a bill to re-landscape these people's yards!"

"Where's the wife now?"

"That's her over there in the white shorts." Harris pointed towards a rather large woman standing on the lawn across the street from the Clark house.

"You know, Tom," Cole began, "there was a time you would have called her 'that fat broad.' Your newfound political correctness is a real tribute to the department's sensitivity training program." Cole slapped Harris on the back as he started toward the woman standing across the street.

"Well, you just keep *your* fat ass out of the way!" Harris chided.

Mrs. Lemoore was in her mid-to-late 40s. She was round around the middle, and her clothes did little to hide the fact. As he neared, Cole could see her eyes were red and puffy from crying. Her arms were tightly crossed across her large bust, and she was chewing on the nail of her right thumb.

"Mrs. Lemoore?" Cole said softly. "I'm Cole Sage of *The Sentinel.*"

The woman turned her head and gave Cole a dazed glance, then went back to watching the house across the street. She didn't respond.

"The police know how to handle this kind of thing. It's going to be all right. What's your husband's first name?"

"Stan," she said in a whisper.

"I hear Stan's quite the man with a barbeque. Dry rub or sauce?"

"Dry rub. Won't ever use sauce. That's for the table."

She neither changed expression nor spoke with any inflection.

"Me too. Except chicken, of course."

"Why don't they do something!" She suddenly became animated and spread her arms out in the direction Harris was standing.

"They're getting ready to have a negotiator talk to Mrs. Clark. I just met him. Seems like he knows what he's doing." Cole had no idea if Varney knew what he was doing or not, but he wanted to comfort this woman. For some reason, he felt a connection to her. He had been on the scene of hundreds of murders, wrecks, fires, and hostage stand-offs and seen and talked to parents, wives, husbands and bystanders-but this was somehow different.

"What will he do?"

"Well, it seems Mrs. Clark..."

"Annie," she broke in.

"Annie...won't answer the phone. So, he will approach the front of the house and try to speak to her. He is unarmed and will use a bullhorn. He needs to get her talking. The more they can get her to do that, the better. It will help her calm down and see what she is doing is wrong and unnecessary. The guy's a pro. She's not a hardened criminal—just somebody who got too upset."

"Hope so. I'm-I'm so scared."

"How 'bout I stay here with you 'til Stan comes out, Mrs. Lemoore?"

"Paula." Again she spoke very softly.

"What?"

"Paula, my name is Paula. 'Mrs. Lemoore' always makes me feel so old. Mrs. Lemoore is my mother-in-law." She seemed to smile slightly.

"I love the name Paula," Cole said to the woman standing by him.

"I don't know what I would do without Stan. I said something this morning I didn't mean. I just want to say I'm sorry." She covered her face and sobbed.

"I bet Stan knows you didn't mean it. He knows you love him. Let's just sit down and wait this thing out."

"Mrs. Clark," the voice from the bullhorn seemed to bounce off every house on the block. "Mrs. Clark, I am Trevor Varney. Can I talk to you?" The young man with the bullhorn stood in the middle of the lawn and spread his arms at shoulder height and slowly turned around. "I'm unarmed. I just want to talk." He put the bullhorn at his side and stood perfectly still.

In what seemed like a slow motion scene from a Sam Peckinpah western, the front windows of the Clark house blew out. The head of Trevor Varney was blown open. Pieces of pink mass, blood, and hair rolled through the air and scattered across the lawn. Cole instinctively pushed Paula Lemoore to the ground shouting, "Stay down, stay down!" as she tried to struggle to her feet.

In the same moment, the body of a gray-haired woman in a blue flowered housedress flew out of the window and sprawled across the flowerbed below. A man in green shorts and a gray T-shirt appeared at the window, then jumped out and grabbed the shotgun the old woman was still clutching in her arms. He took the end of the barrel, spun around and threw the gun across the lawn, sending it sliding and scraping its way across the street, to bang against the curb on the other side.

"Stanley!" Paula Lemoore screamed. She ran across the street and into the arms of her husband running toward her.

The old woman lay motionless in the juniper bushes. From all directions, police ran into the yard. A half-circle of men in blue blocked Cole's view of Annie Clark. An ambulance pulled up in front of the Clark house. Two paramedics hopped out, opened the back doors, and removed a gurney. Stan Lemoore, his arm around his wife's shoulders, walked across the street to the curb in front of his house and sat down.

Cole crossed the street. The paramedics stood over the body of Trevor Varney, and the police got Annie Clark up and on her feet. The blast of the shotgun hit Varney just above the jaw line; his handsome face was gone. The sight of the jagged flesh and shattered bone made Cole feel lightheaded.

"God, I never," one of the paramedics began, then finished the thought to himself.

Cole approached the group of police officers. Annie Clark now faced one of the officers who was reading her rights to her. The other officers seemed to have lost interest in her and were turning their attention to the body on the lawn.

"Do you understand what I have just read to you, ma'am?" The officer, a tall red-haired policeman whose name tag read "McClaron", paused. "Do you understand what you have done?"

"Yes, but he shouldn't have been on my lawn. Alex never let the children cut across our lawn, ever."

The old woman who moments before, so brutally and violently, ended the life of Trevor Varney, now stood small and frail. Her hair and the bun she wore on the back of her head had come undone. The rayon housedress that hung on her small frame was torn and exposed the yellowed fabric of her undergarments. Her shoulders were bowed, and the curving of osteoporosis gave her neck a strained, pulled look as she gazed up at the policeman. McClaron was in violation of department procedure, but didn't have the heart to handcuff the old woman.

"Is there someone we can call for you, Mrs. Clark?" the officer asked gently.

"My Alex is gone, and Stanley Lemoore has killed Mr. Pip."

"Mr. Pip, ma'am?"

"My Persian."

"I see. But is there anyone, your children or other relatives, we can call for you?"

"No, we never could have any children. Alex, you know, meningitis in the Army, couldn't...you know..."

"Mrs. Clark, do you know what you have done here?" McClaron spoke as if he were talking to a young child.

"I was scolding Stanley from across the street for killing Mr. Pip, and he pushed me out of the window! Pushed me! I turned to see what the loud noise was and he pushed me right out the window! I want him arrested and in jail. Why is he gone? He pushed me. He attacked me in my own home."

"What about the gun, ma'am? What about shooting the gun?"

"Oh dear, I don't like guns. Alex always kept that nasty shotgun in the closet. But I never would touch it. He kept it loaded, you know," she said in almost a whisper. "Now that he's gone, I don't know what to do with it. Would you like to have it? I have no use for it."

McClaron acknowledged Cole's presence for the first time. In a stern expression, he shook his head, as if to say "stay back." But in his eyes, there was a deep sadness. He turned to Annie Clark once again. "Mrs. Clark, we are going to have to take you down to the police station."

"By all means, I want to file a complaint. Imagine being pushed through a window. I am an old woman. I could have been hurt badly, maybe even killed, why of all the nerve. And now all this!" Turning to the police and paramedics gathered around Varney's body, she shouted in a high crackling voice, "You there, get off my lawn! Alex might come back soon, and he will be furious!"

"Can I get a female officer over here?" McClaron said into the microphone clipped to his shoulder epaulette.

"Officer, I want those people off my lawn."

"I'll see what I can do."

"Olson is on her way," the radio scratched.

"Let's wait over here, ma'am."

"Oh, I need to lock up and get my things. Oh! I must look a fright. I'll just go in and change."

"No, I'm afraid we don't have time for that. See, Officer Olson is here to give you a ride." McClaron pointed to the black-and-white that had just pulled into the driveway.

"I must leave a note. Alex will be worried if he returns and I'm gone."

"I'll stay to make sure he knows." Cole thought McClaron's voice seemed to crack.

"This her?" a raspy voice female officer asked.

"This is Mrs. Clark. Please transport her downtown." McClaron turned to Officer Olson and said something Cole couldn't hear. Then McClaron turned his attention back to the old woman. "Okay, Mrs. Clark, this is Officer Olson. She will take you downtown."

"A lady policeman? I never heard of such a thing! No wonder people think they can kill your cat and trample your lawn."

"Please come with me, ma'am," Olson barked.

"Remember what I said, Olson. Nice," McClaron snapped.

Officer Olson guided Mrs. Clark to the patrol car. Cole approached McClaron.

"I'm Cole Sage with *The Sentinel*."

"Harris's friend, right?"

"Right."

"I got nothin' to say," McClaron growled.

"What, you have a problem with Harris?"

"No, I got a problem with you. I hate newspaper people. They always get it wrong."

"You ever read my stuff?" Cole asked.

"Nope, why should I? It's all the same. Liberal blather." McClaron turned and walked away.

Cole chuckled and turned to cross back to where the Lemoores were sitting. The paramedics covered Varney's body with a white cloth, and the police taped off the area six feet in all directions around the body. Two detectives were watching as a police photographer took pictures of the shotgun laying in the gutter. About 10 feet away, Paula and Stan Lemoore sat side by side on the curb, holding hands.

"How you doin', Stan?" Cole said, reaching out to shake the man's hand.

"Fine, I guess," Stan said, reciprocating the shake.

"This gentleman stayed with me while you were..." Paula stopped and looked at Stan.

"My name is Cole Sage. I'm with *The Sentinel*. Do you want to talk about what happened?"

"Man, I don't *know* what happened. One minute I'm flat on my back, the next I'm looking down the barrels of a double-barrel twelve gauge. Annie said I killed Mr. Pip and she was going to show me how it feels. She made me go in the house and sit on the couch. I kept saying, 'Annie, put the gun down, you're just excited.' She said that Alex was going to be very angry when he got back. Alex died about five years ago. So I said, 'Annie, Alex is gone.' She started talking about all this stuff I did to her. It didn't make any sense. Hell, I mow her lawn for God's sake. This is crazy."

"What made her shoot?"

"She just kept talking about Alex this, and Alex that, and how he didn't like people on the lawn. She was talking about how Mr. Pip was her only friend and I had taken him from her. About then, the guy started talking on the megaphone thing. That really set her off. She started yelling. Then she just whirled around and fired..." Stan's voice trailed off.

"And after that?" Cole prompted softly.

"She had her back to me, and the window was mostly gone, you know, so I just rushed her and gave her a real hard push. I had no idea she had shot the policeman until after I was outside."

Stan put his head down between his knees and started to wretch. Paula gently rubbed his back. "You'll be okay, honey, you're okay, breathe deep."

"Do you want the paramedics? Maybe they can give you something."

Paula looked up at Cole and smiled. "We'll be fine, thanks. Maybe you should go. Thanks for stickin' with me, you're a nice man, but we need to be alone now, okay?"

"Of course. You take care," Cole looked down at her and smiled back. He stepped down into the street and started back to the police barrier.

"Hey," Stan called to Cole, "don't make Annie out to be crazy or anything. She's a nice lady, just old and confused. I don't think she knows what she did. All right?"

"I'll do my best."

The fire trucks were pulling out and the ambulances started their engines. Many of the police cars were already gone. Natoma Street almost looked back to normal. A young cop removed the yellow tape he'd strung up the hour before. Harris was on the police radio. Cole waved as he walked past him.

"Got a story?" Harris shouted.

"Think so. See you later." Cole waved, but didn't slow his pace.

THREE

Cole stared at the words on his monitor. "Annie Clark, 81, shot and killed Trevor Varney, 29, a police negotiator." *Those are the facts,* he thought, *but they don't tell the story. Eighty-one years, and it comes down to one article in the paper? All over a damn cat? When does a person step across the line between sanity and this kind of madness?* Cole glanced up at the sound of laughter in the next cubicle.

"He just snapped. Started throwing stuff at the City Council. Binders, blueprints, yellow pads, then his briefcase!" The voice in the cubicle again broke into laughter. "Yeah, yeah, cops and everything. Hauled him out screaming and swearing. Walker banging the gavel, what a riot!" Cole recognized the voice as that of Lionel Chun, one of the three who had been at the water cooler earlier.

Why is slipping into madness so amusing, Cole pondered. How close was *he*? Maybe he wasn't at all if he had the presence of mind to wonder about it. Chun irritated Cole, always did.

"Hey Chun, you want to keep it down! Some people actually work around here!" Cole shouted toward the florescent lights.

"Gotta go, Uncle Grump is feeling grouchy again. Okay. I'll see you later," Chun hoarsely whispered into the phone. He never thought Cole could hear his little barbs and slurs, but Cole always did. "Having a bad day...again, Sage?" Chun said in an affected, bored tone.

Cole ignored Chun's sarcasm. He repeatedly hit the delete key on his keyboard and watched the cursor methodically remove the letters on the screen. There was so much more to say than just reporting the shooting. The TV news would handle all the gory details just fine. He wanted to tell the other story: the story of the old widow who, losing her cat, let slip her last thread to reality. The woman who lost her husband and couldn't let him go.

There were no words to explain how she pulled the trigger. None to explain how she went to a closet, and got the "nasty old gun" that had terrified her for so many years, and in one inexplicable moment, took away someone else's husband; someone's father, son, uncle, and friend. All the years of cookies and banana nut bread, all the little Christmas presents for the neighborhood kids, the Easter candy, the Halloween treats and graduation gifts, blown away forever. The little lady in the funny straw hat working in her beloved flower garden was gone, born anew as a murderer. A crazy killer with a shotgun, a babbling old woman led away by the police. Did she even know what she had done?

Cole began to type. Slow at first, then with feverish

intent. The story began to flow, the people came to life, and the old Cole was coming out. He began with the young hostage negotiator, father of three little boys, who had such pride in his job at being able to defuse volatile situations. He told of Paula the wife, her torment at the thought of losing the husband she loved and the unresolved disagreement of the morning. He wrote of Stan, the good neighbor, who, in trying to help, killed a cat, and nearly himself. He's taken hostage, then becomes the hero who stopped the madness. He told of the policeman who looked beyond the tragic violence and saw a little old lady much like his own grandmother. Then Cole began to describe the loneliness of age and the frailty of the mind. He danced around the fine line between Annie as victim and murderer. He couldn't excuse her deeds but was compelled to open a window on an explanation. On a pad next to the keyboard, he was jotting down ideas for expert witnesses, psychologists, social workers and advocates for the elderly when the phone rang.

"Cole, I got a weird call for you a minute ago. The person wouldn't identify herself. I think it might be personal. Didn't want to use a runner."

"Thanks, Olajean, I'll be right up."

The bubble was pierced. Most of the story was completed, though. He could easily finish later. The important thing was that he had captured his feelings. That was something he hadn't done in a long time. He felt good. Cole loved writing; he loved the zone he got into when he was on a roll. This story could make a difference. This was what he needed, and had needed for a long time. Maybe he could write again, write stuff that mattered. He pushed his chair back and hit Save. "Save"- maybe that's what this story was all about. Maybe Cole had been saved.

Back up at the front desk, Olajean handed Cole a pink message. It read "Call Ellie. She needs your help. It's URGENT!" Cole just stared at the number near the bottom of the message. The area code was right, but...it couldn't be.

"Ola, what did the person say, exactly?" Olajean did not answer, already preoccupied once again with her own work. "Ola!" Cole said excitedly as he reached over the desk and punched buttons until they all went dark.

"What in hell you doin'? You lost yo' mind!"

"The person who called—what did they say? Please."

"Damn Cole, calm down. They just said that Ellie—"

"Start at the beginning!" Cole broke in.

"They asked for you. I told 'em you were out. Jus' like you told me to, 'always take a message' isn't that what you said? So, they said it was urgent they get a message to you. I said, 'Okay, what is it?' They said that Ellie needed your help and to call that number. I asked, 'Who should I say called?' and they said, 'Jus' tell him' and hung up." The lights on the phone console were all blinking red. Olajean asked with exasperation, "Can I do my job now?"

"Yeah, thanks, sorry." Cole seemed dazed.

"I hope so! What's got into you, anyways?"

Cole was already headed for the elevator before Olajean even finished her statement. He pushed the up button and waited, he pushed it again. Impatient, he turned and ran to the stairwell and started up to the third floor, reaching his desk a bit winded, and a little red-faced. He sat down in his chair and stared at the message. His heart was pounding but it wasn't from the run up the stairs. Twenty years had passed since the last time he saw Ellie. He knew that she got married. So, why would she need *his* help?

Why me? Cole wondered. He didn't know what to do. Was it a gag? He unconsciously ran the top of the paper between his thumbs and forefingers, over and over again. Should he call? Who would play such a dirty trick? *But then,* he thought, *who would know to play a trick like this?* She must need help. "Oh God, please..." he whispered out loud.

Cole picked up the phone, and dialed the number.

After eight rings, a voice said, "Eastwood Manor."

"Hello, who do I have?" Cole asked.

"Eastwood Manor." The voice sounded slightly annoyed.

"I got a message from Ellie, from this number. They said it's urgent."

"Ellie who?"

"I'm not sure of her married name. Can you check, please?" Cole tried to stay calm.

"Just how would I do that, sir?" the voice said sarcastically.

"Just give me your supervisor. Maybe they can be a little more helpful." Cole felt his anger rising. "Stay calm," he said to himself as he heard the phone click, and music start playing. Time seemed to pass slowly, until finally another voice came on the line.

"Can I help you?"

"Yes, may I have your name please?"

"Certainly, sir, I'm Karen Wallace. I'm the manager on duty."

"Okay," Cole took a deep breath, "I received a message

to call this number. The message was from an old friend of mine named Ellie. I don't know her last name since she married. But the message said she needed help and it was urgent."

"Sir, this is a convalescent hospital, we don't do urgent care here."

"A what?" Cole could feel his throat constricting.

"A convalescent hospital, you know, sort of a rest home. What was your friend's name again?"

"Ellie."

"That short for Ellen?"

"Yes, yes that's right."

"Hold on."

The music-on-hold played Morris Albert singing "Feelings." Cole sat for several minutes; enough time elapsed for the song to change twice.

"Sir?"

"Yes, I'm here."

"Would that be a Mrs. Ellen Christopher?"

"What's her birthday?"

"I can't give out that information, sir."

"I mean how old is she?"

"Umm, about forty-seven, forty-eight maybe. I ain't real strong in math."

"Yes, that's her; can I speak to her please?"

"Sorry, no phone in that room, sir. S'at all you needed?"

"No, I need to speak with her, can you get her?"

"Sorry sir, we don't bring patients to the front."

"Well, at least tell me what's wrong with her. Why is she there?" Cole was becoming frantic.

"Sorry, can't give out private information. Is that it?" Wallace wanted off the phone and she didn't mind showing it.

"No, I need to talk to her!"

"You'll have to just come over then. That's all I can tell you."

"I'm in Chicago, I can't just drive over!" Cole shouted.

"I don't know what to tell you, but I don't need you yellin' at me. I got enough to deal with around here." Karen Wallace hung up, and the sound of the dial tone hummed in his ear.

"What the hell kind of a place is..." Cole slammed the phone down.

"Hey, there's people trying to work around here. Wanna keep it down?" A singsong voice came from Chun's cubicle.

"How 'bout I throw your boney ass out the window?" growled Cole.

He heard the back of a desk chair straighten with a thud, and the sound of footsteps making their way quickly up the hall. Taking a deep breath, he slowly exhaled.

"Relax; don't have a stroke," he said out loud. "One step at a time. Finish the story. It's good, real good. See Brennan, then go to Ellie. Relax, it's cool. Everything will be fine." Cole laid his palms on the top of his desk and took another deep breath. He hit his mouse and the text of the story reappeared on the screen.

About an hour and a half later, the finished story rolled out of the printer. The psychologist and advocates for the elderly were squarely behind the elimination of the death penalty, but the social worker, a Dolores Pena, said upfront that she thought anybody who would kill an unarmed policeman should "fry." Well balanced and full of spark. Brennan should love it.

* * *

"Mick? You in here?" Cole peered around the doorway and into Brennan's darkened office.

"Over here." A very hoarse voice croaked from across the room, "What do you want?"

"What's wrong with you?"

"I don't know, some kind of lung crud, can't seem to shake it."

As Cole's eyes adjusted to the dark room, he could see Brennan stretched out on the dark leather couch covered in a dark green blanket. It was the same one Cole brought him back from Ecuador about 15 years ago. Against the dark paneled wall, he was nearly invisible.

"Here is the piece on the cat killer. There is a whole lot more to it than we expected, could work into a nice series."

"About cat killers?"

"Haven't you heard? The elderly lady the cat belonged to took a hostage and killed a police negotiator. The angle is she just snapped: before that she was just the little old lady on the block who made everybody cookies and stuff. Here's the piece: Three experts giving their read on the elderly and crime and mental illness. I think we could run with this and make quite a good feature series. Maybe even—"

"Hey, hey, hey, I'm not dead yet. Who the hell made you editor?" Brennan cut in.

"I guess I'm a little excited about this thing."

"Jeez, I guess," Brennan croaked and coughed a loose phlegmy rasp. "Well something's lit a fire under you. You're right, sounds like something. Good angle. We need a strong feature piece for Sunday. Work something up and—"

This time Cole broke in, "That's great, but I need a favor." He paused and took a deep breath. "Do you remember Ellie, my..." Cole hesitated.

"Of course, the one that got away. How could I forget? You almost—"

"She needs my help."

"After 20 whatever years, you kiddin' me?"

"I got a message today. She's in a convalescent home. They won't tell me what's wrong with her, and I couldn't talk to her, something about no phone in the room. I need some time. I need to go see her."

"Who called?" Brennan struggled to sit up.

"Wouldn't give Olajean their name, just a number. It was a woman though. I need a week. I have lots of vacation time, sick leave, whatever you want to charge it to. But I'm going tonight."

"You know Cole, this doesn't mean—"

"I know, I know, but she must be in pretty bad trouble to call me for help, don't you think?"

"Hell, *I'd* have to be." Cole couldn't see the concerned look on his old friend's face.

"Funny," Cole said.

"Take whatever you need. But don't get your hopes up about this. I know it's not my place, but time changes stuff, ya know? Who knows what you're gonna find."

"I've considered that. I almost didn't return the call. She needs somebody; she called me, that means something. I've got to know, Mick."

"All right. You're probably right. No, you *are* right. Go, you need to go; this is a book that needs an ending." Brennan threw off his blanket, stood and walked to face Cole. "I know things haven't been going your way. Maybe I'm partially to blame." Cole tried to speak. "No, don't interrupt, this needs said. I don't have many years, hell, the way I'm feeling I don't have many days left. I've always thought a lot of you. I should have given you more, I don't know, encouragement. I'm just not made that way. My idea of help is a good swift kick in the ass, ya know? You're about the only friend I have left. I'm a tired old drunk who needs to retire and is afraid to. Lauren out there is what keeps this place running, keeps me running too. You know she has me eating vitamins? What I'm trying to say don't wind up like me, and that's where you're heading, bitter and alone. If you've got a chance with her again, take it. But if it isn't anything, I mean with her, let it go. Let it go, Cole."

"Thanks, Mick." Cole turned and made his way to the elevator.

Brennan watched Cole's retreating form. Then he turned on the lights, lit a cigarette, and collapsed into his chair. Picking up Cole's printout, he started to read.

FOUR

Cole booked a seat on the 11:45 from O'Hare to LAX. He slept fitfully and ate nothing on the flight. Arriving in L.A., he rented a car, bought a cup of coffee, and embarked on the four-hour drive home. Home: a place you're from, not a place you live. The picture on a Christmas card, the letter from parents, the call from an old friend. There is a saying that you can never go home again. For Cole it had been twenty years. His parents had moved to a small town on the north coast, he never received invitations to high school reunions, and Ellie was all he ever cared about anyway.

Ellie...Not a moment went by that he didn't long for her. Didn't fantasize what his life would be like had he not lost her. What if they had been together? What if he had got her back? These thoughts and a million others had filled his days and restless nights. Countless miles of travel, millions of words written, and yet he had no peace. Now, he was a short drive from seeing her. A wave of apprehension swept over him.

Seldom had Cole felt fear. He had always charged into situations headlong. Damn the torpedoes, full speed ahead! Adrenaline usually carried him most of the way and after the dust settled, he would look back and feel a sense of wonder in either his bravery or stupidity at what he had just done. This, however, was different. He was truly, deeply afraid. Afraid of what he would find, afraid of a problem he couldn't face. Afraid of seeing Ellie's disappointment at what he had become, who he was. Most of all he was afraid for the reality of what life was about to hand him.

The confinement of the heavily populated L.A. basin finally gave way to rolling hills, farms, and orchards. As Cole reached the city limits of "Haley," he saw few things he remembered. A six-lane freeway that bisected the city had replaced the Business District exit of the old highway. There were exit signs for roads, avenues, and parkways he had never heard of. Jolting up from the skyline that used to boast a six-story retirement center as the city's tallest building was a 14-story monolith that was marked by a blazing red star with a yellow tail bearing the city's name in letters nearly a story high.

Cole took the exit that said Civic Center and pulled onto McAlister Avenue, the first name he recognized. McAlister was the main artery of the city, so Cole finally felt he knew where he was. He spotted the McAlister Plaza as he drove along. Once the heart of all the city's shopping, now it seemed small and insignificant among the large stand-alone mega stores.

As he sat waiting for a traffic light to change, he could almost see the signs of the stores that used to front The Plaza: Trains & Planes Hobby Shop, Hilton Floral, Tots to Teens, and the biggest locally owned department store in town, Doolan's. These old stores held a regal place in Cole's memory. All were gone now, replaced by national chains that fronted the center.

Cole remembered the thrill of going to Doolan's as a boy to shop for back-to-school clothes when, in desperation, his mother took him there to buy a coat because the selection of J.C. Penney's was picked over with nothing left in his size. Cole remembered hoping it would last forever; he never had such a coat and swore he would guard it with his life. Sometimes he would leave the house in just a heavy sweater on a cold, stormy day without his mother seeing, just to save his wonderful coat from The Plaza, for days he needed to look his best.

The light changed and Cole crossed a six-lane thoroughfare he had never seen before. Where was the irrigation canal that had bordered The Plaza? Where was the bridge? Cole marveled at all the changes and realized that time had gone on even in his hometown.

He spotted a phone booth in a Burger King parking lot and pulled in. As he got out of the car, he realized that the Burger King was built on the very spot where the trampoline park used to be.

Cole and his cousins had spent countless hours bouncing the summer nights away on the trampolines that covered the park. He tried to recall what the cost had been back then. Fifty cents an hour was his first thought, but he wasn't sure. He didn't hear any trouble, however, remembering the cost of the cold frosty mug of A&W root beer that always finished the evening: 35 cents. The A&W had been right next door, only a few feet from the gate of The Bounce. Now there was a Kragen Auto Parts store.

Cole found the address to the Eastwood Manor Convalescent Hospital and Guest Home in the Yellow Pages. The small map in the corner of the ad had helped and he had a general idea where it was. Turning back to the car, he took a deep breath. The calm before the storm.

Eastwood Manor was in the middle of the block on an older residential street. The houses for most of the block across from the Manor had been torn down and construction on what would become Driftwood Apartments—"A Place to be Yourself" according to the sign—was underway. The Manor grounds were spacious and covered with the shade of majestic oak trees. The building was one story and white. The lawn held the Eastwood Manor sign, way past its prime with paint peeling badly. An elderly man in a wheelchair was parked on the sidewalk with a pale blue thermal blanket pulled to his neck and tucked tightly around his thin body. Cole intended to say hello as he passed. As he approached, he saw the man sat with his toothless mouth agape, his eyes milky blue and unfocused, and on his face an expression that was a cross between pain and fear. Cole shuddered.

He went through the large double glass doors into a reception and waiting room. Several elderly people were sitting in wheelchairs. Most appeared to have no idea where they were. Cole thought of Annie Clark and wondered if a place like this would be her next stop. The air was heavy with cleaning solvent, urine, and air freshener.

"May I help you?" a voice asked from behind the tall reception desk.

As Cole approached, he saw a heavyset woman of about fifty seated behind the desk reading a romance novel.

"Yes, I am here to see Ellen Christopher." The name seemed so foreign to Cole he repeated it, "Ellen Christopher."

"Have you been here before?"

"No."

"I need you to fill out this little form here," the woman said, passing a clipboard across the desk to Cole.

"Why?"

"What?" She responded as if she had just been slapped.

"Why do I need to fill out a form? I'm not checking in."

"It's the rules."

"Well, you don't need my address, phone or anything else. I'm simply visiting Mrs. Christopher on her request." Cole hated forms, and the stress of seeing Ellie was getting to him.

"Look, Mister, I don't make the rules. Why get snippy with me?"

"Then get your supervisor, I'll snip at them if you'd like it better," Cole replied.

"Mrs. Juarez to the front desk, Mrs. Juarez to the front desk," the woman said into an industrial microphone that sent her voice echoing throughout the halls. "She'll be right here." She raised the romance novel so that it covered her face in a quick dismissive snap.

Cole turned and walked to a window and watched the sprinklers spray the far end of the lawn. After several minutes, he heard voices behind him and turned to see a tall Hispanic woman in a crisply starched uniform talking to the receptionist in hushed tones. The receptionist pointed at Cole as he made his way back to the desk.

"That's him," Cole heard her say.

"Can I help you, Mr....?" the Hispanic woman asked.

"Sage, Mrs. Juarez. I'm here to see Mrs. Ellen Christopher at her request."

"Cassie says you don't want to fill out our visitor form."

"Cassie's telling the truth. I will not give you my personal information so you can send me junk mail that I don't want to receive. It is a privacy issue, and frankly, none of your business. Now, which room is Mrs. Christopher in? I would like to see her now." Cole gave Mrs. Juarez a big fake forced smile.

"It is the policy of Eastwood..."

"Look. Mrs. Christopher is an old dear friend of mine and is no doubt paying far more than it's worth to be here. Now if you don't want me to talk to the licensing board about the half dozen or so infractions I've seen already, I suggest you just give me her room number and I'll be on my way."

"You are a very unpleasant man," Mrs. Juarez said in a condescending tone. "Room 128." She turned and walked through an open door behind the desk.

There were two hallways off the reception area. The sign above one door indicated that Rooms 78 through 140 lay beyond. Along the hall, open doors revealed bed after bed of patients simply waiting to die. A few weary old heads turned as he passed. Many slept and a few just stared ahead. One older man called out to Cole asking for cigarettes and muttered curses when Cole said he had none. Televisions were on everywhere. Soap operas, talk shows, game shows, mindless, meaningless, pointless, endless fluff came from nearly every room. Awake, asleep, it didn't matter. The television filled the room with noise.

The thing that struck Cole was the absence of staff. The light above several doors was on which he assumed was meant to call for a nurse. One stooped Asian woman passed him with a pushcart full of brushes, solvents, and cleaning equipment. The fumes of ammonia and body fluids ebbed and flowed with the passing of people and doorways. Slippered feet, unable to push forward, propelled wheelchairs backwards down the hall towards Cole. Catheter bags dangled from the sides of the wheelchairs and omitted their own distinct aroma.

Cole had never been good with sick people. It wasn't a lack of sympathy; it was quite the opposite. He hurt for every person he saw. He ached for their loneliness and despair. Cole suddenly felt claustrophobic, as if trapped in a low-budget zombie movie. He wanted to just run away. Why in God's name was Ellie in this hellish place?

Room 128 was the next room on his right. Cole came to a stop six feet from the doorway. He could hear the television; a game show's bells, and applause, rang out into the hall. He felt like his feet were stuck to the gray speckled tile. Cole Sage was not a coward. He had faced rebels, street gangs, and the soldiers of Cambodian dictator Pol Pot and not given an inch. At this moment, however, he felt a fear so deep and so terrifying he could not move.

Cole laced his fingers and put them behind his head. He looked up at the ceiling and took deep, heaving breaths. He knew he had to go in. His imagination ran wild with images of what lay inside the room. Coma, cancer, paralysis and all manner of illness filled his head. For a fleeting moment, he saw the face of a young beautiful Ellie on the body of a naked, old, withered, motionless woman lying on a bed, mouth gaping, staring at the ceiling.

Cole rubbed his forehead and held his hands over his face for a long moment. He took a deep breath and walked the last few steps into the room. A form sat at the window in a wheelchair of chrome and maroon Naugahyde.

"Ellie?" Cole said softly.

A pair of thin hands took the wheels and, with great effort, turned the chair around to face him. "Hey, big guy," Ellie said in a shaky voice.

Cole could barely recognize her. She was dressed in a light cotton floral print robe. The once statuesque beauty was bone thin. Her neck was long with tendons clearly visible. The face once beaming with life and energy was drawn and etched with the lines of pain. The glorious mane of hair that had bounced and glistened with every step was oily, combed straight back, and laid along her neck. In her eyes, though, he saw the girl and woman he had loved so long ago. The strength and kindness that was so a part of Ellie's being shone through.

"Hello, sweetie."

Ellie reached out a hand to Cole. He took the few steps to her and put her hand in his, kissing it gently. She reached up, placed her other hand on his cheek, and looked deeply into his eyes. With every ounce of strength he possessed, Cole fought back tears. It was no use. He bent down and threw his arms around her. Ellie stroked his hair and softly wept. Several minutes passed and her tears flowed freely. Cole raised his head and tried to speak. Ellie put the tips of her fingers to his lips.

"I have something I need to tell you," she began. "I have Amyotrophic Lateral Sclerosis, Lou Gehrig's disease. I can no longer walk. As you can hear, it has affected my voice and I am losing strength in my arms. Eventually, it will affect my ability to breathe. I know you will have many questions; I have asked them all myself, please understand. I am dying. The only thing I don't know is how long it will take." She took a deep halting breath and let it out. "I am so sorry you have to see me like this. I am so ashamed." She began to cry.

Cole didn't know what to say. He got to his feet and wiped her eyes with his handkerchief. He, too, took shuddered breaths. His mind was having a hard time processing what she had said. Lou Gehrig's disease was something you read about in *People* magazine; the brave soul who paints or writes poetry to inspire others who fought to the end. It did not happen to those you loved. He turned to face Ellie.

"I am so sorry I reacted so badly."

"It's a bit of a shock to see me like this, huh?" She smiled.

"I have missed you so," Cole said without thinking.

"Cole, please sit down. You are making me very nervous." Ellie gave a soft giggle. "Let's start over, what do you say?"

"Good idea." Cole smiled, and pulled up a chair.

The initial shock was over. Cole tried to look either in her eyes or not at all. The sound of her voice was so familiar yet the tremors kept it from being wholly hers. They were sitting about three feet apart facing each other. Cole noticed that her toenails were badly in need of clipping. The room was bare and undecorated: a bed, a small closet, a door to the toilet and the television. Cole stood and took the remote from the stand on the bedside table and clicked off the television. Then he sat back down.

"Oh," Ellie started, "I hardly notice it's on anymore."

"How long have you been here?"

"Little over a year. Allen put me here shortly after I lost the use of my legs."

"Tell me about this disease."

"Gee, I feel like I'm being interviewed. Is this on the record, Mr. Sage?" Ellie smiled. Her wit still sparkled in her eyes.

"I'm sorry, I..."

"You used to take teasing better. I was diagnosed a little over two years ago. They think ALS is hereditary but nobody really knows for sure. At first, I took a medication called Riluzole, but it made me so dizzy I couldn't function. Then I tried this stuff called Baclofen. It gave me these weird muscle twitches. I sound like a pharmacist. There really is no way to stop the disease's progression. It disconnects the nerves where they connect to your spinal column. Little by little as they disconnect, the parts of your body to which the nerves sent signals lose their ability to function. I am one of the lucky ones, they tell me. It went to my legs first. Physical therapy helped a little. Stretching, stuff like that, to keep my muscles from contracting so much, but that stopped when I came here. The thing that's a real drag is the pain. My butt hurts all the time!" Ellie laughed, "Used to be a bigger pain. Not much of it left anymore."

"There is no...?" Cole hesitated

"Cure? Nope. So here I am."

"I am so sorry, Ellie."

"Here now, we'll have no pity parties around here. So, tell me about you. I saw you on CNN when you won that award. I was so proud of you. What have you done lately?"

"Not much. I wrote a piece just before I left, part of a

series I think, about mental health and the elderly."

"You'd have a field day around here."

"Why here, El? Why are you in this place? Isn't there a facility that people who have, I mean, people with..."

"ALS, come, you can say it. I'm not afraid of it."

"ALS."

"Yes, Cole, there is, but Allen, my husband, isn't willing to pay for it. He's a real estate salesman." Ellie did an imitation of Groucho Marx raising his eyebrows and flicking an imaginary cigar. "And a pretty bad one."

"Are you serious?" Cole spoke before he thought.

"Yes, I'm afraid so. So you know about *my* bad choice. Any ladies in your life I should know about?" Ellie said coyly.

"Only you," Cole said softly.

"Stop, I'm serious." Ellie smiled.

"No, no one. There are so many things I want to ask you." Cole changed the subject excitedly, "What have you done with yourself all these years? Do you still paint? I mean, well I guess not in here but..."

"I did for a while, but after I married Allen I became the 'house mom.' It sort of got lost somewhere."

"Mom! I guess I never thought of, well that's cool. Tell me about him, her, them? Boys? Girls?" Cole had relaxed and he felt the old connection to Ellie. It wasn't gone. As they spoke, he had begun to see her through this new form.

"One of each that were Allen's when we got married, and my angel, Erin."

"Wow, I had no idea. Guess I should have figured. So what are they doing? Ages? Tell all."

"Chad is—was—at Desert Community. Ann is at San Diego State, or maybe she's finished by now."

"What do you mean *is*, *was*. That doesn't seem like you, not to know." Cole broke in.

"I haven't seen or heard from them since I came here."

"I'm not sure I'm getting all this."

"My marriage to Allen was in trouble before I got sick, Cole. My illness just gave him an excuse to get me out of the way. I sort of interfered with his social life. I haven't seen him, either. I was sent here in an ambulance during a really bad spell. I really have ups and downs with this. Right now, I'm on an upswing, lucky you." She smiled sadly.

"But you raised those kids, right?"

"If you want to call it that. They resented me from the start and Allen never did anything to ease the strain. I would correct them and he would side with them. By their teens, I had given up. It was like two families in one house: Allen, Chad and Annie, then Erin and me. I'm sorry, Cole, I was trying so hard to keep things, you know, kind of light on your first visit."

Cole laughed. "You still have a gift for understating things."

"We haven't spoken in years, I call for help, and you are on the next plane. And here I sit, wheelchair bound, dying of this damnable disease, with a family that has abandoned me. And the hell of it is, I'm trying to be charming, and I'm so embarrassed and humiliated. I would throw myself out that window, but I can't stand up." Ellie was coming as close to shouting as her shaking speech would allow.

"Now that's more like it! Let it out! That's the girl I remember!"

"Oh shut up! I'm angry."

"Of course you are! You've still got fight left! I was starting to worry about you. I got a news flash, though: we're on the ground floor."

"Please don't make fun of me," she said quietly.

"I never would." Cole stood and walked to the window.

His emotions were like static electricity. Here was the person that he thought was "out in California living the good life," the person he jealously envied and longed to be with, who all along was as miserable as he was. He cursed himself for never contacting her. He cursed his pride. He cursed the life fate had handed them both.

"Cole?"

He realized he had been standing at the window just staring and thinking. What was he to say to her? *I'm sorry I didn't come and rescue you? I was too busy feeling sorry for myself? I'm going to live a long time after you're gone, still loving what you had been?* His heart was breaking, if there was such a thing. All he had dreamed was a lie. He wanted to melt into the floor.

"Cole?" she repeated.

He couldn't face her. He couldn't bring himself to turn around. Why had he come? There was nothing he could do for her. She was sick. He had no cure to offer. He couldn't make her family suddenly love her. Why had she called him? What did she think he could do? There was no hope.

He felt Ellie's hand take his and her head rest against his arm. "Wish I could see out that window. Must be good. There is pretty green paint down here though, kind of."

"Well...," Cole began.

"I have read a lot of things you've written over the years. You always dig up the adoptive mother, catch the city official with their hand in the cookie jar, get the MIA's body back, and that thing with the president you did. You're kind of a detective. What I mean is, you know how to find what you're looking for, right?"

"Yeah, I'm kind of nosey." Cole shrugged.

"Find Erin."

"Your daughter?"

"Yes." Ellie looked down to steel herself. "It's Allen, he..."

"Has he hurt her?"

"No, no not like you think. Please sit so I can see you." She waited until Cole was back in the chair. "When my parents died, an inheritance came to me. I put it in a trust for Erin for college or her wedding or, or something. Anyway, I'm not going to last very long. I want her to get the money. It means a lot to me that she gets what was meant for her. Knowing how Chad and Annie were, my folks, well, they wanted Erin to inherit."

"That seems easy enough. Do you have a will?" Cole asked.

"That's just it. It isn't that easy. You see, when I was really bad, Allen had me sign a, oh what do you call it, a power of attorney. I didn't really understand. Then, later, when I got some strength back, I realized what I had signed. She can't touch the trust until I'm gone. The way it was set up, Erin didn't get it until she was 25 if anything happened to me. So, until then, he could change it. She's 23 and if she can't be found and I die..." She looked up and into Cole's eyes. "Cole, this is important to me, can you understand?"

"Look, these things aren't as easy to do as you think. He can't..."

"Yes, he can. He already sold my parents' home. We had it as a rental. It was in my name, but he sold it. I only found out because I called his office. The secretary congratulated me on the sale.

"Find Erin, Cole. She's my greatest joy. We, we had a ..." Ellie looked at her hands as they twisted in her lap. "I was a fool. I sided with Allen. I thought I should support him as head of the house and maybe he would consider me in dealings with Chad and Annie. It all went wrong. He could have cared less. It drove a wedge between Erin and me. She wouldn't listen to me, just shut me out. One day when I was out, they had an argument and he told her to leave. She did, and I haven't seen her, she hasn't written or called. I don't know where she is. Knowing him, he told her I would side with him. I never would have!" She put her hands over her face.

"I'll find her."

"And bring her back?"

"I'll do my best. But she's a grown woman, El. I can't force her."

"You have to tell her I'm sorry, she has to forgive me, Cole. I was wrong, so wrong and it has driven us apart. It was all my fault. You have to make her see how much I love her, how much I miss her. You are my only hope to get her back."

"I will do everything in my power." Cole knew it was foolish to tell her not to worry, but he could see her strength slipping away as she spoke.

"I know you will. I have missed you so." She smiled, but it was colored with sadness.

"I've missed you too, more than you'll ever know. Are you getting tired? I don't want to wear you out. We will have time to visit later if you need me to go." Cole was becoming concerned with her obvious weakening.

"I don't have a whole lot of 'later,' so you better not leave or I'll chase you down with my wheelchair!" Her smile beamed and the color was returning to her cheeks.

"In that case, I better stick around."

"Can you help me into bed?"

"That's the best offer I've had in years!"

"Aren't *you* the saucy one?"

Cole folded back the covers. He put his hands under Ellie's arms and lifted her from the chair. She wrapped her arms around his neck. For a moment, they were face-to-face and only inches apart. Their eyes met and neither could look away. Cole slipped his arms around her and they embraced. Her cheek against his and his heart against hers they stood, neither wanting to let go. She was so thin, but it was Ellie in his arms again, if only for a moment. He ached to kiss her, but, instead, swept his arm behind her knees and lifted her onto the bed.

"What service! I love to be tucked in."

"Sorry, I forgot the mint on the pillow."

Cole pulled the chair across the room. He sat with his feet propped on the bed rail. Ellie looked much more relaxed, and her voice had smoothed and seemed not nearly as shaky as before. For nearly two hours, they laughed and talked, reminiscing about their youth. She remembered places and people he had long forgotten. He spoke of places and things they had done, some she could not recall. With all the memories and years apart, they still shared the fondness for their lives together. Little was said of their relationship, parting or love. For now, they were just two old friends, together and bathing in the warmth of what had been.

Cole recounted the story of a trip to the coast of Northern California when they became hopelessly lost outside of Petaluma in the winding roads of the coastal mountains. He had been looking out the window as he talked. When he looked back at Ellie, her eyes were closed. He continued to tell the story until he saw that her breathing had become deep and slow.

"And then he told the beautiful girl at his side how much he loved her and always would," Cole said softly. He smiled and rose to his feet. Ellie had drifted to sleep. He kissed her gently on the forehead and slipped out of the room.

FIVE

Cole checked into the Palmwood Motel on McAllister Boulevard. It was one of the older motels but still in pretty good shape. He stopped at a hamburger stand called Lucy's that he was surprised to find still in business. It had been hours since he had eaten, and he couldn't believe how hungry he was. He nearly inhaled the double cheeseburger, fries, and chocolate shake before he was back in the car and headed for downtown.

He was pleased to see *The Daily Record* had expanded, was remodeled and updated from the small-town newspaper he remembered. He made his way through the thick green, tinted glass doors and into the spacious tile atrium. The ceiling was a glass and steel dome from which hung huge baskets of flowers. The late afternoon sun filtered through the green glass of the dome, lighting the floor and giving everything an emerald tint. The receptionist sat behind a curved wall of glass brick about three feet high.

"Welcome to *The Record*, may I help you?"

Cole smiled and, presenting his press credentials, said, "Good afternoon, I'm Cole Sage with *The Chicago Sentinel.* I'd like to speak with your resident research genius, if I could."

"That would be Randy Callen. Let me see if he's in yet." The receptionist spoke into the thin clear tube that curved out from her headset, "A Mr. Cole to see you. He's from *The Chicago Sentinel.*" She paused. "Okay, I'll tell him."

"He'll be right out, Mr. Cage."

Cole smiled broadly and took her card from the small holder on the counter.

"Wenda Brilliams," Cole said.

"Brenda Williams," she said in a matter-of-fact tone.

"Got it."

An elevator door opened, and a young man in his early twenties approached Cole.

"Mr. Cole?"

"Sage, Cole Sage, *Chicago Sentinel.*"

"Brenda has trouble with names sometimes."

"Noticed."

"I'm Randy Callen. How can I help?"

"I need to get some background on a local real estate guy. Thought maybe you could give me a hand."

"It would be my pleasure. Let's go down to my office."

As they entered the elevator, Cole noticed Randy's right hand was badly withered. The fingers were webbed together and came almost to a point at the middle. Randy pushed the B button with his left hand and they began to descend.

"I'm in the dungeon."

"Been there long?" Cole asked good-naturedly.

"I graduated last year from Humboldt State. Saw this gig in *The Journalist* and applied. Seems I was the only one, so here I am. It's cool. Nobody bugs me, and I have the dungeon all to myself. Most of it is the archives. Nobody visits there much since almost everything is on the computers now. So, all in all, it's pretty cool."

As the elevator doors opened, Cole could hear music coming from the right. The "dungeon" was well lit and even a bit on the bright side. As they made their way through a series of gray cloth-covered cubicles, however, Cole noticed the lighting seemed less effective. Then he saw that every other tube was out in the fluorescent lights. As they reached the wall, there were none on at all. In the corner of the room was a long L-shaped table. Six large widescreen monitors faced a tall-backed brown leather executive chair. Three keyboards were waiting between pairs of monitors. Next to each keyboard was a small black disc drive. All the wires were neatly hidden. Curiously absent was any sign of a computer tower.

"Welcome to my little corner of the world." Randy beamed and waved his hand, palm up, like Vanna White revealing a completed phrase.

"Beautiful."

"When I got here, there was only an old IBM 386. Nobody had spent any of the budget for computers down here during the furnishing of the new building. My boss was smart enough to know he didn't have a clue what to order. So he let me do my thing."

"Looks really expensive," Cole offered.

"See, that's where I scored brownie points! Instead of

buying a bunch of towers and processors and hard drives and stuff that would crash, wear out or get outdated, I had all this wired into the mainframe upstairs with fiber optic cables. They constantly tweak and upgrade, so I don't have to worry about my stuff having to be replaced. Saved a bundle. What I spent of my budget was on monitors and cool toys. Nobody noticed, they were so pleased that I only spent half of it. Cool, huh?"

"Very cool." Cole loved the young man's enthusiasm.

"So, what are you looking for?"

"What have you got on a realtor named Allen Christopher?"

"Christopher, huh?" Randy said as he started pecking at the keyboard. "You're the second person in the last couple of weeks to ask about him. What's the deal? He running for something?"

"Not that I know of. Who else was looking?"

"One of the feature writers. She was doing a piece on a survey done of good and bad realtors. Seems his name kept coming up on the bad guy list. That can't be good for business."

"What? He a crook or something?" Cole was surprised by this revelation. From what Ellie had said, Christopher sounded successful.

"Seems so..." The computer distracted Randy. "Here you go. Allen Christopher. Sit down; I'll put it on two."

The second monitor stopped swirling small red-white-and-blue peace signs to open on a screen of text.

"Well, well," Cole said as he pulled up a chair in front of the monitor.

"Here," Randy tossed Cole a mouse. "Cordless and laser."

"Thanks. Looks like Mr. Christopher is a busy boy."

"That's what Carrie said. Tell you what, give me a second, and I'll pull the piece she's been working on. Can't tell her, though; I'll get in hella trouble."

The files on Christopher were in three categories: Articles, Unused, and Research. Under Articles, there was a piece from 1992 when he had received a Board of Realtors award. In 1998. his name was mentioned in an investigation of funding for a city program for remodeling homes for the elderly. For August 2000 there was a piece entitled "Realtor Warned about Padding Escrow" and a follow-up stating no formal action had been taken. Nothing after that in the file.

Research had many filings: fictitious name statements for a couple of businesses, birth announcements, his first wife's obituary, and his license to wed Ellie. Pretty dull stuff, all in all...except for the obituary of the first wife.

"His first wife is dead?"

"O-bit-u-ary. It's newspaper for dead." Randy chuckled at his own joke.

"Slow down, hot rod. What'd she die of?" Cole leaned toward the monitor.

"Mmmm...looks like a car wreck about—what is that?—13, 14 years ago." Randy pointed to a line on the screen.

"Okay, what else you got?"

The Unused file was mostly drafts of articles about the opening of three real estate offices. A copy for an ad announcing "Welcome of Allen Christopher to our office of highly effective agents" was stamped CANCELLED in red. Cole was growing bored with the press releases, most of which were from Christopher about Christopher. Until the last one caught his eye.

> "Allen Christopher is proud to announce his association with Malcor Corporation of Fort Lee, New Jersey. Malcor is exploring the relocation to the southeast section of the city. This multi-million dollar project will bring jobs, a new vitality to the area, and will provide a much-needed anchor for further industrial growth in the area."

Cole scanned the rest of the badly written puff piece until he read the last sentence: "Mr. Christopher is actively involved in rezoning the potential factory site." *Why would it need rezoning?* Cole thought.

"Hey, Randy, can you tell what the date is on this last file in Unused?"

"Looks like it's about six months old. Need an exact date? I can dig deeper."

"No, that's close enough. Have you got anything on a Malcor Corporation?" As Cole spoke, a file folder appeared and blinked in the middle of the screen. "What's this?"

"Carrie's draft of the real estate story. Please delete it after you read it. I'm checking Malcor—"

Cole felt like he was reading somebody else's mail as he skimmed through the article. It was obvious that the writer wasn't anywhere near finished. She had brackets around sentences and phrases, triple spaced sections, paragraphs in red, and spell check hadn't been run in a long time, if ever. She was trying to seem edgy without saying anything the paper could get sued over. Christopher was mentioned twice as *the Realtor with the Most Negative Responses.*

Cole had seen all he needed.

"Here you go. It's not ours. I linked to a news browser that's like an electronic clipping service. Quite a file."

Another folder popped up on Cole's monitor. The first file was all he needed: "Malcor Mob Ties Once Again Investigated." Too much money, too few liabilities, and too few projects in the works had the Feds interested. The article painted a picture of a not-too-cleverly concealed attempt by the mob to filter moneys into a legitimate business. They had purchased Malcor seven years before, then sat on it...until that last couple of years, when it suddenly was turning big profits for no apparent reason.

It's hard to think legitimate when you are used to breaking the law, so why not move west, find some fresh faces, start some new ventures, and hire some clean managers and a board of directors with no ties to the mob? Smart on the surface, but they never think about the origins of the start-up capital. Gets them every time.

"Think I got what I need. You've got a great resource here. I hope they appreciate your talents."

"This is but a stop on the road to riches and fame, Mr. Sage, a stop on the road." Randy did what he considered a good imitation of a wise old philosopher.

"So what's the coolest thing all this stuff can do?"

"Stand back about six or eight feet and watch!"

Cole did as instructed. All six of the 26" monitors went black. Like a bolt of hallucinogenic lightning, the screens exploded with color. The music of a soaring rock band backed by a symphony orchestra thundered from in front and behind in response to the visuals; A panorama of ocean waves, birds in flight, aerial views of the Grand Canyon, sailing on San Francisco Bay under the Golden Gate, skydiving toward earth and then zooming out to a shot of Earth from space. The pictures jumped from screen to screen and did synchronized patterns like the water fountain at the Bellagio in Las Vegas. It was astounding!

Then the monitors all went black again. The silence was almost as deafening as the sound had been.

"That was amazing!" Cole shouted.

"Thought you'd like it." Randy beamed like a kid showing off his new toy—and that's exactly what he was.

"Randy, you are a wonder. It has been a real kick meeting you. If you are ever in Chicago, come by *The Sentinel* and I'll introduce you to some people. I'm not kidding, we've got to get you out of this dungeon." Cole offered his hand to the young man, remembered Randy's misshapen one and quickly offered his left. Randy nodded a look of appreciation and shook Cole's hand firmly.

"You just might see me someday."

"I'll take that as a promise." Cole patted Randy's shoulder. "I'll let know if I dig up anything of interest."

Cole returned to the Palmwood and looked up Allen Christopher in the phone book he found in the desk drawer, scribbling the number and address on a notepad. Tomorrow, he would make a call on Mr. Christopher. As he lay back across the bed, Cole replayed the day's events in his head. He had covered a lot of ground since he left Chicago, and he was starting to feel the effects. His sadness about Ellie had been masked by their talk and laughter for a while. The best thing to do was get busy finding Erin. He wouldn't let himself dwell on Ellie's condition. *She was just sick*, he told himself, but he knew it was more than that. He had a chance to do something for her, something her husband wouldn't. He would not let her down.

SIX

Cole woke late. Dressed in jeans, a Chicago Blues Festival T-shirt and a Cubs baseball cap, he made his way to the street and walked to the McDonalds on the corner. Two Egg McMuffins later, coffee in hand, he walked back to his car in the Palmwood lot. Cole pulled the address for Allen Christopher from his pocket. To his embarrassment, he realized he had no clue where the location was. He went to the motel office and got a city map from the desk clerk. He followed the map toward 1438 Peppertree Lane.

As he drove north, he was amazed at the landscape. Where peach trees and grapevines had once lined the road, now were rows and rows of houses. New building was apparent all over the city, but nowhere as dramatic as in the north end. In the few short miles he had driven, the houses he saw had taken over a dozen family-owned farms. He thought of the kids he had known and rode the school bus with, farm kids who always got on the bus wearing the newest styles. They always had the coolest bikes and wore the coolest shoes. In high school, they proudly wore the royal blue corduroy FFA jackets and took Ag classes. It was assumed they would inherit the farms, grow the peaches, and tend the vineyards. Now the farms were gone. Cole wondered what kind of family history the owners of the earth-toned two-story Tudors and fake '40s retro homes presented to the world.

He stopped at the corner of Tulare and Emmett Roads and marveled at the small shopping center that filled the northeast corner. A small market, video store, take-and-bake pizza, dry cleaner, and a Mexican restaurant sat on the land where his friend Steve had once lived with his aunt and uncle. Old Leo would be spinning in his grave to see what became of his prized orchard of Rio Oso Gem peaches.

Cole thought back to summers in high school and evenings spent with the Padullas. Uncle Leo would bring fresh peaches from the orchard. He grew an experimental variety that were developed at the University of California at Davis. Designed to be frozen, they were sweet, fleshy fruit with, as Cole remembered, an exaggerated peach taste. The thing he would never forget, though, was the size. Aunt Rosa once ran to the copper-toned refrigerator, took out a cantaloupe, and laid it on the table next to a peach. They were the same size. Every night during peach season, the family would gather after dinner and cut a giant peach in half, peel it, and put a single scoop of vanilla ice cream in the cavernous hole left by the pit. Cole's mouth actually watered at the memory.

He also recalled how Rosa was always reading a book

when he'd come in. Cole's strongest image of Rosa was the day they came in as she was reading *The Godfather.* He could see the slightly bent Italian lady, arms waving, dentures slipping, spit flying, telling how the Mafia in Sicily had threatened her father's brother and somebody-or-other, and that's why they had come to America. "La Cosa Nostra, La Cosa Nostra," she repeated over and over throughout the story. She was absolutely convinced that the story of the Corleone family was a thinly disguised account of a real Mafia family in New York that was still looking for her descendants who had escaped Sicily by the grace of Saint Teresa.

A truck's air horn blasted Cole out of his reverie. The light changed and with it his memories. No longer in the quiet countryside of his youth, the unforgiving traffic reminded him of that. Jolted back to the present, Cole floored the accelerator, shot into the intersection, and made the left turn toward Vintage Glenn Estates.

The one constant in the landscape was irrigation canals. Every mile or so, there was a small bridge over a concrete river. As a kid, Cole and everyone he knew swam in them. Now, they looked very small and dirty, and would be the last places he would take a cool dip on a 100-plus summer day.

The reality of where he was going and what he was about to do began to form a knot in Cole's stomach. His first thoughts about meeting Allen Christopher were violent and colored in blood. Cole knew that was not the path he would take, but playing through scenes of bludgeoning Christopher with various objects helped vent his anger. He tried a litany of curses and profane names in his mental role-playing that helped hone the edge of his hatred for what this man had done to Ellie. What he would actually say and do were as much a mystery to Cole as the reason he was driving "out in the country" to see him.

Ahead on the left, Cole spotted a tall stone fence that curved into what the sign called "Vintage Glenn Estates, The Place to Be Who You Really Are." This place would be who Allen Christopher really was, because it wasn't the house he shared with Ellie. When they were first married, Ellie told Cole they had bought a single-story Victorian house built in the '20s. It was on a tree-lined street in the old part of town, across from a large park. Ellie described the things she had done with it, the way she had decorated. She was so proud, that she always had a Charles Dickens Christmas party during the holidays. She had confided to Cole that, as bad as her marriage was, she still took great pride in her home and her lovely things. Cole was sure she didn't know that Christopher had sold the house.

Cole drove through the stone gates of Vintage Glenn Estates and found Peppertree Lane with no trouble; 1438 was in the middle of the block. The garage door was up, and the interior was nearly void of the stuff that usually crowds out all but the smallest car. The landscaping was obviously new; there were lines in the sod where it hadn't grown together. Cole pulled up across the street.

A young man in a pair of baggy shorts and a faded blue T-shirt was coming out of the garage. An early '80s BMW was parked in front of the house behind a fairly new Mustang. In the driveway was a new Mercedes Benz. A young couple with a stroller passed Cole on the sidewalk and gave him a less-than-neighborly glare. He waved and smiled.

A door on the rear wall of the garage was open, giving

Cole a straight shot into the backyard. As he watched, a young woman in sweatpants and a tank top walked by the door several times with a shovel. The young man who Cole took for Chad pushed a wheelbarrow full of peat moss behind the young woman who must have been his sister Ann. Then, there he was, Allen Christopher, carrying a sapling tree in a five-gallon pot.

Cole got out of the car and crossed the street. He had never seen such an empty, sterile garage in his life. The walls were taped and textured, but not painted. A small stack of paint cans, probably for touch up, sat in the corner. A recycling bin was on the wall opposite the water heater, and a snowboard and two pairs of skis were hung on the right wall. On the wall next to the rear door was a white plastic sign that said "Mercedes Benz Parking Only." The floor was swept clean, the broom leaning strangely out of place next to a door that led into the house. Cole walked into the backyard.

"When'd you move in?" Cole said, trying to sound friendly.

"We're not buying anything!" Christopher called across the yard.

"Not selling anything." Cole's tone cooled.

Christopher set down the tree he was carrying and removed his leather garden gloves. The children gave Cole a blank, disinterested glance and went back to spreading peat in the planter. As he crossed the yard, Christopher shoved the gloves into the back pocket of his cargo shorts. Allen Christopher was not what Cole had envisioned. He was taller than Cole, thinner, and had more hair.

All his life, Cole had found too-neat people very suspect. Maybe it was a vanity thing— theirs, not his. Cole always felt haircuts were a nuisance, something that you did a couple weeks after it was absolutely necessary. Allen Christopher, in Cole's eyes, was coiffured. He had a George Hamilton tan and the look of the guys at the gym who watched themselves in the mirrored walls as they jogged on the treadmill. Christopher approached, pushing his sunglasses back on the top of his head, holding back thick, probably dyed, hair. (Yet another pet peeve of Cole's. Men just didn't do that.) Even without his resentment of Christopher's treatment of Ellie, Cole wasn't going to like this guy.

"What do you want?" Christopher asked coldly.

"That's not very friendly."

"I don't like strangers in my backyard."

"Not very neighborly, either," Cole said, trying to appear friendly.

"Are you my neighbor?" Christopher's confidence seemed momentarily stalled.

"No, but I might have been. If I had been, I would have been very disappointed in my reception. My name is Cole Sage, I'm an—"

"Cole Sage? I know who you are," Christopher cut him off. "Same question. What do you want?"

Cole considered the overwhelming urge to punch Christopher in the nose. He flashed back on all the things he had said when he had role-played this scene in his head. Then he thought of Ellie and resisted both.

"I saw Ellie yesterday."

"So?"

"You know, I thought I was just going to pay you a friendly visit. Try to sort a few things out."

"We're not friends. You mean nothing to me. Neither

do the mythical romantic adventures I've been forced to endure hearing for years."

Cole took a deep breath and let it out slowly. "Ellie and I are old friends. She seemed in some distress and called me for some assistance," Cole said, trying to remain calm. "I simply wanted to see—"

"Ellen is none of your concern. She is my wife. She is terminally ill and is being taken care of. Whatever she told you is no business of yours, and I would thank you to stay away from her." Christopher's voice was now just below a shout.

"Like you've done?"

Out of the corner of his eye, Cole saw Chad approaching on his left. He had none of his father's concern about appearance. His thin wispy hair came almost to his shoulders and needed to be washed. From his temples to his chin ran the raw, over-pinched signs of untreated acne. Chad wore a sweaty faded T-shirt with the words "Island of LESBOS—Every Man's Dream" across the chest. Cole thought he looked sweatier than his activity could have produced. As Chad got closer, Cole recognized the acrid stench of a methamphetamine user.

"This guy givin' you trouble, Dad?" Chad said, trying to stand with a threatening posture.

"So, you must be Chad."

"That's right. Who are you?"

"He's no one," Christopher barked. "I think it's time for you to leave."

"Yeah, leave," Chad echoed.

"How long you been a tweaker, kid?"

"You think you're so smart. What makes you think I use meth?"

Allen Christopher looked from his son to the stranger in his backyard but didn't speak.

"Well let's see. Your skin looks like hamburger, your gums are swollen, you're skin and bones, you smell like a chemical plant, and you're sweating like it's a hundred degrees out here. Should we look for tracks, tin foil and lighter, or bags of pills?"

"Chad, what is he talking about?"

"Rehab."

"Shut up. Who are you, anyway?" Chad shouted.

Across the lawn came Ann. She must have taken after her mother. She was neither tall nor slim like her father. Ann was no more than five-two and about 50 pounds overweight. Her tank top was too small, and the top of her sweat pants was rolled down, exposing a flabby belly like the white underside of a fish. She had small breasts, and her stomach protruded beyond them. Unlike her brother, she had clear, smooth skin and a nice color. Her eyes were light brown, almost golden. When she reached them, she planted her feet, and folded her arms across her chest, where they seemed to rest on her belly.

"What's going on?" Ann said, nervously uncrossing arms and pushing her hair behind her ears with both hands.

"Hello, Ann. My name is Cole Sage, and I'm talking to your father about your mother and her condition."

"My mother's dead!"

"He's referring to Ellen." Christopher still seemed stunned from Cole's exchange with Chad.

"She's not my mother!" Ann said angrily.

"Ellie is an old friend of mine, Ann."

"I want you off my property. Now!" Christopher shouted.

Cole reached up and took Christopher by the collar. He twisted the shirt around his hand until he was sure he had Christopher's attention. Christopher grabbed Cole's wrist but then released it when he looked into Cole's eyes.

Chad immediately dropped to his knees and sat cross-legged on the grass. He had a noticeable twitch in his right cheek.

"Are you going to behave and listen to what I have to say?"

"Just don't hurt my children."

Cole laughed. "It's your ass I'm about to kick, but nice sentiment anyway."

Christopher nodded. Cole released his shirt.

"I came here," Cole began, "because a dear friend of mine said she was in trouble. How she ever got tangled up with you three, I will never understand. She wanted my help, and now I see why. I will help her any way I can. First, I want to know where Erin is."

"I don't know." Christopher spoke first.

"Not good enough."

"Who cares about that stuck-up little bitch?" Ann snarled.

"I do and her mother does. Do you know where she is?"

"Hell, I hope," Ann sneered.

Chad chuckled. "Good one."

"How about you, zit face? You know where she is?"

Chad started to get up until he saw the look Cole was giving him. Then he twisted, pulled at the grass and re-crossed his legs. "I don't care where she is."

"I don't even know her, but somehow I think she is very lucky." Cole shook his head in disgust. "You had Ellie sign a power of attorney when she got sick. She wants it back," Cole said looking straight into Christopher's eyes. "She's going to seek legal counsel to help straighten out her affairs," Cole bluffed.

"And you think I'll hand it to you?"

"Could save you a lot of money and trouble."

"She has nothing."

"California law says she owns half of the proceeds from the house you sold. So, I guess that means this one, too."

"Without my support, they would've put her in County Hospital. She'd be a welfare case."

"And you would let that happen?"

"I have my family to look out for."

"She's no longer part of your family?" Cole said in amazement.

"She chose to go to the nursing home. She—"

Cole suddenly whipped the back of his hand across Christopher's face with all his strength. "Next time you lie to me, it will be my fist. Your treatment of Ellie is, is—" Cole couldn't think of a strong-enough comparison. "She gets sick, you dump her in a home. Hell is too good for you."

"Not that I owe you an explanation," Christopher began, "but I work hard for my money. It is *my* money and I will spend it how, and *on whom*, I choose. Ellen made her choice. I took her in. I gave her a home, and her spoiled brat, too. She's not even my kid. With everything I'd done for her, she chose Erin over me and my children. After that, I had no desire for her, no need for her. Frankly, what happens to her now is not my concern. I've let her stay on my insurance and haven't divorced her, just out of pity. If she wants to play the ingrate, I'll cut her off without a cent. Do you have any idea what it costs to care for her?"

"And Erin's inheritance? How do you justify that? It's from her grandparents, and as you so plainly admit, no relations of yours. You need to give up power of attorney. You are on dangerous ground here."

"This is none of your business."

"I've made it my business. Hear me and hear me well: I am not a sick woman confined to a wheelchair. I have little in life that matters to me more than those I love and who need my help. If you do anything to harm Ellie or make her life unpleasant, you will answer to me. God help you if you put me in that position. Am I clear?"

"Are you *threatening* me?" Christopher glared.

"I am *promising* you."

"You heard that. You're my witnesses." Christopher turned toward his children, who sat gazing up at him.

"A dope addict and a neurotic, overweight, nail-biting daddy's girl? They'll look great in court." Cole almost laughed.

"Get out of here! Now!" Christopher screamed.

Chad started to get up. Cole shot him a look, and he sat back down again. Ann was crying and biting her nails. Blood was running down the side of her palm from chewing too deep on her little finger.

"I'm going. I'll find Erin. You will give me power of attorney. You had better not go near Ellie. You abandoned her, and you're going to pay for that."

Cole started to leave, then stopped and turned back to face Christopher. "I can almost understand a self-centered pretty boy like you turning his back on a sick wife, I really can. God knows what you have turned these two into. But if you are any kind of a man at all, you'll get that kid into rehab. And look at her, look at her hands, her weight.

They both need help. Don't you see that? Or are you going to dump them, too?" Cole threw his hands up in a gesture of total exasperation, turned and walked away.

"He can't talk to you like that, Dad. I'm going to kick his ass!" Chad jumped to his feet and started toward Cole.

Christopher blocked Chad's movement with an arm across his son's chest, stopping him with little resistance. "Oh, for God's sake, Chad," Christopher said in a dismissive sigh, "you're not going to do anything."

Cole got in the car and sat looking out the window. Had he been wrong about Ellie? How could she have chosen to be in the lives of those people? The adrenaline that had been pumping so furiously was starting to subside. He felt a bit shaky as he turned the engine over.

"What a bunch!" Cole said aloud as he pulled away from the curb.

The meeting with Christopher had gone badly. He didn't expect to be welcomed with open arms, but it was worse than he imagined. There were issues far deeper than he thought. Christopher clearly resented whatever Ellie had told him about Cole. The daughter was a basket case and the boy was in a dangerous spiral. Christopher had rationalized what would be considered in any divorce proceeding as improper handling of community assets. It was, in his eyes, the natural course of things.

Cole realized he had no legal grounds to pursue Christopher or insist that he relinquish power of attorney. He probably had broken a couple of laws in the last few minutes, not the least of which was assault. He didn't understand the dynamic of their relationship. Ellie still held some regard, misguided as it was, for Christopher's keeping their marriage contract in her absence. Christopher, on the other hand, saw himself free to do as he pleased. This attitude, Cole was sure, started long before Ellie's illness.

There wasn't much else he could do today, so he decided to have a look around. In a town this size, Cole was sure gossip would be plentiful, and there would be much to learn about Allen Christopher.

SEVEN

The one consistent thing Cole kept hearing as he asked around town about the zoning, real estate, and the poorer side of town was reference to "the old preacher out there". Like the guy said, "When you ain't got nothin' you got nothin' to lose." Cole was pretty sure he knew where to find the preacher people kept referring to. Hopefully, he knew something that would shed some light on Malcor.

The gravel's crunch under the tires made a throaty sound as Cole pulled into the parking lot of the Friendly Tabernacle. Except for the splotches of graffiti paint-over, it looked just like he remembered. A remnant of World War II, the jumbo Quonset hut was a strange corrugated metal building—a perfect half dome with a flat front and back, like someone cut a tin can in half long ways and stuck it in the ground. The sign in the front sputtered and crackled its neon message, JESUS SAVES. A worn, faded canvas banner proclaimed REVIVAL NIGHTLY.

At one time, this odd little building was the neighborhood movie theater, home to several thousand Dust Bowl refugees. The Del Rio showed cowboy serials, pre-War "B" romances, and Buck Rogers-style science fiction. That was before the city passed an ordinance declaring the little gravel parking lot too small for the 200-seat tin movie palace. The fact that most people walked to the Del Rio was of little consequence to the city fathers, who didn't like the looks of the "Okie firetrap" anyway.

Then Edwin Thessalonians Bates came back to town. The little Quonset hut had sat empty for three years when the traveling Evangelist saw a "For Sale" sign nailed to the front door. To him it was a sign from God and, upon this rock, Brother Bates was going to build his church. Not one to take "no" for an answer and certainly not one to hesitate to speak on behalf of the Almighty in His absence, Brother Bates struck quite a deal: Not only did he get the building for no money down (30 years before infomercials) but upon assuring the owner his "Eternal real estate holdings" would be determined by the outcome of the transaction, there was also to be no payment due for six months. Nearly 40 years later, E. T. Bates was the unofficial mayor of "the poor side of town."

Tonight, about a dozen cars occupied the lot. At the rear of the lot, under the single light bulb that glowed over the back door, sat a red 10-year-old Cadillac. Brother Bates would be present for the services this evening. The gravel crunched underfoot, and Cole made his way to the front, remembering years before when his grandmother would take him to her church as if it were St. Peter's in

Rome. Of course, she would have never compared this sanctified ground to "the dwelling place of the Scarlet Woman." Nevertheless, she had puffed out her bountiful chest, lodged her well-worn Bible under her arm, and led them in to wait upon the Lord.

"Cole, get ready for a blessing!" she had told him. "The fire is falling, and His Spirit has come to dwell in this place! Blessed be the name of the Lord! Hallelujah!"— before they even got out of the parking lot.

The front of the tabernacle still sported poster boxes from the old Del Rio. Now instead of "Cattle Queen of Montana" and "Lady of New Orleans" one sheets, there were hand-lettered butcher paper signs reading:

Services Nightly 7:00

Lay Your Needs Before the Lord!

Miracles! Healing! Prophetic Messages!

Edwin T. Bates, Evangelist

Not much had changed.

The lobby still had the thick red carpet of the Del Rio, now threadbare in spots. Silver duct tape held some of the seams together, and dark sections told the tale of a leaking roof. The snack bar now displayed tapes, books, and pamphlets by the featured Evangelist. Cole wondered if Guinness had a record for the longest running nightly revival.

"Good evening," chirped a woman in her 80s. Her hair was curled tightly and held in place by a thin black hairnet. It almost glowed from the bluing that once made the white brighter but now had dyed her thinning hair a pale azure tint.

"Good evening to you!" Sage said brightly.

"Your first time with us?" Her pale gray eyes sparkled behind frameless gold wire glasses. Memories of his grandmother swept over Cole as he took in the old lady smell of flowered soaps and inexpensive dime store perfume, probably purchased before he was born. Her dress was a shiny rayon floral print, just like his grandmother used to wear, and was accented with a yellow-and-orange-colored glass broach. True to his memory, her feet were squeezed into a pair of black lace-up shoes that her ankles overran. Sage smiled at her warmly.

"Have you been around here long, ma'am?" *Ma'am? Where had that come from?* He hadn't called anyone "ma'am" in 30 years.

"Oh mercy," she reflected, "about 35 years, I expect. I came to one of Brother Bates' meetings the first week he was here. Mercy me, that's more like 40! My husband, Jack, was still working at the cannery when I first got the baptism. Mercy, mercy, he's been gone 12 years now. Emphysema. Lord love him. He wasn't saved 'til the last, but we'll walk the streets of glory together now."

"Maybe you knew my grandma, Zelma Park?"

"Mercy sakes, I loved Sister Park! You're her grandson! How long has she been gone now? Oh, how I loved to hear her daughter Minnie sing and play the guitar! Mercy, mercy, 'Mansion Over the Hill Top.' Oh, what a blessing they were!"

The thought of his Aunt Minnie playing guitar and singing brought an uncontrollable chuckle from Cole. The longstanding family joke was the way his dad would say, "Minnie, I'd rather hear you sing than eat. I've heard you eat!" At that, she would always slap her brother on the shoulder and squeal "Yoooou."

The last time he saw her was at a hamburger stand when he was in college. She bought a Coke and, when the girl handed it to her through the window, the foam had receded to leave the cup's top inch-and-a-half without soda. Minnie smiled and said as only a 77-year-old Pentecostal spinster could, "You must be a Baptist."

"Why, yes I am, how did you know?"

"Because your cup's not full!" Minnie said as she turned and winked at me.

The poor girl never knew what hit her. She knew her theology had just been insulted, but she wasn't quite sure how. As Cole watched his aunt cross the parking lot and take a seat on the bus bench, he knew the performance had been for him. Minnie had a stroke not long after that and lived out her days in a convalescent hospital full of other old men and women unable to move or speak. Cole had gone to see her with his parents once. She had just lain, eyes wide, lifeless, staring at the ceiling. He never went back. When she died, he got her guitar, a 1950 Harmony Monterey.

"Gomes is my name." The words brought Cole back to the smiling face in front of him. "Kate Gomes."

Cole took the hand offered him and said softly, " Cole Sage is mine." He was suddenly struck with emotion. Perhaps it was the mortality of everything around him. Maybe he just remembered too much. He slipped past the old woman and through the swinging doors with their big circular windows and into the sanctuary.

Everything was just the same. The gold glitter cross hanging from picture frame wire still hung in an unplanned tilt toward the pulpit, kind of like a model airplane on a kid's ceiling. The pulpit with its stained plywood still proudly bore the three crosses cut from pine and stained walnut. Two pots of silk flowers wrapped in bright green and red foil and tied with satin bows stood in front of the pulpit. The stage was covered in the same thick red carpet of the foyer and proudly displayed a metallic blue set of Slingerland drums, a Fender bass amp, a Hammond B3 organ, and a row of acoustic and electric guitars. Off to one side sat a small beige tweed Fender amplifier that probably hadn't been moved in years.

Scattered throughout this musty auditorium were about 50 or 60 people, some chatting, some staring, and some just there to get into the air conditioned building and out of their sweltering houses for an hour or two. Cole took a seat on an aisle about three-fourths back. There was no sense trying to see Bates until after the service. The Reverend had his hand in a little of everything in this part of town. Not that he had any direct power or influence, but he was a force to be reckoned with. If there was something to know, he knew it.

The tabernacle had been feeding the homeless out of the back door since Bates came to town. When the weather turned bad, the aisles and foyer were turned into a makeshift shelter. There was a trust and sense that Brother Bates was watching out for "the least of these." His love for the lowest of the low was real, and on more than one occasion, he had raised his booming voice at meetings when the city council members thought some new ordinance or other would help clean up the streets. He usually won, and the street people knew it.

He could help the police without being a snitch, and he could just as easily look the other way when he felt like it. He had an Ecclesiastical sense of right and wrong and would not be swayed left or right once his mind was made up.

Cole nervously flipped the pages of the worn hymnal from the rack on the pew. Cole had never quite got religion. He knew there was a force out there much greater than himself, but what was he to do with it? That was the question that had always been with him. He was raised in a very conservative God-fearing, Bible-believing, church-going, and almost-Pentecostal-but-not-quite family.

On some level, he believed, but he had just seen and heard too many things that didn't agree with what the folks sitting around him would call his "spirit." As the organ softly played and the faithful quietly chatted, Cole thought of all his questions about this place and a dozen others he had been to.

The dull hum of the ancient air conditioner and the syrupy lull of the organ took Cole far away to memories long forgotten. He thought of preachers and songs, pulpit flowers and the sharp creased edges of Sunday bulletins, and he closed his eyes and let his memories take him away.

At 13, Cole had heard a traveling preacher talk on the subject, "The Day the Moon Turns Red." For an hour and a half, the man in the navy blue suit and blazing white shirt spun tales from the Old Testament prophets, enthralling and terrifying his Sunday night crowd. With the authority of Samuel of old, he made his case for the end of the world. The sign would be the face of the moon turning scarlet like the sins of man. He went on to explain that you had better repent or you would be left behind in the horrible day of the Lord. The thing that terrified young Cole was that the moon might turn red that very year! For several weeks, without revealing what he was doing, he would go out in the back yard and gaze up at the moon. On the nights the orb hung in the night sky a pale white, he went back inside relieved that he had a little more time on earth. The thing that sent him into a real panic was the night he went out and there was no moon.

As calmly as he could, with his breath shallow and slow, he asked his father where the moon was.

"Dark of the moon. Only the people on the other side of the world can see it," his father had replied.

What if it were red? Cole had thought.

Time passed and several full moons occurred before Cole forgot the prophet's message, only to remember it one night driving home when he was 16. It hadn't happened. A slip of faith. A false prophet.

Near his 17th birthday, a revival was planned at his family's church. Cole was asked to run a closed-circuit TV camera so the overflow crowds could watch in grainy black-and-white in the fellowship hall. Cole was so proud he could hardly sleep the night before. The big day arrived. Several hundred people packed the main auditorium and, indeed, seats were occupied in the overflow.

It was like no church service he had ever seen. The Evangelist had brought in professional lighting, sound, and a full band, just like on TV—guitars, bass, drums, piano, organ, horns, and four black backup singers. Suddenly, the room was cast into total darkness. A drum roll slowly built, then a voice like the clap of thunder from above announced: "Brothers and sisters, saints and sinners, open your hearts, open your minds tonight, you will be a witness to a miracle! Tonight! Right here, the fire will fall from heaven and God will anoint his servant. The lame will walk, the blind will see, the deaf shall hear! Raise your hands, raise your voice! Welcome God's man of the hour, God's man for America, God's man for *you*, the man who will revive this city, Ben Tanner!"

The lights exploded in white light! The band erupted into a crescendo of "This is My Story, This is My Song, Praising My Savior All the Day Long." From the right side of the stage came a man in a red velvet, gold-zippered jumpsuit. From the wide bell-bottoms, you could barely see the tips and heels of a pair of flamenco boots. His arms were raised high over his head. A Bible in one hand and the other, fingers spread wide. "Give God a handclap!" he shouted, and the audience was on its feet!

The band blasted hot rocking rhythms that no band in Las Vegas could have touched. The people clapped, stomped, and sang. Old ladies with their hair in tight buns on the back of their heads twirled and danced a Holy Ghost jig in the aisles, eyes closed, hands reaching for heaven. Cole didn't know what to think. He had been fighting a pitched battle with his parents over rock-and-roll since the Beatles were on "Ed Sullivan." Now, he was peering through his black-and-white lens at a full-blown rock-and-roll concert. He had a vision of the Israelites dancing around the golden calf in "The Ten Commandments."

For nearly an hour, Tanner led the crowd in old hymns, favorite choruses, and new "songs of praise." Each song built on the last, the band sailed on a sea of bass and drums. Building, ever building, each song louder than the one before, if that were possible. Men Cole had never seen out of their Sunday best were peeling off suit coats and tearing off ties. Women who were always dressed to the nines, every bouffant hair sprayed carefully in place, now sweating, swaying, and moving like go-go girls. Cole laughed out loud several times. At first, he caught himself remembering where he was, but later realized no one could hear him and certainly no one was watching him.

With a wave of his hand and a signal to the band, Ben Tanner took the pulpit. "Give God a handclap!" The place again roared with applause. He raised his hands like Moses over the Red Sea and said, "Please be seated."

For just short of 30 minutes, Ben Tanner pranced, stomped, and waved his Bible. For the life of him, though, Cole couldn't remember a single thing he ever said. What he did remember was very clear: At the end of his sermon Tanner called for the sick, lame, blind, afflicted in any way spiritually, physically, or financially to come to the front of the auditorium. "The power of God is in this place!" Tanner declared and urged those in need to make their way forward to get a "double dose" of what God had in store for them.

Out of the door on each side of the stage came men and women with a stack of black clothes about the size of a bath towel draped across their arms, standing at the ready like a small army of waiters and waitresses. As people came forward by the dozens, the band struck up Tanner's theme song, "This is My Story, This is My Song." As the audience sang and swayed, Tanner made his way through the throng massing at the front of the stage. His mic was turned off as he touched and spoke to various people across the front of the group.

On some preordained cue, the mic came back on, and Tanner began muttering and sputtering out something that appeared to be "speaking in tongues." Then, to the amazement of everyone in the building, he spun around on his heels and slapped his palm to a rather large woman's forehead. Down she went. Like an old-time silent comedy, bam!, flat on her back with a slight bounce. One of the waiting attendants ran up and covered her from the waist down with one of the black cloths. Bam!, bam!, bam!, one person after another was "slain in the spirit" as Tanner continued to slam his palm against forehead after forehead. When the last person lay flat on their back on the floor, some babbling in an unknown tongue, some twitching and trembling, some dead still, Tanner threw his hands over his head and cried, "Give God a handclap" and—just like Cole would later see James Brown do many times—Tanner's knees seemed to buckle. He was grabbed and supported by one of his assistants, the band kicked the volume up two notches, and Tanner was led off to a side door. Elvis had left the building.

The Ben Tanner Revival went on for 36 weeks. Cole's family gave up after the second week. His father never said anything, but Cole got the distinct impression he wasn't buying it. Such showmanship didn't play well with his father's conservative outlook and demeanor. Cole was replaced as closed-circuit cameraman at the end of week six when the crowds and money dictated that actual TV cameras be brought in and operated by "professionals." Cole was unceremoniously relieved of duty.

The month-long revival that ended up lasting almost nine stopped as abruptly as Cole's camera job. Turned out Ben Tanner had an eye for the boys. One afternoon, before, during, or after the sound check and band rehearsal, Tanner was found with the very effeminate Teen Choir pianist, a pimply faced 16-year-old that the guys all called Larry the Fairy. It seems the Pastor of Visitation paid a visit to the fireside room and found Larry bent over the back of a couch, pants around his ankles and Tanner giving him what the English might call an old-fashioned "buggering."

The revival ended that night with Tanner announcing

that the Lord was calling him to Orlando. Larry was swept off to Bible School in Kentucky. The few in the know decided not to let this "sin of the flesh" destroy all the good that had been done. Cole found out when a family friend told his dad over coffee and didn't know that Cole was reading in his favorite spot on the other side of the kitchen snack bar. The Great Ben Tanner Revival of 1969 was never mentioned again. A second slip of faith, another false prophet.

Three years later, as a college student, the final slip of faith occurred. Cole had found great comfort and excitement in the College Bible Study at the little Assembly of God Church not far from the college. A big deal and much to-do was made about a guest speaker who was to speak on Satan and Witchcraft in Modern-Day America. The announcements promised startling revelation as to how the devil used rock music, art, and the movies to lure young people into witchcraft and devil worship.

In a burst of uncharacteristic Evangelical zeal, Cole invited his friend Chuck and a girl named Robin from his art class. Robin had often told those around her that she was a white witch. She often described Wiccan rituals and her worship of trees. *If anybody ever needed to get "saved" it's her,* Cole had thought. To his surprise, she accepted the invitation and promised to come to the meeting.

Cole and Chuck sat near the back on the side so they could see people as they arrived. The speaker was introduced but no sign of Robin. The speaker began a history of witchcraft. He talked about Anton LeVay and the Satanic Bible. At 7:15, in walked Robin, her boyfriend, and another couple Cole didn't know. The speaker seemed to watch them take their seats. He appeared to lose his place and shuffled through his notes. The speaker began to sweat. He stammered and twice took sips of water from a glass on the pulpit. The next few minutes, the man rambled disjointedly about the history of witchcraft, revival in America and something to do with the meek inheriting the earth. The conviction of his talk and the boldness of his speech seemed to diminish as he went.

About fifteen minutes after they came in, Robin and her friends got up and filed out. As she passed Cole, Robin made a hand gesture he didn't recognize. It was a fist with her index and little fingers extended. Years later, he would learn that this gesture—now a staple at heavy metal concerts—was "the goat's head" or sign for the devil. Even without knowing its meaning, the gesture and the look in her eyes gave him a shiver.

As the back doors clanged shut, the speaker wiped his brow with his handkerchief and said, "There has been a repressive spirit in this place. I have never been so attacked by the powers of darkness. It has been lifted, and now I feel I can go on. Let us pray."

The man at the pulpit lifted his hands heavenward and beseeched his Creator to give him strength to finish his talk. Cole felt he had lost the battle. The idol of Baal had not been toppled, the Red Sea had not parted, and this man seemed to have shrunk. Where was his God? Was it his lack of faith, or had good failed to triumph over evil? How could the college girl witch have reduced this warrior against Satan and witchcraft to this sweaty, quivering coward that stood before him? Cole knew if God were indeed up there, He was embarrassed by the lack of faith in His mighty power this little man professed. Cole left that night and never returned.

"Hallelujah!" a voice that shook the tin walls jolted Cole from his memories. There he was, older, a bit thinner and grayer, but still a giant of a man. Brother E.T. Bates was about to begin the service.

For 60 minutes, Bates shouted, stomped, whispered, sang phrases from old hymns, joked, cried, and pled the blood of Jesus on the sinners in the pews. He was a wonder to watch. His delivery was honed to a razor's edge from years of services just like this one. There was no emotion, no fear, no hope of glory left untouched. He knew all the buttons to push and in what order. When he pulled his huge white handkerchief from his breast pocket and wiped the sweat from his scarlet face, it punctuated the point he was making as no words could ever do.

The closing story of the man who had sat in the third row from the back, left hardly a dry eye in the place. It told how many years ago, a man sat in the third row from the back and struggled with the decision to go forward and be saved. "He knew he needed the Lord! That small voice tugged at his heart. His hands sweated and his heart pounded! Just like many of you tonight. He knew, hallelujah, that God was calling him into the family. 'Behold I stand at the door and knock,' Jesus said, oh, hallelujah. This fellow heard the knock, but did he answer, my friends? Oh no, he stifled his feelings, he blocked the calling of the Holy Ghost. 'Tomorrow,' he said, 'tomorrow I will be saved.' But how many of us know if we will have a tomorrow? I remember the look of joy on his mother's face as the young man stood to his feet. I remember how she looked, hallelujah, thinking her wayward boy had come home. I remember how she saw her family restored and her prodigal's name written in the Lamb's Book of Life, hallelujah! But oh, my dear ones, I, too, remember the sorrow and heartbreak as he turned and made his way out the back door. I remember that mother burying her face in her hand and sobbing, knowing her baby, her boy, had turned his back on the Savior's gift of eternal life. I shed a tear as well at that scene, beloved, I had done everything this poor preacher could do to show him the way, but he turned his back on the Word. I wish I could tell you he turned and took the Savior's hand, I wish I could tell you a story of a life redeemed, I wish I could tell you of a family raising a new generation walking in the path of righteousness. But I can't.

"You see, that young man left this place that night, he left having heard the small soft voice of the Holy Ghost, he left that night with the invitation song still ringing in his ears, but he didn't go home, no sir, it breaks my heart to tell you, he sought out his old friends, he sought out those so practiced in sin, so controlled by worldly things, and Satan was right there to welcome him back! To drown that voice deep in his heart, he joined his friends in drink, he joined in their laughter, and to dull the aching need to the Savior, he got drunk!

"When the bar closed that night, he staggered to his car. Barely able to stand, he climbed behind the wheel! Swerving back and forth across the lanes of the highway, he never saw the car stranded on the side of the road. He never saw the father trying to start the stalled engine, he never saw the mother gently rocking her precious baby in the front seat. He never saw the three little ones peacefully sleeping in the back. But, the saddest thing of all, my dear friends, he never saw how the life was crushed out of them when his speeding car hit them from behind, exploding in a ball of fire. That beautiful family snatched from this life and sent into eternity. Now, I don't know their hearts, I don't know if they were ready to meet the Savior on the streets of glory. I pray with all my heart they were, and that they are seated at the feet of Jesus tonight, hallelujah! But I do know one thing: I stood by the side of a casket, I stood by the still silent body of a young man who had sat on the third row from the back, and cried tears of sorrow. I cried for that mother. I cried for the choice that young man made, because they would never have a reunion in heaven. For he had made the choice to refuse the gift of eternal life.

"Don't you do what that young man did, my friend, don't you refuse the Savior. As our dear sister Maria begins to play 'Just As I Am,' you, too, slip from your seat, I want you to answer God's call and come down to this old-fashioned altar and meet the Savior. You know who you are, you know you need the Savior, come on, come pray with me tonight. And don't be like that young man in the third row from the back."

As the organ began to play, Bates walked to the edge of the platform and stood, eyes closed, hands raised heavenward. People began to stream forward. Some to be saved, some for the third or fourth time, but they came forward. Cole sat and watched as old men and women made their way forward and put their hands on the shoulders of those kneeling at the front.

Bates prayed, over and over, for those who had heeded the call. There was a rousing round of "hallelujah"s and "praise the Lord"s, and then the meeting was over. A loud joyous rendition of "In the Sweet Bye and Bye" boomed from the band. They had returned to the platform unnoticed as Bates slipped through the side door.

Cole made his way down the aisle and shook hands with several people. "Lord Bless You this Week" was offered by at least six. He felt a bit apprehensive about using the platform door, but he didn't want to run the risk not being able to find Bates. The door opened into a hallway lit only by a small fixture in the ceiling. It should've had two bulbs but one must've been burned out. Cole could hear the sound of coughing coming from an open door down the hall.

"Good evening," Cole said softly as he tapped on the doorframe.

Inside, Edwin Bates stood, suit coat off, pouring hot water from a kettle heated on a hot plate into a mug. "Good evening. Cup of tea? The old throat isn't what it used to be," Bates said with a slightly questioning smile.

"No thanks. My name is Sage, Cole Sage. Mind if I ask you a few questions?"

"That kind of comes with the territory. What is it, son?"

"I understand you have been speaking out against the Malcor project," Cole began.

"Now, see here, I will not be threatened or intimidated by you or anyone else! I'm an old man and—"

Cole cut him off. "Whoa, whoa, whoa, I'm on your side! I'm just trying to get some information."

"I'm so sorry," Bates said with embarrassment. "I'm getting a little edgy. Been getting threatening messages left on my answering machine. Some pretty nasty letters, too. I guess I look at everybody a little suspect lately. I'm sorry." Bates set the mug of tea on the table. "Have a seat. Let's start over."

"I work for *The Sentinel* in Chicago."

"My, my, I had no idea that our little problem drew national attention," Bates puffed up a bit.

"Well, not exactly. You see, I'm in town helping a friend with some legal troubles and—"

"You're a lawyer, too?"

"Nope," Cole smiled, "but she hasn't got anybody else. I'm kind of pushy and not afraid to stick my nose in things. That's why I'm here. Do you know a guy named Christopher, Allen Christopher?"

"He's a real estate agent. Represents Malcor. Been buying up every house he can get his hands on 'round the airport. I hear he has one of the zoning guys in his pocket. That's probably rumor."

"How did you get involved in all this, Reverend?"

"Please, call me Ted. I'm just a country preacher. No college, no degree, just love the Lord."

"All right." Cole felt very uncomfortable being on first name basis with E.T. Bates. It seemed to take away the aura, like being a kid again and seeing your favorite teacher in their bathing suit at the lake.

"A lot of my flock comes from the airport district. I was born and partly raised right there on the corner of Hedges and Kent Streets. Our house was originally downtown. It was a little diner called the Three Little Pigs, and my dad bought the building for $100 and had it moved onto our lot. That was in 1934." Bates realized he was drifting, "Sorry. I get off track sometimes. Anyway, lots of folks out there have been there since the Depression. They own their places, humble as they may be, free and clear. Place to live out their lives. If this zoning change happens, they will get pushed out. Not by choice but by their greedy kids, relatives, and bad counsel."

"They don't have to sell, I mean these aren't 'forced' sales are they?" Cole wasn't getting where Bates was going.

"Well, once one or two take the bait, the others will follow. Trouble is, a big block of houses have been bought up over the years by William Brecker."

"I know the name. Real estate agent? Got his own office? That guy?"

"Yessir! Becker must own 50 or 60 houses in the district. If he sells, we got problems. If the zoning changes, we got problems. He's got a lot of pull downtown and 'for the good of the community' the city might just force sales of the holdouts."

"How can they do that? Aren't the deeds honored under the old zoning ordinances?"

"Not if the properties around them are torn down to make way for future construction. Then we have part ghost town, part neighborhood. It will happen, but then what? These little houses aren't worth much. Even if they are paid for, what will that dab of money get for them? This is the cheapest section of town. These folks won't be able to pay the deposit to get into one of those retirement centers on the north side. The renters will be okay. They'll just find another place. But it's the older folks I worry about, and that's who I'm fightin' for."

"So, Christopher approaches the homeowners about selling?"

"Yes, Lord forgive me, and there's a crook if I ever saw one. 'By your fruits ye shall be known' and his are plenty rotten. He has told people every cock-and-bull story you can imagine. He even had one old fella who was nearly blind sign a sales agreement and told him it was a refusal letter! This man has no shame. These folks can't afford a lawyer, so they turn to me and a few of the pastors in the district to see what we can do, and I can tell you, it's not much. Malcor's got big bucks and bigger plans, and God help anybody who gets in their way. Check the record for fires lately? Dramatic increase in electrical and attic fires. That's no accident. I know what you're thinking, and you're right, we can't prove it, but doesn't mean it isn't so. As a newspaperman, you should know that."

"The thing I don't get is the zoning people. They can't just go from residential to commercial on a whim. There are laws governing things like this."

"There surely are. That's our biggest problem. Back in the Depression when this area of town got started, it was a tent city of Dust Bowl refugees. Bottomland by the river that nobody much wanted. So, willing to make a cheap easy buck, a couple of the farmers who owned the land—Bronson and Kerr by name—rather than kick off the squatters, decided to sell. They broke the land into lots and sold it off. No zoning laws back then, and who cared about the Okies anyway? Everyone figured they would drift out just as they drifted in. Some of the folks were tradespeople back home, though, and decided to set up shop out here. My dad was a blacksmith, and his shop was next to our house until he died, and that was during the Korean War. There were mechanics shops, grocery stores, churches, and a veterinary hospital. Later on, there were welders, cabinet shops, all kinds of businesses. There's still the big lumberyard on Park Street. No one ever bothered to zone the area. Then it was incorporated into the city back in the '50s. Nobody paid any attention. That's why there's no sidewalks or fire hydrants. Just poor folks with no say-so downtown. Malcor has petitioned to have the whole area east of the river zoned industrial commercial. Since it isn't zoned at all, it doesn't really have to be changed. Word is, Christopher has been spreading some money around downtown to get it done quicker."

"Doesn't sound too hopeful for the homeowners. But bribery is still a crime, even if it is a done deal." Cole realized there wasn't much more Bates could offer.

"We need some press on this thing. Can you help?" Bates knew the answer before he asked.

"I'm not sure it would help, being written up in *The Sentinel.* Maybe the *Ledger*, huh?" Cole stood to go. "I appreciate your time, Brother Bates. I'll let you know if I find anything out that will help."

The big man stood and extended his hand. "I'll be praying for you."

"Thanks. Say one for my friend Ellie, too, would ya? She needs it a lot more than me." Cole thought if there was anyone worthy of God's ear, it was Bates, and welcomed the help.

"We all need prayer, son. God bless you real good."

"I hope so."

EIGHT

The Zoning Department was housed in a marble mausoleum referred to as the Court House. It actually served as the home to most city offices. The City Hall, built in the early '50s, was a shortsighted project built too small even before construction was finished. The functioning Court House had moved to a new building in the late '60s while the old building filled with the overflow from City Hall.

Green marble went up the wall four feet high and seemed to make the long hall nearly come together at the far end. Cole loved old buildings and the coolness that the marble floor and walls seemed to give off. The double doors were frosted glass and said "Zoning Department, Myron G. Hearst, Commissioner" in gold leaf lettering. A small piece of paper was taped to the left door reading "Please Use Other Side" in block letters with a blue felt tip pen. The door whooshed as it opened into a large office filled with old-fashioned gray metal desks, all of which were piled high with stacks of papers. A young woman with a distinct lack of chin and large dangling earrings sat behind a sign on the counter that read "Judy Oscar, Receptionist."

"Hi Judy." Cole smiled. "Cool earrings! Did you make them?" Cole could see upon a closer look that they had been somebody's idea of a craft project. They looked like they were made out of Play-Doh and macaroni, then splashed with nail polish.

"No, my niece did. Like 'em?"

"Love 'em!" Cole lied.

"What can I do for you today?"

Cole held up his press credentials. "I would like to speak with Mr. Hearst if I may."

"No can do. Mr. Hearst is out on medical leave." Then in a whisper Judy said, "Brain tumor, probably won't make it. It's really sad. He was so nice."

"I'm sorry."

"Mr. Elias is the Acting Commissioner. He's in."

"He'll do." Cole matched Judy's whisper. "What's he like?"

Judy wrinkled her nose like something smelled bad. "Let's just say I like Mr. Hearst a lot more."

"Got it. Young or old?"

"'Bout 35, I guess. Changing everything, nobody likes him. Likes to be the boss." Judy sighed.

"I'll let him. Wanna tell him I'm here?" Cole smiled.

Judy picked up the phone and punched in three numbers. The conversation was mostly one sided. Judy made faces and winked at Cole during the pauses. She hung up the phone and pointed at the far corner of the room.

"Just follow your nose." Judy smiled.

"Why, does he stink?" Cole grinned and went through the swinging half door at the end of the counter. Judy was still laughing as Cole made his way to the back of the office.

A tall man with thinning hair and the scars of adolescent acne stood in the door of the office. He wore a white shirt with a thin black tie, loose at the neck. He watched Cole as he made his way through the maze of desks.

"Mr. Sage," the thin man said, smiling. "Sven Elias. How can I help?"

"Not sure you can, I'm just on a fact-finding mission. I sure appreciate your taking time to see me."

"My pleasure, please come in." Elias gave a wide genuine smile showing the faint shadows of the new-style clear braces.

"I was sorry to hear about Mr. Hearst. Big shoes to fill," Cole bluffed. "But I hear you run a tight ship. Good for you. Can't be easy."

Elias frowned and cleared his throat. "I'm doing my best. A lot of resistance to somebody new taking over, you know how it is. Myron Hearst was loved by everybody. Did you know he had been Commissioner for 33 years? Lot of pain people don't know how to deal with, so the new guy is the easiest target. I understand how it works, but that doesn't make the transition any smoother. You know what they say, 'It's lonely at the top!'"

"You look like you're up to it." Cole liked this man.

"Thanks, so what brings you in?"

"Well, it is this Malcor thing," Cole began slowly. "What's the straight dope on this zoning change? There are so many stories going around I thought I would come to the one who really knows what's going on." Cole waited; Elias showed signs of needing somebody to talk to.

"Oh, boy." Elias took a deep breath, stood up, and crossed the room to close the door."You're from Chicago, Mr. Sage?"

"Please, call me Cole. Yes, and I'm a Cubbies fan, no jokes please."

"No jokes. Look, I'm a small town guy. Went to the community college and a small Methodist College in Indiana. Big cities are like foreign countries to me. Can I ask you something?"

Cole nodded.

"Are there still mobsters in the big eastern cities?" Elias was dead serious.

"Well, yeah, I guess. Why do you ask?" Cole sensed real uneasiness and it wasn't from Elias reading the papers.

"I've heard that the Malcor people are connected with mob guys. Do you know anything about that?"

"It was said that they fix union problems. Organized crime has a long history of union involvement. The mob was the money and muscle behind them. Why?" Cole wondered where this was going.

"This is off the record. That's what it's called, right? When you can't print what I say?" Elias said earnestly.

"Yes, that's what it's called." Cole smiled.

"I was approached by a local real estate salesman." Elias paused, staring at Cole for several seconds, while trying to decide whether to go on. "He tried to bribe me. He said he wanted the zoning changed and that his friends at Malcor could be very generous." Elias's face flushed a bit.

"Allen Christopher?"

"Do you think he's connected to the mob?"

Cole looked at the young man in the out-of-date tie and realized this was not the story he had come looking for. Christopher was more than the sum of his shady parts.

This wasn't stealing sales or—bad as it was—hustling old people. This was felony criminal intent. There was something more than the bribe, though. Elias was not just worried, he was scared.

"Sven, I don't think you need to worry about the mob. I don't see Christopher as a mob type, do you?" Cole tried to sound reassuring.

Sven Elias needed a friend, and Cole's big-city confidence and matter-of-fact way of dismissing Christopher made Cole the friend Elias had been praying for. Elias was honest and inexperienced—a combination Cole was smart enough to know was dangerous.

"You're right, that's right." In that moment, Elias decided to let Cole have it all. "Why is he trying to bribe me then? It is illegal to even suggest payment to a city official. I feel guilty just having been offered the diamonds."

"Diamonds, what diamonds?" Cole was caught completely off guard.

"I didn't mention that? Let me start over." Elias suddenly stood. "He brought out a package of diamonds from his briefcase," he recalled excitedly, "and you never saw such sparkle." Elias took a small waxy paper envelope from his top desk drawer. "He said he would give me this diamond if I would go to the City Council meeting and propose the zoning change. He said when the zoning was recorded as commercial/industrial. It was all mine! I nearly peed my pants. Who else but a gangster gets little envelopes of loose diamonds? You should have seen them! I bet there was maybe 50 in the little wax paper thing they were in. Any one of them was bigger than my wife's engagement ring, and that cost me almost $3,000. And you know what?" Elias lowered his voice, trying to stress the importance of his next statement. "I saw, gosh, I don't know, maybe 10 more of those little packets in his briefcase. That's a lot of money, Mr. Sage."

Cole wasn't quite sure how to respond. He just sat quietly and watched Elias thinking as he squeezed the top of his well-worn leather chair. There was a lot more to Allen Christopher than he had thought. Where *did* he get a bunch of diamonds? Why the bribe? Anybody in real estate, industry, even with rental properties knows a zoning change is easy to get done.

"Sven, who have you told about this?"

"My wife Karen and now you. There aren't too many people around here I feel I could confide in. We only moved here three months ago. And I'm not exactly Mr. Popular."

"Let me ask you something. Bribe or not, what was going to be done about the airport district zoning?"

"Nothing. Legally, Malcor or anybody else could do just about whatever they wanted out there, provided it doesn't violate any state environment or safety laws. There actually isn't any zoning designation. So many different kinds of usage have all been grandfathered in that unless the whole area was scraped clean, there's no way to get it straightened out."

"Who knows about the status of the zoning?" Cole asked.

"It's no secret. Public records are open to anyone."

"I know, but is it public knowledge? What I mean is, does everybody know it's a mess?"

"Probably not. It's not a very desirable area as I see it. Sales out there are usually small—old houses or duplexes. I checked with records, and there have been no new businesses started or old ones sold in over five years." Elias had done his homework.

"So, there is a good chance the Malcor people wouldn't know it from a casual visit. They would entrust their real estate representative and lawyers to investigate usage, permits, and stuff like that, right?"

"Probably." Elias frowned, not quite following Cole's line of thought.

"Christopher stands to make a bundle if he can put together a major industrial complex. A bribe to make it look like he can get things done in town would be a good investment, for him, right? So the zoning is a moot point. It wouldn't affect the homeowners or small businesses that are already there. The Malcor people see Christopher as the guy who can get things done. If he can bribe you, necessary or not, on paper he comes through looking like he has people on the "inside", implying he can handle *anything* that comes up, right? I think the zoning is just a way to make Christopher appear to be a big shot. I bet if you check the records, a guy like Christopher has made lots of sales out in the airport district. He knows the zoning situation going in. Makes a big deal of it and figures he can seal the deal with industrial zoning for the project. You with me?" Cole realized he had been thinking out loud.

"I think so." Elias knew he was out of his depth.

"I have an idea. Don't mention the bribe thing to anybody for a while. Let me do some sniffing around. I think this might just be a piece in a puzzle. Let's see if we can figure out the whole picture before we do anything. What do you think?" Cole knew this was a hot potato that Elias would love to toss to somebody else.

"You mean the diamond."

"Yeah, that just doesn't smell right. Where does a guy

like Christopher get a bunch of diamonds? From what I gather, he's successful, in a lowbrow kind of way, but at the price of popularity. The bribery thing can wait for a bit. Just sit tight and let's see what else we can find out. Here's a number where I can be reached. If he shows up again, let me know. Just stall him, tell him whatever you want but don't agree or disagree, get it?" Cole stood and handed Elias a piece of paper he had taken off a desk pad and scribbled his number on.

"I tell you, Cole, I am just not used to this kind of thing. I really didn't mean to dump all this on you. I sure appreciate your help, I don't have anyone I can really talk to."

"I think dealing with Mr. Christopher will suit both our purposes. If we do this right, it will bolster your credibility with the doubters around here." Cole jerked his thumb over his shoulder, signifying the office behind him. "See ya around."

"Thanks."

"And Sven, don't worry. I've helped trap rats a lot bigger than Christopher." Cole made his way out of the outer office and through the swinging door.

"You see what I meant?" Judy waited for the conspiratorial reinforcement from Cole.

"No, actually I think you got the guy all wrong. Don't let that nerdy look fool you. You've got a bit of a tiger back there. He certainly showed me what's what. Lot more to your Mr. Elias than meets the eye. If I were you, I'd let him get to know you. Could pay off big time for a talented girl like you." Cole knew a butt kisser when he saw one and with this new information, Judy was all ready to pucker up for her new boss.

"You think so?" Judy said, somewhat amazed.

"Hey, in Chicago, I have to deal with hard cases like Elias all the time." Cole was afraid he was laying it on a bit thick, but Sven needed all the help he could get.

"Thanks, I had no idea."

"No reason you would, my dear, no reason you would." Cole winked and walked away.

Out on the sidewalk, Cole flipped open his cell phone and hit "7" for Precinct 51. "Lieutenant Harris, please." Cole never called his friend's cell phone.

After what seemed like a hundred rings, a familiar voice said, "Harris."

"Tom, it's Cole."

"Hey, where you been? I thought we were playing poker Friday night?"

"You won't believe it, I'm back in my ol' home town." Cole tried to sound lighthearted.

"Why? What's wrong?" Harris knew his friend far too well to know this wasn't a case of homesickness.

"It's Ellie. She—"

"Ellie? You kidding me? What's the matter? Is she okay?"

"No Tom, she isn't," Cole felt a catch in his voice. "I need a couple of favors."

"Out of my jurisdiction," Harris said, trying to relieve the tension.

"I need to find somebody. The name is Erin Christopher. She's believed to still be in the state but that's about it."

"Got a middle name?"

"Uh, no. I'll have to get it."

"You all right?"

"Just a little overwhelmed. Look, Ellie is very sick. Erin

is her daughter, and they haven't spoken in a couple years. Ellie needs her."

"She called you? It's been a long time, Cole. I am a little surprised by this."

"Join the club. The other thing is a little weird. I'll fill you in later. I need the names of a couple of small-time crooks around here. Think I'm onto something that involves her husband."

"Her husband? God, Cole, what's he up to?"

"I'm not sure exactly, but how about bribery of a city official for starters? Here's the weird part, he offered the guy diamonds."

"Diamonds?"

"Yeah, evidently he's got a sackful. This guy is a real bastard. What he isn't is big time. He's a cheap sleazeball, in hock up to his eyeballs. I can't figure out this whole diamond thing. I figure it's somebody else's deal and he's riding along. Just a hunch. That's where the locals might help. I don't think they're hot, couldn't be. Too risky, he wouldn't be flashing them around."

"Brother, what you don't get into. I'll try the girl first. How old is she?"

"About twenty-three. Ellie thinks she may have gone into nursing."

"Did you ask her dad?"

"Less than helpful."

"That old Sage charm?" Harris laughed.

"Something like that," Cole answered softly. "Tom, this is important to me."

"I know. I'll do the best I can."

"Thanks, be in touch."

The line went dead and Cole stuck the phone in his

pocket. He had always been ready for the chase, Sherlock Sage, "the games afoot" and all that. His reputation was built around his ability to ferret out information. To him it was like a game. Watching the pieces move around the board. He got paid to find the story, dig the dirt, and expose the bad guys. This time it was different. This time it was personal, and that devil-may-care approach to success seemed shallow. As he stood on the corner waiting for the light to change, he was jerked from his thoughts as a silver Mercedes came slowly around the corner. Allen Christopher was driving it.

NINE

The wind blew hot and dry through the car window. The air conditioner worked just fine, but this was the "summer" Cole remembered. He enjoyed the radiant glow of the heat. Like a dry sauna, burning, roasting, in a slow bake. It was the summer of soft hot pavement in shopping center parking lots, the mirage of distant water on the road, rotten fruit, humid irrigation, orchard roads, and tumbleweed dust fields. As he rolled along, his thoughts drifted slow and disjointed.

Harris found Erin within 12 hours. Wouldn't say how, just that it was magic and he never gave away the secret. For all of Ellie's worrying about her whereabouts, she was only a two-hour drive away.

The radio played loud and bass-y. Classic Rock. Cole always thought of classic rock as doo-wop "oldies but goodies" stuff he didn't hear the first time around, but now, "classic" was the music of his life. Crosby, Stills, Nash and Young wailed, "Four dead in O-Hi-O, Four dead in O-Hi-O." He drifted to a picture, black and white, a body laying on the ground, a girl with long dark hair, mouth open in a shocked wail. Kent State, "Four dead in O-Hi-O."

How many people hearing this song now knew the pain? How many remembered the grief? Television documentaries, Hollywood blockbusters, and books dulled the rage, the ache, the frustration that was Vietnam. It seemed so small now. Bosnia, Afghanistan, Iraq I and II, Afghanistan again—each slowly overshadowing Vietnam. Where was the outrage now? Where was the movement? Movement? How many people hearing Ohio even know there *was* a Movement? Where were the voices of dissent? America had been lulled into a media hot tub of materialistic complacency. The Movement. Cole wasn't a member of anything. You don't need a weatherman to know which way the wind blows. But he had seen, he had heard, and he had felt the open wound that was Vietnam. And he remembered April 24, 1971, San Francisco and the Moratorium against the War!

As the highway hummed, he rolled back in time. It was as though it were yesterday. In fact, it was so clear, it could have been today. Cole remembered the bluest sky he ever saw and, and clouds, my God, the clouds were so billowy, so white, so huge. That day God smiled down on his children of peace and gave them a glorious day to march. Cole was back on the Bay Bridge, the top down on his white Triumph, while the sun shone bright overhead. Ellie was beside him, an off-white muslin scarf tied around her head to control her curly brown hair. She wore big black sunglasses, like Sophia Loren. The eight-track was chuggin' out "Lookin' Out My Back Door" by Credence Clearwater Revival. No wonder he remembered.

The March changed his life. Not in some great cosmic awakening, not a rebirth to an antiwar firebrand, nothing so great and cathartic. But he changed. He saw thousands and thousands of people marching, all in one accord, all with the same commitment to stopping a war. Not just stopping a war but the government of the United States of America. The free expression of their right to freedom of speech, the right to gather, and the voice of the people, by the people, and for the people in the streets and on the rolling hills of San Francisco. Long hairs, short hairs, men, women, nuns, and rabbis clad in black, framed against the saffron of Hare Krishna robes. Drag queens, businessmen, and G.I. Joes side by side, a hundred thousand, two hundred thousand, half a million, who knew? Together chanting, singing, waving signs; an ocean of bodies, human waves on a sea of protest.

"Hell no, we won't go!"

"Ho Ho Ho Chi Min!"

"One, Two, Three, Four, we don't want your dirty war!"

And they sang, "All we are saying is give peace a chance...."

"And it's one, two, three, four, what are we fightin' for?"

Cole's strongest memory was of Ellie, though. *That* is what changed him. As they crested a hill, ahead all they could see were people all the way to the bay. Behind them, even greater numbers. She turned and, with a smile that would have paled the glow of an angel, she said, "We can do it, Cole, we can stop the war. I love you!" It was the first time she ever said it. In a world gone mad with war and protest, he found peace. She wrapped both arms around his and squeezed. There were thousands of people on the street, but for those few moments there were really only two.

"Crosby....Stills...Nash.....and Neil Young here on the Rock Pile 106.5, your classic rock station. Coming up, Zeppelin, Bowie and a top of the pile classic from the Beatles right after this—"

Cole snapped off the radio and glanced at the low-slung black Corvette passing on his left. The road sign said 94 miles to Jessup. Cole forgot how much he enjoyed the open road. Since moving to Chicago, there were very few occasions to drive any great distance. The road before him acted as a tonic.

The town of Jessup was nothing to brag about. Population 15,890 according to the city limits sign. The new highway passed by about 12 miles away, and the space between the off ramp and the town was brown, dry, and pretty much uninhabited. As he pulled in, he realized it could be any little town in any state. A hardware store, a cafe, a boarded-up movie theatre, a video store, and a Mexican restaurant lined the main street.

Cole pulled up in front of the Hillside Cafe and went inside. One young mother and her toddler sat in the corner booth. A tiny little woman no more than four-foot-ten came sprightly out from behind the counter. Atop her head sat a beehive of carrot red hair. As she approached, she smiled a smile that Cole couldn't help returning.

"Hi, Hun. By yourself today?"

"Yes, ma'am!" Cole shot back. *I did it again,* he thought. *Where is this ma'am thing coming from?*

"I'm Mickie, and I'm your only choice for a waitress

today." Mickie was at least 60, maybe more. Women half her age would kill for the spring in her step.

"I wouldn't have it any other way. What's good?"

"Everything but the cook's reputation," she giggled.

"Thanks for the tip." Cole grinned.

"That's my line after you pay the bill. Haven't seen you in here before. Passing through?" Mickie inquired.

Cole realized that beneath the perky smile and bouncy step laid the heart of the town gossip. You would have thought they installed Mickie at the Hillside Cafe the same day as the grill. Her crisp powder blue uniform and white nametag probably hadn't been updated in years. This was her domain, and she reined over it with love and a definite sense of control.

"Actually," began Cole, "I'm here on family business."

"That right? Well only about 10,000 people here anymore, no matter what the city limits sign and the silly city council says. Anybody I know, you suppose?" *Sly old fox,* Cole thought as Mickie waited for a reply.

"A friend of mine is very ill and the last anyone knew, her daughter was here in Jessup. So, I'm doing some Sherlock Holmes work to find her. Her mother would really like to see her," Cole hesitated, "before she goes."

He suddenly felt like he would throw up. The reality of looming death, Ellie's death, had been suppressed beneath the need to find Erin. Now he made it real, he spoke the words, and somehow sealed Ellie's fate. Cole realized he was staring out the front window, but he couldn't blink, he couldn't move. *My God,* he thought, *I'm going to start crying.* He clenched his teeth until they ached, he felt his eyes begin to blur. He willed himself to not blink. His broad shoulders began to shudder. With no control over his body, his hands flew over his face, and he began to sob. The booth and table shook with the force of his quaking. He was nearly silent in his grief, which only added to the force of his tremors.

Mickie slipped behind the counter and returned with a terrycloth hand towel and gently laid it across Cole's head and hands. She quietly moved to the back booth and scooted the young woman and child out the back door. Like a little elfin spirit, she noiselessly glided across the floor, flipped the Open sign over to Closed, and flicked the left panel of lights off over the booths where Cole sat.

Cole had no sense of being. A black hole just swallowed him up as he fell deeper and deeper into his grief. He had no sense of the time when he finally inhaled a deep lungful of air and let it out in jerking bursts. He pulled the soft white towel from atop his head and held it to his burning eyes. It was then he came to the realization where he was. Weak and still shaking, he lowered the towel to look around him shamefully.

"You gonna be okay, Sweetie?" Mickie said softly. A glass of water and a cup of coffee sat between them. She had slid into the booth across from him unnoticed.

"Yeah," Cole whispered. He felt a panicked need to run but was too embarrassed or ashamed to move. He wiped his face.

"Sometimes it just comes out. We can't control it. It's okay. Just sit still, nobody's gonna bother you. Have a sip of water."

Cole put the soft damp cloth back up to his eyes. He felt like such a fool, yet this little waitress across from him knew his grief. Mickie had probably heard a million and one stories of heartache and pain, and yet, knew each one mattered. He lowered the towel and looked at her. Lines unseen before crisscrossed the face beneath the beige pancake makeup and bright red bee-stung lips. *How old is this woman?* he thought.

"Ya know, my Will never cried that I saw," Mickie said. "He was a man. Men don't cry. Big joke. Many a morning his pillow was wet with tears. When my Mikey got killed in Vietnam, Will was like a rock. But at night sometimes our bed would shake to where I thought I would fall out. He thought I slept through it, the silly goose. But I knew. He was broken. Never got over it. Mikey was his boy. Sometimes I think I should have let him know I knew he was cryin'; I should have held him and we should have cried together. Of course, he would've had none of that." She paused and looked down at the top of the Formica table.

"I had a customer in here last week who died. Right over there in number six. He was 82. Came here from the hospital. Just minutes after his wife passed away. We didn't know. Came in and ordered a chocolate milk shake. I teased him about a second childhood. Strangest thing, he wrote a sweet little note on a napkin. Said how much he loved his Gwen—and he just died." She smiled and said, "Finished his shake, though. Yep, finished his shake."

"Thanks, Mickie," Cole said.

"You want to talk? Don't have to. Tell me to scram and I will. You just sit there as long as you need to. Ain't no business this time a day, so don't worry about it."

Cole looked across the table and wanted—no, needed—to talk. For more than an hour, he told this little coffee shop confidante about Ellie. It was a celebration of her as he had loved her. How they met, favorite dates, trips together, it was a stream of consciousness flight through the treasured memories he carried so close for so long. To his amazement, he even told her of the last time they made love. Cole felt a glow as he told how afterward Ellie held onto his arm with both of hers as they walked back up the beach to the car, and how she fell asleep on the way home still holding his arm in hers.

He told his new friend how in college Ellie disappeared for almost a year after the first time they broke up. She just vanished. He asked everyone who knew her where she had gone. No one knew a thing. Not being on the best terms with her parents, the call to her family was met with a curt, "She's away for a while, she's fine, thanks for calling."

Then, one day while he was crossing campus, there she was. Of all his memories of Ellie, this was his greatest regret, far more than losing her when he went on the Asian assignment. He knew what fate's hand dealt him. This memory, so vivid, so real, that as he told Mickie the story, he even saw the colors.

It was spring, not just the month of April or May, but the spring of rebirth, blossoms, sunshine, and life. And there she was. After a year of wandering, there she came, 100 yards away, walking towards him. But not just walking, she literally bounced. Dressed in a kaleidoscopic ankle-length skirt that billowed like some psychedelic pop art poster and exploded with blues, reds, greens and purples that seemed to shoot out color with each jump and twirl as she raced towards him. Her hair had always been cut short, now it was falling, cascading over her shoulders in big flowing curls. As she drew closer, he saw her beautiful smile. Beaming and laughing, she twirled again. She jumped up and wrapped her legs around his waist, her arms around his neck. With her cheek pressed tight against his, she giggled, "I've come for you!"

The momentum of her weight caused Cole to drop his books and do a spin in the middle of the commons.

Ellie jumped to the grass and again said, "I've come for you, Cole!" For the briefest moment, he thought she had lost her mind. Her smile told him otherwise. He looked at her up close and realized she was wearing a very thin, gauze peasant blouse. She wore no bra and her nipples showed clearly through the see-through material.

"Where have you been?" Cole demanded.

"Everywhere! New York, California, Toronto, and a million other places! I've been everywhere and now I've come for you! We're going to Mexico." Ellie's glee was like a child discovering the butterflies in their own backyard.

"Mexico! How can I go to Mexico?"

"My friends have a van," she replied.

"No, no, wait. Are you nuts? I have four weeks left this semester. I have finals. I might get an internship. I can't go to Mexico." Cole nearly stuttered from the absurdity of her suggestion.

"I have traveled six hundred miles out of our way to get you!" Her tone was a mix of hurt and astonishment.

"You have been gone almost a year! I have been worried sick. Nobody knew where you went. You parents wouldn't tell me where you went! Now you just drop out of the clouds and say 'Let's go to Mexico'? And what the hell kind of hippie getup are you wearing? The whole world can see your tits! Have you lost your mind? What am I supposed to think? Who's in the van, the Manson Family?" Cole's voice was rising with every question.

"When did you become my father?!" Ellie screamed.

"And when did you become so uptight? You are the one... you are the one who always goes with the flow. Take chances, reach for your dreams... was that all bullshit? Who *are* you?"

"Who am I? Who the hell are you?" he shot back. "Ellie, are you strung out?" His voice and tone softened, "I'll get you help. We can beat this thing. I love you. I'm here for you."

"You think I'm high? That's it? You're here for me! I am here for you! I came to get you! I am here to save your soul. Free yourself of this material obsession you have. Join us! Live life for a while, free your mind. Get high on life. That's where I'm at. Dance in the grass, swim in the sea... each day, Cole, take each day, make love to it, caress it. Tomorrow it's gone. You don't own it; you just get to use it. It's not yours. Come with me. We're leaving at 4 o'clock. Please."

"I want to be a journalist. I want to write. The Sun is reviewing my internship app. That could mean a job, a real job, on a real paper. You know that's what I have always dreamed of. I can't just drop it and go dance in the sun! Get real."

"I *am* real. Realer than I have ever been. I have friends who love me for me. Not some clique, but real thinking, living, loving people. Everything is shared, everything is free. If we run out of money, we stop and work for a while. I cooked during wheat harvest. We boxed shoes at a factory in New Hampshire, cut cane in Louisiana, and danced in the cane breaks at night. We painted apartments in Bakersfield and picked hops in Oregon. We got dirty, we felt the earth, and we discovered America. Not the one in books or on the 6 o'clock news but the real America, with real people, beautiful people. People with families who sing while they work, who laugh at the end of a hard day because they are free. At night, around fires in the fields, they play guitars and banjos and little accordions and sing and dance and tell stories and—"

"What next? How long can you just ramble and pick fruit? You sound like a commercial for the Woody Guthrie Travel Agency. Okay, let's sing 'This Land Is Your Land'! Come on, Ellie, come home. You have lived the great experiment, you have touched the land. I need you here. Please let your friends go on without you, and you and I will go later. Next month, school will be out. We can take off after finals."

"That won't happen."

"Sure it will. We can have a whole month if you want."

"You are part of the machine. You have—"

"Where did you get all this crap? Me? Part of the machine! I have always been more involved than you. I have marched more miles, given more money, manned more tables, passed out more flyers. I have even been arrested for fighting the Imperialist War Machine. But I want to really change things, not just make a lot of noise, and I can do that through the press. I've got a real chance with this internship. If they like me, who knows where it will lead. Come on, Ellie, think."

Tears streamed down her beautiful tanned cheeks. "This time is for me. If you really care about me, you'll come. You can always get a job. You can always finish school. But now, right now, this is for me. You decide. We need this. If we are going to be together, we need this time. Free, free to get up and lay down where and when we want. To touch, to feel, to really live life and see life, together. Don't you see?"

"I guess not," Cole said softly.

"I really thought you'd come. I don't know you anymore." She turned and took about five steps, before turning to face him again. Without taking her eyes from his, she returned to where Cole stood motionless, and softly put her arms around his neck. She kissed him. With all the warmth of her being, she kissed him deeply, as if to speak from her soul to his. Then she turned and ran back across the commons. Ran like she was being pursued by a pack of dogs. All the colors seemed to have dimmed, the joy and beauty gone. Just a dark-haired girl fleeing the scene of an accident.

Cole watched her go. He finished the semester, did well. He made the Dean's List. The internship at The Sun fell through. He didn't see Ellie for almost a year.

"You marry her?"

"Nope," Cole said matter-of-factly.

"Boy, howdy, you sure can tell a story." Mickie laughed.

"It has tumbled around in my heart for so long it's polished like a stone." Cole smiled for the first time. "Now, doesn't that sound like a writer?"

"Yeah, a bad one," Mickie teased. "But you're a good man to come looking for the girl. And Jessup is the end of the trail?"

"Erin is here, I think. She doesn't know her mother is ill. They haven't seen each other in about four years. Ellie's husband was pretty rough on the girl, and she bolted. I need to let her know Ellie's sick and try to get her to come back, before it's too late. Three years ago, she called her mother on her birthday. Wouldn't say where she was. A friend of mine, a cop in Chicago, traced her here. He said she's a nurse. Funny, Ellie trained to be a nurse."

"The hospital is just up the road. Shouldn't be hard to find out."

"That's my next stop." Cole smiled. "Mickie, you're okay."

"Stop. Don't be getting all grateful on me. Been enough cryin', don't get *me* started." She gave a theatrical giggle and covered her mouth with a napkin like the ingenue in a melodrama. "Just part of the service here at the Hillside Cafe."

"Just the same..." Cole's voice trailed off and he looked out the front window. "Looks like you've got some customers."

"Oh yeah, Ben and Ruby. They come in every day about this time for coffee, and they share a doughnut. Better let 'em in." Mickie slid out of the booth.

Cole took a business card from his wallet and a $20 bill. On the back of the card, in pencil, he wrote, "For psychological services and thoughtfulness above and beyond the call of duty" and signed it "Cole." He slipped it and the $20 under the corner of his water glass, slid out of the booth, blew Mickie a kiss, and left the cafe.

TEN

The hospital was only a mile and a half outside of town. The three-story red brick building sat on a slight rise surrounded by acres of grass, trees, and small ponds. Sprinklers chattered back and forth across the broad stretches of green. It was like a little oasis in the dry, dusty surroundings. A large old-fashioned white sign with crisp black lettering on the front lawn read "Santa Felicia Regional Medical Center."

Welcome to Happy Acres, Cole thought as he parked facing the front entrance. The sign said "Visitors, 30-Minute Limit.' He hoped he wouldn't need much more.

The tall glass doors glided open with a modern efficiency you wouldn't expect from such an old building. The air inside hit like an Artic blast and made Cole shiver. The walls in the lobby were covered with overblown enlargements of the hospital in years past, former directors, and a big map of the service area provided by the hospital. Green chairs and couches surrounding short sterile chrome and glass tables looked like they had been there since opening day.

In a chrome stand was a hospital directory and map. "Cafeteria and food service, follow the yellow line." At Cole's feet were six colored stripes painted on the floor. He followed the yellow line with his eyes to where it rounded the corner of the lobby. He pursued it down corridors, around corners, through swinging double doors, across a breezeway, and arrived at a sign that read "The Gardens Cafeteria and Coffee Shop."

Inside the cafeteria were round tables with white tablecloths, each one topped with a vase of fresh-cut flowers. At the rear was the service area, and at the register sat just the kind of person Cole was looking for. One look and he knew she was a fountain of information.

Since he hadn't eaten, Cole picked up a turkey sandwich and a bottle of grape juice. He mustered up his best smile and made his way to the register.

"Good afternoon." He beamed.

"Good afternoon to you. Will this be it?" The woman sitting at the stool must have weighed 300 pounds. Her salt-and-pepper hair was covered in an industrial strength hairnet. Her white uniform was starched brittle, and her nametag said "Biddy."

"Well, you look like the lady who knows what's going on around here. I could use your help."

"I don't know about that." Her smiled faded slightly.

"I don't need to know what doctor's foolin' around with what nurse or anything like that." Cole winked, and he could have sworn her cheeks colored a bit. "I'm looking for a friend of mine's daughter. I was passing through town and thought I'd say 'hi' if she was on duty."

"Who might that be?" Biddy frowned.

"I'm not serving papers, not a private detective, or signing people up for Amway. Just a social call. Her name is Erin. Don't know her married name." He didn't know if she was married or not but needed a reason for not knowing her last name. "She's a nurse."

"Erin Mitchell, she's the only Erin here. What a sweetheart. Always brings me peanut brittle. She makes the best peanut brittle you ever tasted, with me trying to diet, too."

"Diet! What on earth for? I always say a girl isn't worth huggin' without a little meat on her bones. Do you think she's here?" Cole grinned.

"She was in here for 10 o'clock break. Have you seen her little girl? What an angel. She brings her in sometimes and gets her an ice cream. I don't charge her, but don't you tell."

Cole made the motion of turning a key on his lips and tossing it over his shoulder. "What department is she in?"

"Why, maternity, of course. She just loves the babies." Biddy pulled a drawer out under the register and took out a Ziploc bag of peanut brittle, "You just have to taste this." She opened the bag, took out a piece and put it on Cole's tray. "No charge."

"Gee, thanks." Cole smiled at the round-faced woman.

"Way to a man's heart, ya know."

"You are a charmer, Biddy."

"A girl's gotta have a few lures in her bag if she wants to land a big one."

"I gotta come here more often. The service is great." Cole was slightly embarrassed of his shameless flirting, but it always seemed to work. *Besides,* he thought, *it always brightens their day.*

Cole made his way to a table just far enough to end all conversation, ate the sandwich absentmindedly and downed the grape juice. He thought of the times he ate meals with Ellie while she was in nursing school. He used to set his alarm so he could get up and go have lunch with her at four in the morning. Now her daughter was a nurse. *Ellie will be proud,* he thought, and smiled. *She doesn't even know she's a grandmother.*

Maternity was at the end of the blue line on the second floor. Cole approached the nurse's station. He felt a little shaky and wasn't sure just what he would say to her. "She's Ellie's daughter, so it shouldn't be tough. She's a caregiver. That says a lot," he whispered to himself.

"Yes sir?" A woman in a pink flowered uniform looked up from behind a computer monitor.

"Hi. Is Erin Mitchell on duty?"

"Yes, she is."

"I would love to say 'hi' if I could." Cole once again turned on his best smile. This time it was met with a cold stare.

"She gets off at 3."

"I need to speak to her. It is very important, and will only take a minute. Suppose you could let her know I'm here. I'm an old friend of the family."

"We had three deliveries this morning—"

"Boys or girls?" Cole broke in.

"Two boys, one girl."

"I don't have any kids of my own. Sure wish I did. Is Erin a delivery nurse?"

"Natal care, and she does the new mother training."

"I've come a long way—"

The woman behind the desk keyed a microphone, "Nurse Mitchell to the desk, please. Nurse Mitchell to the desk." She unkeyed the mic and pointed to a small waiting room across the hall. "You can wait in there." Her expression still didn't change.

"Thanks a lot."

Cole went across the hall and took a seat in the waiting room. He couldn't see the desk from where he sat. It didn't matter, though. The stress wouldn't let him sit still. He got up and went to the window. The view of the grounds was quite beautiful from the second floor. He cracked his knuckles and rubbed his hands together.

"Hello," came a voice from behind him.

Cole turned slowly to see a face he knew. For a moment, he couldn't breathe. His heart felt as though it would explode from his chest. Standing right in front of him was Ellie, just as she looked when they were together. It was as if time stood still. The last 24 years never happened. He laughed.

"God in heaven."

"Sorry?"

"It's just...it's just—"

"Do I know you?"

"I'm sorry. My name is Cole, Cole Sage. I'm—"

"You're kidding." The young woman's expression changed to one almost as thunderstruck as Cole's.

They both stood and looked at each other for the longest time. She was tall and on the thin side. Her curly brown hair was pulled back and clipped just above her ears with pink barrettes that matched her uniform. The bridge of her nose wrinkled just like Ellie's used to do as she studied the man in front of her. A smile slowly curled her lips and then broadened to show the same amazing smile he loved so much. She was beautiful.

"My mother used to speak of you. What on earth are you doing here? How did you find me? I mean, what brings you here to see me?"

"Can we sit?"

"Sure." Erin's voice conveyed a sense of concern.

They made their way to a small bench.

"Uh, I don't know exactly how to begin," Cole rubbed his hands together nervously, "So I guess I'll just spit it out. I have some bad news. Your mom's real sick." Cole paused and looked down. He could feel tears building. He would not allow it. He steeled himself. "I know that—"

"What is it? Please, is she going to be okay?" Erin's hand was at her throat and Cole saw a glimpse of what she must have been like as a little girl.

"She's very ill. Has been for almost three years. She has Lou Gehrig's disease, ALS."

"Oh my God." Erin put her hand over her mouth. "Where — what, what hospital is she in?" she stammered.

"Your father—" Cole began.

"He's not my father!" Erin stood suddenly.

"Allen Christopher, your mother's husband—" Cole paused, not quite sure how he wanted to respond to her statement, "—put her in a nursing home. She is not doing well at all, and I'm trying to get her moved, but he has power of attorney. She contacted me to help find you. She needs to see you before—"

"She's not—What do you mean?"

"She's dying, Erin. She wants to see you. Your brother and sister won't even go see her. Christopher hasn't been there in a year or more." Cole's voice was rising with emotion.

"Can you help her? Can you do something for her?"

"The thing she needs most is you. She loves you very much and misses you terribly. She knows she was wrong in not being there for you."

"It's a little late for that! She threw me away. For that—" Her hands flew up to her face and she spun around. Her shoulders shook in her attempt to contain her silent sobs.

"Look, I don't know what happened between you two, but your mother is very special to me." Cole hesitated, then said softly, "Can we go for a walk?"

"Just wait. Please, I can't think. This is all so much to take in."

Cole stood and walked over to Erin. "Here," he said as he handed her his handkerchief. He reached out and put his hand on her shoulder.

"No." She shrugged it off. "I won't go back."

"Okay, okay," he whispered," can we get out of *here*, though? The charmer at the desk is staring a hole in the glass, come on."

Erin blew her nose and slowly turned to face Cole. "Yes, let's get some air. I would like to talk to you."

Crossing to the desk she said, "I'm going to lunch, Rose."

"Should I call security?" Rose said in a faked whisper.

"No, Rose, Mr. Sage is an old family friend, and he has just given me some bad news. I just need to get some air. We're going for a walk."

"I don't like his looks. Are you sure you're not being kidnapped or something?"

"No Rosie, really he's fine. Don't worry." Erin smiled

and Cole thought she might have giggled. Turning to Cole she said, "Let's go to the garden."

They rounded the corner and went to a side exit door. Outside was a walled courtyard. Ivy covered the walls, and there was a pond with a waterfall that gently trickled down mossy rocks. There were several benches with dedication plaques on their back supports. Tall willows surrounded the far walls, their wispy branches swaying along the red bricks.

"This garden is part of the chapel. I just love the peaceful feeling here. Nobody ever uses it. Would you like to sit down?" Erin regained her composure and spoke with an almost affectionate tone.

"Yes, that would be nice."

They made their way to a cement bench under a tall cottonwood tree. Cole was once again aware of how very much Erin looked like her mother. Ellie had never been as thin, but her face, hair, and coloring was Ellie over and over. The sensation was dizzying. He tried not to stare, but he simply couldn't help it. He wondered how he could feel so at ease with someone he just met. It went beyond the resemblance; it was as though he knew her. Her manner, her speech, it wasn't Ellie, but it was so familiar. The pain and anger she showed, oddly didn't put him off, it seemed to draw him closer. After her outburst in the waiting room, she seemed to relax and take him in as well.

"You know, Mr. Sage," Erin began.

"Cole, please. 'Mr. Sage' always makes me feel so old." Cole smiled.

"Okay, Cole," Erin returned the smile, "I've always wanted to meet you."

"Really?"

"Oh yes, Mama always spoke of you with such, I don't know, affection maybe, that I always wondered what you would be like."

Cole was studying the young woman with such intensity he was almost scowling.

"Is something wrong?"

"I'm just kind of blown away that she would mention me," he said with a sincerity that surprised Erin.

"You need to understand something. Growing up in our house was very hard. There was so much fighting. Allen was so cruel to Mama, and he hated me. I have never understood why she stayed with him. I begged her to leave him many times, and she would just say, 'He's been working so hard' or 'He really needs to get away for a while.' I realize now it was a pretty classic case of an abused woman, but she is so strong in so many other ways, I just don't understand why she was so afraid to leave.

"I remember once when I was in the sixth grade, I had this mad crush on a boy on my school bus, and I asked Mama what love was like. She told me about this boy *she* once had a crush on. She talked about how serious he was and how he didn't even know she was alive for the longest time. Then, one day he just came and sat down by her and started talking to her and it was the start of a beautiful romance. It's funny now, but she was so shy and sweet about it. She wouldn't tell me the boy's name. You know how when you're young, you just think of your parents always being together and how they were the first and last love they ever had? It came as a real revelation that she once had someone she loved besides my father. But I finally teased and pleaded until she said your name...Cole." Erin smiled coyly.

"In my defense, I did notice her. The first time I ever saw your mom, I was smitten." Cole seemed to beam at the memory. "Your grandparents bought the house down the street from my aunt. I saw her the day they moved in. She wore a gray sweatshirt that said 'NAVY' on the front and a pair of khaki shorts. The thing that got me was her hair. It was so curly, and it bounced as she carried a box down the ramp from the moving truck. What a cutie. She was in the seventh grade. Your mother is very generous. She didn't mention that it took me four years to get up the guts to go and sit with her. That was a long time ago."

"We spent many hours alone. It was like we had only each other. Chad and Annie never accepted us." Erin sighed deeply.

"What do you mean, 'accepted' you?"

"I was about five when Mama met Allen, and his kids were 8 and 10, so I was always in the way, and they resented Mama."

"So, who was your mom's first husband, your father?"

"I was hoping you would know." Erin looked at Cole hopefully.

"We lost touch you might say. I didn't know she had been married before," Cole stammered.

"She would never talk about it."

"Didn't you ask your grandparents?" Cole questioned.

"By the time I was old enough to want to know, they were really old. Grandma died when I was seven, and Grandpa had Alzheimer's. It was a forbidden subject. All I know is, he died when I was a baby and she won't talk about him. It is the meanest thing she has ever done to me. I think I have a right to know, don't you?"

Cole certainly wanted to know. He couldn't imagine Ellie married twice.

"What does your birth certificate say? You have one, don't you? You must, right?" Cole hoped he wasn't pushing.

"Oh sure, but all it says under father is: 'Eric Brockett, place of birth Taos, New Mexico, date of birth 12/13/48.' I have searched, written letters, made calls—all nothing. Mom said he died in Mexico working in the oil fields. That's it. She wouldn't say anything else, ever."

"I'll be damned," Cole said almost to himself.

"You're still a reporter, right?"

"How did you know that?"

"Oh, I know all about you. All the adventures in Southeast Asia, interviewing radicals, tobacco trials, that thing with the president. Mama always read me your stories. She would always say, 'Did you know that I used to know him?' She knew I did, but I think she just wanted to say it." She paused. "Could you help me find out about my father?" Erin suddenly looked down, knowing she had crossed a line between them. "I'm sorry, that's rude."

"Gee, after a buildup like that, how could I refuse? I'm surprised she kept track. Funny, I figured after we broke up, I was long forgotten. I was not very chivalrous in our parting, and have always regretted the way it happened. I guess they're right: Time wounds all heels." Cole smiled sadly.

"Did *you* ever marry?" Erin inquired.

"Nope." Cole changed the subject. "What's this I hear about you having a little girl? Does Ellie know?"

"No, I'm ashamed of that. I met my husband, Ben, just after I moved here. We married a year later. He's an intern here at Santa Felicia. He just adores Jenny. Oh, here." She handed Cole a set of keys with a picture keychain of a little girl in a powder blue jumper with white tights.

"Well, I can see where she gets her looks. She's a doll." Cole smiled.

"You know, it's so weird to talk to you. You are not what I expected."

"How so? What *were* you expecting? More like Tom Selleck, less like Ed Asner?" Cole grinned.

"That's exactly what I expected. My mom always said how funny you were." Erin smiled.

"I haven't felt very funny lately."

"When I was in high school, I got stood up on Prom Night. No explanation. The boy just didn't show. I was devastated. Actually thought about just killing myself so I wouldn't have to face the kids at school. Allen laughed, Chad said something nasty. I'm sure Ann would have said something nasty too, but thankfully, she was away at college. Mama came to my room and cried with me. She said the same kind of thing happened to her. She told me how you just went away and left her wondering why. That was the last time she and I were close. She fell asleep in the chair next to my bed.

"Allen burst in around midnight, screaming and calling her names. Saying how sick he was of her neglecting him. He swore at her, called her terrible things. I tried to defend her, and he slapped me across the face. She didn't say a word, just ran out of my room. That hurt worse than getting stood up. I won't go back, Cole, I can't. She chose Allen over me. That's what she wanted." Erin stood up and moved behind the bench.

"There's something else," Cole said firmly.

Erin didn't look up; she slowly traced a crack in the top of the bench. Cole weighed what to do next. He felt so inadequate. This wasn't an investigative interview. This was for Ellie. This was his chance to redeem himself somehow.

He cursed himself for agreeing to do this. His face felt like it was on fire. He could find no words.

"Your inheritance. The money and property that should go to you is going to go to Christopher and the other kids. Your mom doesn't want that. The money was her parents' and needs to go to you. To her, them getting her parents' money is the final insult."

Erin stood straight and flashed a fiery look at Cole. "Grandpa's money? That's what this is about? She can't buy me back!" Erin's anger caused her words to spit out from between clenched teeth. Then, with a rage that unleashed years of resentment and hurt, she lashed out at Cole. "Why are you here, some mythic hero from mother's past, to raise the flag of love lost and all will be forgiven? Don't you get it? I don't need her or her money." She took a deep breath. "And I sure don't need you coming here trying to shame me into something I said I would never ever do!" Tears streamed down her cheeks.

"Erin, please sit down. I have some things to say and then I'm out of here. Please."

"I think you should go," Erin said icily.

"Sit down." Cole's voice was harsh and cold as steel.

Erin blinked and rounded the bench. She stood in front of him, rigid, fists clenched at her sides.

Cole suddenly laughed. "What the hell are you gonna to do, hit me?" The sight of the beautiful girl dressed in pink ready to do battle struck him as funny, and he couldn't contain his laughter.

"What is it with you? Are you nuts?" Erin hit her sides with her fists.

Cole laughed all the harder. He slapped the bench seat and said, "Sit down, come on." He rubbed his eyes with the back of his hand as he tried to contain his amusement. His reaction was partly humor at her reaction and partly nervous emotion.

Erin sat, and in a calm, even voice said, "I'm not amused."

"I'm sorry. Maybe I *am* nuts, but I need to say a couple of things. First, I'm sorry I can't get through to you. I see the hurt and anger, and I know I'm not the one to make it go away. I just wish I knew how to let you know how wrong you are about you mother's motivation in all this."

"You don't understand—"

"Let me finish... please." Cole was now in control of himself and his thoughts. "You're right, I was the wrong person to send, and it must seem foolish to you to have a long-lost boyfriend of your mother's come to plead with you to come back home, but I am all she has. Do you understand that? I got a message she needed help, and I came. Now the only person she *really* has, her own flesh and blood, is turning her back on her. I admit I don't understand why, and I'll admit I'm angry as hell. But you're an adult. How old are you anyway, 22, 23? No one can make you do anything. It's sad, though, that you can't forgive your mother when she's dying. It isn't pretty. She has lost all control of her body. It's humiliating, frustrating, and a pretty shitty way to die. I am not trying to shame you into anything. The shame is yours, you named it, not me.

"Let's clear the air, okay? Yes, I left your mom without saying goodbye. She had been back from Mexico for almost a year. We took a long a weekend at a small resort on the coast. It's one of the sweetest memories I have. We argued on the way back. I'll be damned if I can remember what we fought about, but when I got home, I had a message. I landed an assignment in the Philippines to write an article on the New People's Army. They were communist guerrillas and there was fear they would take over the country. It was my first big break. I thought, 'I'll show her' and left that night. I didn't know that I would be bouncing around Southeast Asia for three years. How could I know it would ruin my life?

"Listen, we will probably never see each other again after today. I have met Allen Christopher and would and could kill him for what he's done to your mother," he paused and looked Erin in the eyes, "and to you.

"She made me promise I wouldn't hurt him. You see, I have nothing left to live for. I know that sounds melodramatic, but it's true."

"I know you think—" Erin tried to interrupt.

"I have loved your mother every day, every hour, every minute of the past 30 years. Losing her, well," Cole cleared his throat, "she was everything I ever wanted, and I threw her away in an act of selfish stupidity. When I realized what I had done, it was too late. I called and she was gone. Your grandparents, who were never big fans of mine, wouldn't tell me how to reach her. I was going to have her join me in Cambodia. Today, I learned she'd married. I can't believe she found somebody that fast. You want pain—try that one on."

"I had no idea what you meant to each other, but..."

Cole straightened, "Now she's dying, and all the silly hopes of someday getting back together are dead, all the 'what ifs' and 'if I had onlys' are all that's left. When she goes, so does my heart and soul. The thing that hurts the most is I missed all the years when she was growing older.

She has gone from the beautiful, wild, passionate girl I worshipped to a poor emaciated shell I don't recognize. Even her voice that haunted my dreams all these years is gone. Now it's just a shaky whisper. The only thing that is Ellie is her eyes, her beautiful eyes. When I sat with her, they were all I could look at."

Erin sniffed hard and wiped her eyes with her sleeve.

"All I'm saying, Erin, is regrets are hard to live with. I know; mine outweigh everything I have ever done. None of the awards, prizes and so-called fame ever meant anything because the one person I loved in life wasn't there to share it with me. And, believe me, there are no substitutes. She is the only mother you will ever have, and she loves you very much." Cole put his hands on his knees and rose from the bench.

"I wish she could have been with you." Erin smiled. "You're probably right, but I won't go back. When I left, I swore I would never ever go back. I just can't do it. I'm sorry for the mean things I said to you. I had no way of knowing what she meant to you. I see it now, she felt the same way. But she should never have chosen him over me. I just can't forgive that."

Cole looked down at the young woman on the bench. She was so much like Ellie. Her hands were between her knees and she gently rocked back and forth. Her head bowed, Cole could no longer see her face. The meeting was over. He had failed.

ELEVEN

The drive back seemed twice as long. Cole didn't turn on the radio. He replayed the time with Erin over and over in his head. He played the I-should-have-said game until he finally yelled, "I give up!"

Back at his motel, he showered and changed clothes. As he sat on the bed to tie his shoes, his cell phone rang. The number belonged to Tom Harris in Chicago.

"Cole, I found you some new friends."

"What have you got?"

"Talked to a detective named Mark Wilson. He's your man out there if you need help. His first choice is named Perez, Anthony Perez, street name Whisper. Dope, cars, small-time fence for stolen goods. Vato malo. Hangs out at a bar called La Perla. Rough place, be real careful, Wilson says.

"Number two is a guy named Terrell Le'ney Jefferson,

AKA Tree Top. No criminal record, but Wilson says he's into everything but drugs. If it will turn a buck, he's in. Drives a green and orange Acura with lots of flashy stuff on it. Likes to park on Filbert and watch the world go buy. Lots of flash and cash. A lover not a fighter but has some muscle behind him. "

"Whisper and Tree Top, got it."

"Hey, you find the girl?"

"Yeah. Ellie's a grandma. Doesn't know it. Tom, you wouldn't believe how much she looks like her mother. Took me way back. She's a nurse like you said, like Ellie wanted to be. Married to a doctor. I couldn't get her to come back though. Lots of anger. I don't know how I'll tell Ellie."

"Tell her the truth, Cole. It will hurt, but it's the only way."

"I guess."

"Hey, I got a call. When will you be back?"

"I don't know. Be in touch, thanks."

"Later."

Cole stood and went to the window. A strong breeze came up and the curtains flapped hard. The trees in the parking lot swayed and the flag above snapped. He watched a Burger King cup roll and bounce across the pavement. Reaching in his pocket, he counted his money: six twenties, three tens, two fives and seven singles. The alarm on the nightstand flipped over to 4:30.

La Perla occupied a free standing building, on a short street with the sign missing just off of Market. It sat between an auto electric place and a boarded-up shoe repair shop. The sign on the building looked fairly new, but the twenty year old faded coral pink paint chipped away from the brick and the eves was peeling badly. The attic ventilator on the roof clicked with every rotation. Cole remembered the bar next door to his friend Manuel's house growing up.

Manuel, a Mexican kid, always held the distinction of being the fattest in class and Cole's best friend. Cole befriended him one day when he traded his tuna sandwich for Manuel's burrito. In the early '60s, most gringos in California confused a burrito with a small donkey, but even at 10 years old, Cole possessed an adventurous palate. Homemade tortilla, refried beans, chunks of boiled potato with a little green chili sauce. It exploded with a spicy sparkle and Cole knew he just discovered a whole new world.

The next day, he traded peanut butter and jelly for a chili relleno. When they discovered a common love of Wolfman Jack on the radio, the bond was sealed. Manuel lived in a small, unpainted wooden house on the old highway next to a bar called Dee Dee's. Dee Dee, the original owner of a cowboy bar, died of liver cancer years before. Since then, the place changed hands a dozen times, but always stayed a watering hole for Mexican farm workers on their way home. None of the parade of owners bothered to change the sign out front.

Manuel and Cole found great sport in shooting at the revolving vent on the roof with BB guns. Somehow they always stopped just before they incurred the wrath of the bartender or, worse yet, Manuel's mother. Cole always addressed her as Senora Jaramillo. She stood well under five feet and must have been nearly as big around; short in stature, but a giant in the kitchen.

The Senora spoke no English, yet Cole certainly understood what displeased her. She never hesitated to give him a slap on the back of the head if he did anything she didn't like, then using Manuel as interpreter, she would explain the infraction. Muddy shoes, teasing her little dog, running in the house, and being too loud always got a bop on the head. Fast to scold or slap, and just as quick to give a hug or a fresh hot tortilla sprinkled with cinnamon, sugar and dripping with butter. Senora Jaramillo loved Cole, and he knew it.

Cole and Manuel remained the best of friends through grammar school and high school, until their junior year. Cole got a pale green 1963 Volkswagen from his parents and drove proudly over to show Manuel. When he arrived, he found the front door of the little house standing wide open. Inside, not a stick of furniture or picture on the wall remained, only dust balls and a few sheets of paper swirled around the floor. The rectangles on the wall where the few religious pictures hung for so many years almost glowed against the faded wallpaper. They were gone, without goodbye or warning. Cole stood in the kitchen where the table once sat, where he spent hours doing homework and shared hot tortillas and butter that Senora Jaramillo so lovingly made, and cried.

He heard nothing of his friend for fifteen years. Then Cole ran into an old classmate from grade school that came from Capitiro, Manuel's hometown in Mexico. He said his uncle knew Manuel's father. Manuel and his family returned to Capitiro because his father lost his job. Someone falsely accused him of stealing. The shame proved too much for Armando Jaramillo, and he returned home where such a thing would have been laughed at in its foolishness. In Capitiro, no one would ever question his honesty.

After graduating from high school, Manuel enlisted in the Mexican Air Force. His English helped him get into the Medical Corps. He'd trained in Texas with the Air National Guard as part of a "Friendly Neighbor" exchange. This led to Officer Training School and enrollment in medical school. Over the years, he climbed up though the ranks and finally received a promotion to Colonel. Now Doctor Jaramillo, he held the title of Chief Administrator at a military hospital near Mexico City. He married an important politician's daughter and they became parents of three little boys. Over the years, Cole never ate a burrito without thinking of Manuel.

The glass front door of La Perla appeared to have been painted white with house paint and a wide brush. Inside it smelled of cigarettes and beer. A yellow Corona sign blinked and flickered above a fish tank behind the bar. One old man sat at a table in the center of the room. Several groups of men sat in booths that lined the walls. There were no women in the place.

Cole fingered the bills in his pocket as he approached the bar.

"Good afternoon."

"No hablo ingles," growled the bartender.

"That so?" Cole slipped a $10 bill across the bar.

"Not completely, no." The bartender smiled. He wore a faded brown T-shirt that advertised a brake shop under a white dress shirt.

"I need to speak to Whisper," Cole said casually.

"Don't know him."

"That's too bad, he would have been very grateful."

"For what?"

"For you introducing me." Cole smiled.

"That so?" said a soft raspy voice behind him.

Cole turned to see a small dark man, with a freshly shaved head and a very sparse moustache. He wore tan chinos and a pair of brand new suede work boots with no laces. His white T-shirt bore sharp creases down the center that spoke of someone taking great pains to iron it just so.

Over the T-shirt he wore a red checked shirt several sizes too big, unbuttoned, stiff with starch, and showing the same careful ironing. Just above the collar of his T-shirt ran a thick, jagged, pink horizontal scar.

"Whisper Perez?"

"Maybe." The man spoke with the definite sound of vocal cord damage.

"I'm Cole Sage." Cole stared into Whisper's eyes, the small man blinked. "From Chicago."

"Chicago? What the hell are you doing in a shithole like this?"

"Looking for you." Cole smiled.

Whisper laughed but made little sound. "This is either real important or you crazy."

"Little of both."

"Beer?"

"Coca-Cola, please."

"Javie! Cerveza y Coke." Whisper pointed in the bartender's direction. "My sister's husband. Come, sit."

Cole followed Whisper to a booth where a thick heavily tattooed man sat spinning a Miller High Lite bottle with his index finger. He wore dark Ray-Ban sunglasses.

"This is Luis." The man in the sunglasses looked up but didn't speak. "He's not very friendly." Whisper smiled and bobbed his head at his own joke.

"I need some help." Cole jumped right to the heart of the matter.

"From me?"

"I heard you could help."

"Who told you that?"

"A cop in Chicago."

Whisper looked at Cole for a long moment. His eyes gave away his obvious pleasure at this. "What's his name?"

"Tom Harris, he's a detective. Know him?"

"Heard of him," Whisper lied. "What you need to know?"

"First, I'm not a cop or any other kind of law. Second, I don't want to know anything you don't want to tell me."

"I don't get it."

"You believe in love?"

"You come here to ask me that! Luis. You hear this shit?" Whisper laughed and wrinkled his brow as he took a long look at Cole, "Yeah, I believe in love."

"The woman I loved more than anyone on earth is being done a deep wrong. We parted a long time ago, long story, big mistake. She's sick, dying." Cole paused. "She called me to help her, asked me to do two things. The first thing, I've already blown. I only have this final chance to do one last thing for her before she dies. I can't let her go knowing I failed her." Cole looked Whisper straight in the eyes.

"What can I do?"

"Somebody is flashing a lot of diamonds around town. Even tried to bribe a city official with them. I don't care *where* they are coming from. I just want to nail a guy named Allen Christopher. You know him?"

"No."

"Ever heard of him?"

"Luis?"

The big man shook his head. Whisper took a stack of business cards out of his shirt pocket and slowly shuffled through them. Several times, he turned a card over and read a handwritten note on the back.

"These are the cards of people who we have done business with one time or another. Kind of a—what you call a Rolla...whatever." Whisper flicked the cards towards Cole. "No Christopher here. What'd he do?"

"The woman I love is his wife. He put her in a rest home, like where some people throw away their old parents. Hasn't even gone to visit her, just left her there to die." Cole could feel his face reddening as his temper rose. "He's trying to steal the inheritance meant for her daughter. Ellie, my friend, wants her daughter to get her grandparent's money. Christopher tricked Ellie into signing a document, a power of attorney. Do you know what that is?" Whisper nodded. "I have to get it back. If I can get—"

"So, you want us to kill him? Luis could do it easy."

"No," Cole said calmly. Whisper was dead serious. "I need to find out who is helping him get diamonds then screw it up for him. I figure if I can let them know he is looking at a felony bribery charge, they will cut him loose."

"If it were *my* woman, I would kill him." Whisper looked at Cole, his brow deeply creased, and Cole knew this fierce young man saw no reason for Christopher to still be alive.

"I promised Ellie I wouldn't hurt him."

"When she dies, then." Whisper kissed the crucifix that hung around his neck and crossed himself.

"Maybe," Cole said coldly.

"This sounds like niggas to me. You heard of Tree Top? Flashy nigga, lots of money, cars, and shit. He's a fool." Whisper nearly spat with contempt.

"Where can I find him?"

"Look man, he ain't civilized like me. He'll hurt you before you can speak. His crew don't care, they'll hurt you bad. Bunch of white guys who think they're black."

"How do I get to him then?"

"Luis, what is that skinny fool's name, you know, the guy who's with that puta gorda Felicia."

"Andre."

"Yeah, yeah, you got his number?"

Luis took a cell phone from his pocket and hit a series of buttons. He handed the phone to Whisper.

"'Dre, that you? Whisper. Fine, fine. Hey, what you know about diamonds? Don't matter who told me. How can I get in?" Whisper smiled at Cole. "No, still don't love me? Okay, okay, so what's up with this diamond thing? Who? Anderson, who's he? Tree's into this? Yeah? Damn, that's a lot of money! Shit, I'll sell you my ol' lady for that! Oh well, I thought maybe I could play, too." Whisper laughed hoarsely. "How's Felicia? Cool. Cool. Ah right, later." Whisper clicked the phone closed and handed it to Luis, "Ain't that some shit!"

"What'd he say?" Cole asked slowly.

"He says there is this white guy named Richard Amber—"

"Anderson?"

"Yeah, yeah Anderson. He's got a line on cheap diamonds. Tree's people been buyin' cars with 'em. Then sellin' the cars. He's payin' lots of money to do it. Dre's made 10K already. Oh yeah, he said Tree still hates my ass." Whisper smiled. "I should have whacked him when I had the chance. You give me an idea! Maybe I will anyway, you know, I—"

"Thanks, but you don't need to," Cole interrupted.

"It's all right. I tell you something, I don't like those people. You know what I read the other day? In *Newsweek* or *Time* or one of those doctor office magazines you know? They want to be paid for bein' slaves. What kind of shit is that? There ain't a slave alive anymore.

"You want to pay somebody, pay my abuelo. He came here in World War II. Joined up, fought the Nazis. When he came home, he worked the fields. You know what parathion is? The government says it's the most dangerous poison ever used on crops. My grandfather sprayed it for 20 or 30 years. No mask. He would come home looking like a snowman, covered with that shit. He got cancer. Lungs, liver, and something wrong with his blood, too. He couldn't die in peace, though, because it screwed up his nerves and shit. He twitched and shook so hard at the end they tied him down to his bed. How come we don't get money for him? He just died at Christmas. Slaves got beat and shit, but none ever died like that."

"Not much right in this world anymore." Cole stared down at the table.

"My people don't ask for nothin'. We work hard, Okay, maybe we don't," Whisper jerked his head at Luis and grinned, "but regular folks do. It ain't right. I say no money for no slave families. I'm a citizen, I even vote. But that money for slaves thing, that just ain't right."

"I don't think it will happen," Cole said somewhat amazed at Whisper's interest in reparations.

"Good."

Cole slid out of the booth. "Here, let me buy the drinks." He reached in his pocket as he turned toward the bar.

"You already did with the money you gave Javie."

"Ah, come on Whisper," the barman protested.

"You can keep the change."

"Thanks for your help." Cole offered his hand. Whisper took it.

"You come back sometime so we can talk politics and shit. These guys don't keep up with things like I do. Gets boring."

"I'll do that next time I'm back in town."

"No you won't, but it's the thought that counts, huh?

"I might surprise you. Vaya con Dios."

"Spanish! See Luis a man with class. Que dios los bendiga hermano."

Luis smiled for the first time.

TWELVE

Cole decided on a low-tech approach to finding Richard Anderson. Taking a phone book from the dresser drawer in his motel room, he turned to A. There, he saw Richard and Eloise, 2118 Meadowview Court. He jotted the address on a motel notepad and fell back across the bed, falling into a deep, exhausted sleep. The next morning he rolled into a bright shaft of light that leaked through the curtains, and awoke with a start. The cheap plastic clock on the nightstand read 9:30.

At a quarter past eleven Cole pulled up in front of the Anderson house on Meadowview. Located in an upscale development of custom homes, the lawn showed the crisp edge of being freshly cut, and the bushes were all newly trimmed, but the house nearly shouted "no one home."

Several minutes passed after the doorbell rang out "The Entertainer" before Cole heard the sound of footsteps approaching. The large oak and stained glass door opened to reveal a large, fleshy woman. She wore a white sleeveless knit top stretched over the large stomach that protruded far past her breasts. The black shorts that stopped just above her dimpled knees weren't the best choice to achieve the "black is always slimming" look. Her large legs ended in bare feet and toes stained from freshly mowed grass.

"Sorry I took so long. I cain't hear the door bell in the backyard. I needed to rake. The gardener left grass all over the lawn. What a mess." Her soft voice betrayed a Southern lilt.

"Mrs. Anderson?" Cole asked.

"Yes, what can I do for you?"

"I would like to speak with your husband if I may. Don't worry, I'm not a salesman." Cole turned on his best smile.

"He's not here." She said unfazed by the smile. Her tone turned cautious and unfriendly.

"Oh, okay." Cole scrambled for an approach."Will he be back soon? A friend said he might be interested in buying my wife's car. Original '65 Mustang; it's a cutie, belonged to her mom. The original little ol' lady who only drove it to church and the grocery store. My wife wants one of those big ol' SUV things." Cole pointed to his own vehicle." That's a rental, mine's in the shop."

"Richard is uh, he uh..." Her eyes filled with tears.

"He's gone, isn't he," Cole said softly. "Look, I'm not here about a car. Can we chat a minute?"

"Are you a policeman?"

"No, just trying to get some information before somebody gets in trouble."

Eloise Anderson lifted her chin and looked deeply into

Cole's eyes. "You're not a con are you." She offered this as a statement more than a question.

"No, I work for the *The Sentinel* in Chicago." Cole knew the truth would be his best bet.

"Guess you better come in out of the sun." She opened the door wide and stepped back. "I'll get us some lemonade. We can talk in here." She pointed to a large, high-beamed room.

The room, as well as its furnishings, was very large. Heavy, overstuffed leather sofas lined the walls and a floor-to-ceiling fireplace dominated the far corner. The wall closest to Cole contained a gallery of several dozen photographs of a much younger, much thinner Eloise and a tall, handsome man he took for Richard Anderson. In the pictures, they stood with presidents, politicians, musicians, movie stars and televangelists—the rich and powerful smiling, arm-in-arm with the handsome young couple. On a small shelf at the center of the gallery were two Grammy awards and three Dove awards for gospel music. To the left of the shelf were three gold record awards, all presented to Eloise Anderson.

A Steinway grand piano stood majestically to the left of the fireplace. Next to a bench stood a small mahogany table covered with what looked to Cole to be sheet music, blank sheet music.

In the center of the ceiling, suspended from a dark walnut stained beam, hung a projection TV. The room was everything Cole always dreamed of; dark, masculine, and comfortable. He traced the beams with his eyes, trying to figure out where they hid the screen for the TV, when he heard footsteps behind him.

"Here we go, Mister..." Eloise looked at Cole quizzically.

"I'm sorry, forgot to properly introduce myself. Sage, Cole Sage. What a great room! I have always wanted a room like this."

"Make me an offer," she said softly, almost to herself.

"Your piano is magnificent. Are you doing some writing?" Cole grasped for something to put Eloise at ease. "I saw your awards. Wow, you're famous!" He felt like a babbling idiot.

"A long time ago." She took a deep breath and seemed to straighten herself. "Mr. Sage, my husband is gone. Three days ago I came home to find his clothes missing and a letter on the kitchen table. He won't be coming back."

"It doesn't have anything to do with you, does it?"

"No," Eloise said softly.

"Is he in trouble?"

"He will be if they find him. Do you know about him? His history?"

"Until last night I never heard of him. Look, I'm not after him or looking to turn him in. Quite frankly, I don't care what he's done. I mainly want to find out his connection to a man named Allen Christopher. Does your husband's disappearing act have anything to do with him?" Cole could see her need to talk.

"In the letter, Richard said he made the score of a lifetime and he loved me but he could never see me again. I'm not sure exactly what he did, but he said he paid off the house and left a key to a safety deposit box. He said I would be set for the rest of my life." Tears began to stream down her cheeks. "He *is* my life. I would rather visit him in prison than never see him again."

Cole took a long drink of his lemonade. "Did you see the diamonds Mrs. Anderson?"

The large woman shifted her weight on the couch. She stared at the fireplace and didn't speak for nearly a minute. "Richard always thought I knew nothing of his business. He said if I didn't know anything I would never get in trouble. Then he would tell me little bits and pieces here and there. He just can't keep a secret. Did you know he used to be a preacher? The devil got a hold of his heart, though. He's not like other men; lust of the flesh isn't his problem. He has always been faithful to me. Richard fell for another love, the root of all evil. He promised me he would give me the world. When he found he couldn't do it the right way, he did it any way he could. I never wanted to be rich." She began to sob softly.

Cole felt deeply saddened as he watched her thick shoulders move up and down. Her pudgy fingers covered her face. She wiped her eyes and let out a shuddering sigh. "He told me the diamonds were legitimate. 'Bought and paid for', were his exact words. Were they stolen?"

"I don't think they were stolen. At least," Cole paused, "until he took off with them."

"Who do they belong to?"

"I have a feeling that Allen Christopher may have financed this scheme somehow."

"Why are you involved in this?" For the first time Cole sensed her suspicion. "Who is this Christopher guy to you anyway?"

"He has hurt someone I love almost as much as Richard has hurt you. Look, I need to connect Christopher to these diamonds somehow. Not any of this is my business. I am very sorry your husband is gone. I know how it must hurt, really I do. A long time ago I loved someone very much, but I let her get away." Cole took a deep breath.

"She has a horrible disease killing her inch by inch. Christopher is her husband. He got her to sign a power of attorney order playing on her weakness. She really didn't know what she signed. He put her in the filthiest rest home you could imagine, to die. She asked me to protect her daughter's inheritance. Christopher is trying to get it.

"With the power of attorney, when Ellie dies, he gets everything. He can rewrite their will, change documents, bank accounts, whatever he wants. All she wants is to go knowing her daughter will get her inheritance handed down from her parents. I have got to do this for her. I have failed her in so many ways. Do you understand?" Cole felt this thread to the diamonds slipping away.

"I don't see how Richard fits in."

"Did he say how the diamonds were paid for? Please think, is there anything you remember? Whether you understand it or not. Anything?"

"One night Richard told me that a real estate agent helped him buy these diamonds. He would front the money; Richard planned to buy cars, boats, motorcycles, anything of value with the diamonds. He said the beauty of it is that the diamonds were bought and paid for. He said there is a huge mark up in their value, so when they bought the stuff with them they made even bigger profits when they resold it."

"So why did he leave, do you think?"

"Because he is Richard. He put one over on somebody."

"Like what? What's his game? How could he con Christopher?"

"Leverage."

"I'm sorry?"

"Using other people's money. Richard has never learned

that if you borrow you must pay back. He must have built up the purchases then used the track record to get a line of credit. He makes several purchases, pays on time, then lowers the boom."

"He has done this before?"

"Oh, Mr. Sage, my Richard has spent many years behind bars trying to find the perfect ways to leverage other people's money to be able to get someone else's money."

"So, you think he bought the last bunch of stones on credit, then took off?"

"Probably with your Mr. Christopher's credit."

"Did you ever see any diamonds?"

Eloise smiled."Richard has a good heart, really. But down deep he is a show off, like a little kid. One night, he spread diamonds out on a black velvet skirt of mine. 'Know how much these are worth?'" she said in a deep throaty imitation of her husband, "'A million dollars!'"

"So how much of a mark-up is there? Three, four-hundred percent?"

"Six," Eloise said flatly.

"So, if Richard takes off with a million in stones, Christopher is left holding the tab for, what? A hundred and...?"

"One hundred and sixty something thousand. Math's always been my strong suit." She smiled in a girlish way.

"How long did he do all this diamond swapping?"

"About six months, maybe a year. Like I said, I only get bits and pieces of Richard's business."

"So he paid for your house out of the profits from the ones that were paid for. Slick."

"He said we could take this business anywhere. But I like it here, it's home. Our boys are here. I didn't want to leave."

"Will you play me something?"

"What?"

"On the piano, something you wrote. It isn't every day I meet a famous songwriter."

She stared at Cole for a long moment. He looked away as she struggled to lift her weight from the low-slung couch. As she crossed the room, she turned and gave Cole a puzzled look, then smiled. The heavily padded leather bench creaked softly as she seated herself. Flipping through the notes and sheet music on the table next to the piano, she chose a doublewide sheet and placed it on the piano. The music that rose from the Steinway, as she began to play, was so light and airy it seemed to float around the room. Such a sentimental melody, and yet somehow familiar, like something from a 1940's musical. As she played, Eloise Anderson's spirit rose with the notes and, as she closed her eyes, Cole quietly slipped out the front door.

Finding Tree Top Jefferson wouldn't be nearly as easy as finding Richard Anderson's house. Cole knew people like Jefferson only came out at night, so he drove to Eastwood Convalescent to see Ellie. She dozed softly, the effect of a strong pain pill to help her lower back pain. Hours of sitting in her wheelchair took a toll on her spine and hips. Cole sat for almost three hours watching her sleep.

With her head softly raised by the pillows, Ellie looked peaceful and completely at rest. For the first time since he arrived, Cole saw in this still face the girl and woman he loved. Her face was now smooth, free of the grimace of pain, and the labored twist of muscles as she fought for breath was relaxed. Cole thought of times she napped under a tree in the park when they were supposed to be studying. He drifted back to when she slept after making love and the sound of her feathery breathing on his shoulder.

THIRTEEN

The air outside Eastwood Manor was cool and sweet with the smell of fresh mowed lawn and sprinklers as Cole made his way to his car. The sun was starting to set, and the breeze of evening had started blowing in from the east. A blast of captured afternoon heat greeted him as he opened the car door. He started the car and hit the switch to roll down all the windows.

"Hey, Mister, hey!"

Cole turned to see a heavyset woman in a white uniform running up the walk towards him.

"Are you Mrs. Christopher's husband?" she panted.

Cole shut off the engine and got out of the car. "No, is something wrong?" He hadn't been out of Ellie's room for more than a minute or two and couldn't imagine she was having a problem. She had been resting so peacefully.

"Well," the woman hesitated, "it's the—"

"What is it, is she all right? What's the problem?"

"It's the billing, sir. We haven't received payment in three months. Are you family? We would really like to get this cleared up." The woman spoke in rapid bursts almost as if she were reading from note cards.

"No, I am not family, just an old friend. Have you called her husband? Of course you have, I'm sorry, silly question. How can I help?" Cole tried not to show his fury.

"Perhaps you could review what we have in her file. I'm sorry to bother you about this, but Miss Ellie is so sweet and I would hate for us to have to...." The woman looked down at her feet and handed Cole a thick file folder with a blue tab. "This place ain't the greatest, but the County Hospital is a whole lot worse. Maybe you could see if there's a mistake somewhere."

"I'll do what I can." Cole gave the woman a thin smile. *That rat bastard Christopher had already stopped paying when I saw him*, Cole said to himself as the woman turned to go back inside.

The file on Ellen J. Christopher wasn't very thick. The address and date of birth were correct, and her diagnosis in black and white looked harsh and unsympathetic. Next to "Contact Information," someone had made a note in the margin: "number changed." Toward the bottom of the sheet in a bold hand were the words INSURANCE CANCELED in red pen.

The reception Cole got from the woman behind the "Billing and Insurance" counter was a clear signal that money matters were taken very seriously at Eastwood Manor. After several questions, that received sharp, short, unfriendly answers, Cole decided to change his approach.

"When was the last time you heard from her husband?" he said without looking up from the file.

"The day he checked her in," the woman said curtly from behind the computer monitor. "Everything was fine until about three months ago, then we got notice of her insurance bein' canceled. Called the husband's number and it had been disconnected. We have sent a couple of letters, too, but no response. He dumped her. Happens all the time. Usually parents or an old aunt or something, not a wife."

"So, what happens?" Cole moved to face the woman.

She was thin, about 50 and had eyes with dark circles that were magnified by her thick glasses. Her nametag identified her as "M. Skillings, Office Manager." She wasn't mean or particularly nasty, just matter of fact. Her detachment obviously came from too many bills unpaid and too many relatives who didn't care about those left to their care. Cole knew charm, wit, or heaven above wouldn't move this woman from her assigned duty.

"We will file papers on the first. That will give her about three, maybe four weeks, and then it's off to County."

"Just like that?"

"Just like that. Unless someone steps forward, pays the back billing, and provides confirmation that payment will be secured for at least 12 months. Her condition is terminal, so the company watches billing pretty closely."

"Eastwood Manor, First in Care." Cole read aloud from the brochure on the counter.

"Care isn't free, sir."

"Respect for your patients is," Cole growled from clenched teeth.

"I'm sorry if I have been too frank, sir. I'm only following company procedures."

"I'm sure you are." Cole took a deep breath. "Look, this isn't a pleasant situation for either of us. Give me the forms or whatever it takes and I'll take care of this. I do not want Ellie bothered about this, do you understand?"

"Of course, sir." Skillings gave Cole an icy glare as she spun around to a rack of papers behind her. "Fill these out and return them with a cashier's check for the amount attached." She shuffled some papers together, slammed the stapler down and handed the papers to Cole. "Since you are not immediate family, we will require a six-month advance on payment."

Cole turned and left the building.

As he drove downtown, Cole tried to figure out if he had enough money to cover nine months of Ellie's care. He lived a very simple life and sometimes put his entire check into a savings account. He couldn't remember the last time he checked the balance and had no idea what he might've put away. It didn't matter; whatever it took, he would pay. So would Christopher.

Filbert Avenue in the 1950s and '60s was the heart of the city. Sears, Penney's, Woolworths and half-a-dozen jewelry stores anchored the heart of downtown. The city's only two elevators were both on opposite corners of Filbert and Sixth Street. That was a long time ago.

Now there were nightclubs advertising "Oil Wrestling" and "Amateur Iron Man Fights" on Budweiser banners. The jewelry stores had become Thai restaurants, and the Penney's building was home to a Mexican nightclub and a Subway sandwich shop. Police cruisers patrolled from dusk until 3 a.m. In the summer, the sidewalks were crowded with club hoppers, hustlers out to sell drugs and thugs out to give anybody they decided to a hard time. The street glowed and sparkled with flashy signs and taillights.

Cole felt completely out of place as he stepped from the public parking garage and onto the street. He saw no one even remotely close to his own age. He unconsciously pulled in his stomach and tried to walk taller. Scanning both sides of the street, he made his way along through the Friday night throng. Doormen and bouncers gave Cole a nod as he passed, and he was approaching the fourth club before he realized they thought he was a cop.

As he crossed Seventh Street, he spotted the green and orange Acura at the curb. At each end of the car stood two very big, very bald, very white guys in sunglasses. The one at the tail end of the car wore a shiny black tank top. His arms were massive and completely covered with colorful tattoos. The man posted at the front of the car wore a white long sleeve T-shirt and had the jacket of a warm-up suit tied around his waist. They both wore nylon jogging suit pants and high-top tennis shoes. No one passed within four feet of them on the sidewalk.

The light at Filbert and Seventh changed to green three times before Cole crossed to the Acura's side of the street.

"Nice car. Take a lot of diamonds to buy something like that," Cole said to the guy with the huge parrots tattooed on his biceps.

There was no response. The guy in the white T-shirt shifted his weight from one leg to the other.

"Lot of upkeep on a car like that. And two bodyguards, now that takes some serious cash to maintain that kind of security." White T-shirt looked straight ahead. Tattoo crossed his arms. Cole bent down and tried to see through the black tint of the window. "So, is he in there or what?"

"It's time for you to leave."

"That's not friendly. Could get someone like you in a lot of trouble. It sounded a bit threatening."

"He's a cop," said White T-shirt.

"So?" replied Tattoo.

"I get the distinct feeling you don't like me. And that is just not friendly. So where's Jefferson?"

"Not here," T-shirt offered.

"Good, good that's a start to a nice conversation," Cole said smiling.

"You're right, I don't like you. I'm not friendly, and I'm tired you buggin'." Tattoo stepped forward.

"See, there you go again. Your body language projects a definitely hostile message. I warned you about getting in trouble. I was being nice. I really don't understand your unfriendly attitude toward me." Cole gave him a big forced smile.

The sound of laughter across the street made all three men turn. A tall black man was in the center of a group of about eight in the crosswalk. He was head and shoulders taller than the women he held in each arm and a full head taller than the men in front and behind him. He wore an LA Lakers jersey with a long-sleeved purple turtleneck under it. As the group stepped from the street to the curb, the tall black man gave a quick jerk of his head in the direction of Cole and the two men guarding the car. From Cole's vantage point, he saw the tattooed man shrug his broad shoulders.

The tall man broke from the group, saying something Cole couldn't hear. He walked with the loping swagger of an NBA star. Cole knew this was his man.

"What's goin' on here?" The accent was on *here*.

"You must be Mr. Jefferson." Cole smiled.

"You know I am. Who are you?" Tree Top Jefferson didn't smile.

"I'm the guy about to cut off your meal ticket."

"That so."

"Yep, that so," Cole said with his head slightly tilted to one side.

"Who is this fool, and why he standin' right up by my car when I told you nobody gets next to it!" Jefferson stared at Tattoo.

"He jus' now come up, Tree. I don't know who he is!"

"How rude of me," Cole interrupted. "My name is Cole Sage. From *The Chicago Sentinel*, you know, the newspaper. I would like to interview you, Mr. Jefferson. It could save you a lot of grief."

"An' what if I don't want no interview?"

"Like I said, I could make things dry up around here. That is, if you are unwilling to help me out."

"You talkin' big shit. Why a newspaper in Chicago care 'bout what I do?"

"Look, I don't want to put your business out here on the street like some two-bit pimp. Where can we go to talk? Your friend Mr. Anderson has skipped town. How's that for starters?"

"Who's he?"

"Okay, I tried to be helpful." Cole started walking down the street. "One, two, three—"

"Yo, hold up a minute!" Jefferson's voice had gone up almost an octave.

Gotcha, Cole said to himself as he continued walking.

"Yo, ho'd up!" Jefferson jogged up next to Cole.

"You like coffee?"

"Whatever."

The two men went into a small coffee shop and took the last table down the narrow alcove. Cole sat with his back to the wall, folded his hands, and placed them on the small table. Tree Top Jefferson looked almost comical trying to get his long legs to adapt to the cramped surroundings. In his constant effort to be cool, he finally stretched them out to the left of Cole and crossed them at the ankles.

Tree Top eyed the waitress who had just left with their drink order. "What's yo' game?"

"Just trying to help out a friend."

"Who?"

"No one you know or would care about. Listen, pretty soon I'm going back to Chicago. When I'm gone, I don't care what you do or to who. But we got a problem, and it isn't with each other. Tell me about this diamond scam. How did you get in? Was it Richard Anderson?" Cole leaned back.

"How I know you ain't police?"

"Don't you know most of the cops around here?"

"Yeah."

"Well, don't I look a little old to be a rookie?"

Jefferson laughed and laced his long fingers behind his head. He was doing everything he could to give the appearance of being calm, but the little beads of sweat on his upper lip and forehead were giving him away.

"You gotta be big city. Nobody around here would be messin' with my boys out there. I usually don't go off and chat with just anybody, you know. Not good for my image." Jefferson turned and faced Cole head on. "How you know Anderson's gone?"

"His wife told me this afternoon."

"Ain't that a bitch?" Jefferson looked at the tabletop for a long moment deep in thought before he spoke again. "So, what about Christopher?" Jefferson paused and, as an afterthought, said, "You know him, too? Will he still give me the stones?"

"How deep are you into them?"

"Me? No, no I'm cool."

"Here's the deal. Game's over. Anderson took the ball and ran off. But it's the other guy. He's the one I want to get to. What do you know about Allen Christopher?"

"I don't know him, like, *know him*, you know? He was Anderson's guy. But why should I tell *you* anything. What's your game?"

"Look, Christopher tried to bribe a city official with some of these diamonds you been buying cars with."

"How do you know about that?"

"That's not important, the thing is—"

"To me it is!" Jefferson interrupted.

"Mrs. Anderson has been left behind. She told me what little she knows, hoping I'll help her find her husband. On the surface, it's a legitimate scheme. Anderson got a little greedy. Christopher is the money behind the stones. You know that, right? He's a real estate salesman. He put up the money to buy the diamonds. Anderson got you and some other people to buy and resell stuff. He scammed Christopher and took off. No more diamonds for you and a hell of a bill for Christopher to pay. Thing is, Christopher doesn't have any money."

"One double mocha and one decaf. Anything else for you gentleman?" the bubbly blonde in the green apron turned and left before either man could even look up at her.

"You seem to know an awful lot. How you get on to me?"

"Chicago cops," Cole said flatly.

This was a revelation to Tree Top Jefferson.

"Man, I don't need this. Anderson said this was a straight deal, no problems. I don't need no cops."

"I don't care about any of this. What you do is your business. I'm all about getting Christopher. You hear me? Next week I won't even remember we met. Let me ask you something," Cole paused. "What should I call you anyway?"

"People call me Tree."

"Thank you. Tree, is your mother alive?"

"You leave my mama out of this!"

"Relax, I don't mean any disrespect. Is she alive?"

"Yeah, she lives 'cross town."

"What if she got sick, real sick, and was dying. And her man dumped her in a rest home and stopped payin'. How would that make you feel?"

"He'd be dead. That's how I'd feel."

"Well, Christopher did that to his wife. She and I were once very close. I let her go. You see where I'm goin'?"

"You gonna kill him?"

"No, but he'll wish he were dead. I want him put behind bars for a long, long time."

"Man, I don't need any of this. Sorry about your friend, but I don't need this. I got a good thing goin' on. I don't need this shit at all. Chicago cops, shit, I don't need this, man." Jefferson was on his feet. "You don't need to wait 'til next week, you forget we ever met now—you hear me, right now!" He was screaming at Cole.

Cole took a long slow sip of his coffee. "You may need my help later," he said softly.

"I don't need nothin'! You hear me, Chicago? Don't be comin' to my town and be tellin' me I need yo' help!" Jefferson grabbed the back of his chair and threw it against the wall. The chair hit the tile floor with a clang, slid and thudded against the windows.

"Suit yourself," Cole said in a matter-of-fact tone.

"I suit me fine! I'll suit *you* if you ain't careful!" Jefferson's long legs had got him out of the alcove and into the main area of the store.

Patrons put down their books and magazines and watched as Jefferson ranted and screamed, waving his arms about as he hit the front door. Then every eye in the store turned to Cole. Standing, Cole lifted his Double Mocha Venti and, with a broad smile and a light bow, silently toasted the gaping crowd. As he passed the counter, he slipped a $5 bill into the tip jar and left the store.

On the sidewalk, Cole shuddered. He hated confrontation and felt like he'd been playing tag with a cobra. Whisper had been easy. Tree Top Jefferson was a whole different thing. He was dangerous and unstable—it could be chemically induced or maybe he was just plain crazy. Either way, there was a volatility that made Cole's stomach knot up. He had just jumped into the deep end of the pool.

FOURTEEN

Cole rolled and tumbled most of the night, finally falling into a deep sleep around dawn. He hadn't gotten what he wanted from Jefferson. Richard Anderson, for whatever reason, had shielded Allen Christopher from Tree Top and probably anyone else involved with turning the diamonds into cash. Had Anderson planned on skipping town from the start? How hard was Christopher feeling the squeeze? Did he even know Anderson was gone? *Only one way to find out*, Cole thought.

He sat on the edge of the bed. It was nearly 10 o'clock. He rubbed his eyes and thumbed through a stack of business cards on the nightstand. He dialed the number for John H. Brazil & Associates.

"Mr. Brazil, please. Bob Borsma from Denver calling."

"Just a moment, Mr. Borsma."

"John Brazil, how can I help?"

"Good morning. My name is Borsma, Bob Borsma. I'm with Coloco Properties here in Denver. Got a minute?"

"You bet, what's up?"

"I understand you're the broker?"

"Yep."

"I need to get some info on one of your agents if I may. He's listed as a principal investor in a project our office is trying to put together. I don't need facts or figures or anything like that. We're just trying to get a feel for the players."

"So, who's your man? Oops, sorry—or woman. Gotta be PC."

"Man. Allen Christopher. What can you tell me about him?"

"Allen's been with us about a year, maybe a little less. Came from an office 'cross town. You say he's an investor?"

"Yeah, it's a general partnership we're putting together. Why, would that be a problem?"

"Well." The line went silent.

Cole smelled blood, and his shark was in full-on. "Big producer, is he?"

"I wouldn't exactly say that. Tell me a bit about this project, Bob." Brazil was being far too careful. Cole could almost hear the man ask himself, *How much do I tell this guy?*

"Sure, are you looking for a project, John?" Cole decided to soften his approach a bit.

"Ah, no, no—just curious."

"Eagle Rock is in its second phase. The Remco Investment Group pretty much controlled Phase One. We're looking at about 800 homes in Phase Two. Median of about $450,000. The thing with Phase Two is the shopping center, and that's where Allen has really shown an interest. We have Wal-Mart and Albertson's on board so far. Starbucks and Blockbuster are pretty sure things. Couple in negotiation that I probably shouldn't talk about quite yet. We figure right around $42 million after we split the cost of the highway refigure with the State. It's a bit of a bear. We need to add an overpass. Solid project, John. We still need a couple of investors to tie it up."

"Allen has bought in?"

"Not yet. We haven't signed docs on Phase Two partners. John, do I sense some hesitancy on your end of the line there? I really need the straight dope. You see, Allen is the only out-of-towner in this deal. Unless I can bring *you* in." Cole gave a slight chuckle. "Little humor there, John. So, what's up? Is there something I should know?"

"Well, Mr. Borsma..." Brazil began.

"Bob, please."

"Bob. I just don't know where Allen would get the money for this kind of a project."

"All tied up with stuff out there?"

"Not exactly. Hold on a second, can you?"

"Sure."

Brazil got up and Cole heard the thud of an office door closing. "I'm back. Look, Bob, Allen Christopher is not a big producer around here. He's pretty near the bottom, actually. I loaned him $4,500 about four months ago. Seems he couldn't pay for his wife's care in a rest home. I guess the insurance would only pay so much. So far, I haven't seen a cent."

Cole felt his jaw tighten.

"Here's the weird part. He pulls up yesterday in a new Mercedes, now you call. I'm getting a bad vibe here."

"Tell me something, John, just between us. He's not

involved in drugs, is he?" Cole thought he would throw Brazil a curve ball.

"God, no, at least—no, I can't see that."

"This is really upsetting. I was counting on his five mill to—" Cole paused for effect. "I'm sorry, please try to forget I said that. Guess I was thinking out loud. Hey, I've kept you long enough. Thanks for your help. Seems I need to have a little chat with our Mr. Christopher."

"Bob, I, well, I feel there is something else you should know."

"What's that?" *Here it comes,* Cole thought.

"My receptionist came to me a while back and said a friend of Allen's had been receiving packages from a jewelry wholesaler. She didn't think anything of it the first time it happened. Allen explained the friend was a business associate and that was that. Thing was, he started getting about one a week. So, she came to me asking if it was all right. I got busy and then was gone on vacation. You know how it is. When I asked him about it, he said his friend needed the packages to be signed for and sometimes paid for, and since he was usually around, he didn't think it would be a problem. I asked him what he was doing, and he basically told me it was outside of work and none of my business. I still get steamed when I think about it."

"John, I appreciate your candor. I have a funny feeling Mr. Christopher hasn't been on the square with me. Thanks again. I hope we get to meet someday." Cole hung up before Borsma had a chance to respond.

In Ellie's file at Eastwood Manor there had been a copy of a check Christopher had written. When the office manager wasn't looking, Cole had jotted down the account number on the back of the form she'd given him.

He looked up the phone number for the Century Banking Company.

"Bookkeeping, please," Cole said in a cheerful voice.

The sound of laughter and talking preceded a woman's voice saying, "Hi, this is Brenda. How can I help?"

"Good Morning, Brenda. Phillip Potter here, I'm with People's Credit Union in Oxnard. Sounds like your day's going pretty good so far."

"I'm really armpit deep in alligators," she giggled. "One of the girls just got engaged, so we've been sort of celebrating. I am so behind! How can I help?"

"Got a check here drawn on an account with you folks. Can you tell me if it will clear?"

"You betcha. Account number?"

"O2-34-6792, belongs to an Allen Christopher."

"Oh," Brenda said flatly.

"Ooo, I don't like the sound of that," Cole said mockingly.

"How much this time?"

"Forty-six hundred and change."

"Oh, brother. I don't even need to look, Phil. No way, Jose."

"Great. Tell me something. Does this guy have a history of this?"

"He keeps just enough in the account to keep from having it closed. Got a big overdraft, so some of his checks roll over. It drives me crazy. I'm always on the phone either declining payment or trying to get him to make a deposit. Argh," Brenda growled.

"Yeah, I've got a second one here for another of $3,200. My customer was going to sell him a car or truck or something, then he came back and was buying a trailer. Customer dropped off the checks, so I'm checking while he's at the teller window. He's not going to be happy. What's the bride-to-be's name?"

"Jessica."

"Well, tell her congrats from me. Thanks, Brenda." Cole hung up. That was too easy.

He loved to stir things up. Maybe it was just a mean streak. Being able to get the information he needed was a skill, but then being able to add a little poison to a bad guy's life was a pleasure. Everybody likes to be sneaky, but Cole relished it, savored it, and replayed it over and over. In less than five minutes, he found that Allen Christopher was broke, had a bad track record with his bank, and had driven a very large wedge between himself and his boss. To sprinkle gasoline on the fire, Cole made the inquiries as a dignified real estate mogul and a friendly, thoughtful bank employee. Any denials by Christopher would only reaffirm people's preconceived notion of what he was all about. Cole smiled at the thought of Christopher being confronted by his boss as to how he thought he was going to invest in a huge building project when he still owed him $4,500.

Cole remembered first learning the art of the anonymous payback. When he was about 10 years old, he had made a trip to the county library with his teenage cousin, Michelle. She had told their parents they were going to do homework, but she taught Cole something he remembered far longer than anything he learned in the third grade. An old lady down the street had told Cole's aunt that Michelle was with a bunch of girls in a car smoking. The woman had seen them cruising downtown on Friday night when Michelle was supposed to be at the home of a sick friend. The plan now was payback.

For more than an hour, Cole and Michelle removed the subscription cards from nearly every magazine in the library. Then, using their left hands and pens in a dozens colors—so, as Michelle believed—no one would be able to prove it was them, Cole and Michelle filled in the old lady's name and address. For months, the old lady received dozens and dozens of magazines in her mailbox, followed by requests for payment for subscriptions she had no clue why she received. Cruel? To be sure. Payback? Gloriously so. Most importantly in Cole's eyes was that the secret wasn't revealed until long after the old woman's death.

In the years that followed, Michelle honed her ability to torment. Pizzas arrived at the door of some unsuspecting offender, subscriptions to three or four record clubs, and orders for gas, water, or electricity to be turned off. The closing of bank accounts and balances sent to a victim's home was her final victory. With the account closed and the balance spent, seven days' worth of checks bounced all over town like little rubber balls. Shortly after the bank stunt, Michelle married a law student and found out she was dancing very close to a felony. At the funeral of Cole's aunt, his cousin had shared this revelation with him and thus ended one of the great careers in revenge.

Cole's years of undercover newspaper research had always seemed a bit more rewarding when accompanied by a bit of venom. He wondered many times how the little light he shed on a foul deed, otherwise unexposed, helped tilt the balance just a little in favor of the good guys. He did just enough to cause a lot of aggravation to unpunished villains who hadn't broken the law but just caused an innocent person pain: The current address of a deadbeat dad who owed child support sent to a welfare mother's caseworker; a tenant a poor landlord couldn't get rid of who just happened to have an outstanding warrant tipped to the police; the restaurant owner who cheated waitresses out of their fair share of tips and whose sanitation violations the health department was happy to hear about. Cole seldom, if ever, disclosed his little role-playing episodes to anyone, and he liked it that way. Just like the Lone Ranger or the Bob Dylan movie, he like being *Masked and Anonymous.*

Thumbing through the cards on the nightstand, Cole found the one for Sven Elias.

"Sven? Cole Sage. Any word on our friend?"

"Hello, Mr. Sage—Cole. Yes, he phoned yesterday. He asked if I had changed my mind, and I did just as you said. I told him I was still thinking about it. He became quite curt with me. Said he didn't have all the time in the world. I think he's under some kind of pressure." Sven laughed softly. "I played dumb and said my wife wanted to know how many karats and what grade the diamonds were. Then he really got mad. It was pretty funny."

"Sounds like I've created a monster. Good job. Just don't scare him off. I think I'm going to pay Mr. Christopher a visit. For now, it might be a good idea not to take his calls. Looks like this is going to come together real nice. Thanks for letting me in on the action." Cole couldn't help making Elias feel important. He was always a sucker for the underdog.

"Thank you, Cole. I'm not real creative about stuff, and you have really helped me a lot."

"Take care, Sven."

Cole showered, dressed, and had breakfast with the help of the McDonald's drive-through. It was a bright, warm Saturday morning, and on his way to Allen Christopher's office, Cole passed three or four schools with soccer fields packed with brightly colored teams surrounded by lines of parents.

As he pulled into the parking lot, Cole noticed a group of men in matching red jerseys gathered in front of the office. Four of them were playing catch. The others just stood around talking. Cole parked and approached the group. He could now see that the fronts of the jerseys said "BRAZIL REALTY" in bold white letters. The backs said, "HUMP DAY LUNCH LEAGUE."

"Beautiful day for a game!" Cole called to two of the men playing catch.

"Sure is!" a tall, good-looking black man called back.

"Mind if I borrow this a minute?" Cole said as he pulled an aluminum baseball bat from the canvas bag lying on the sidewalk.

He didn't wait for an answer and went through the double glass doors into Brazil & Associates Realty.

"Allen Christopher's office?"

"The end of the hall." Cole was already halfway there as the receptionist tried to protest, "but he's on the phone. Sir, sir!"

Allen Christopher sat behind his desk, one hand across his brow, the other tightly pressing the phone to his ear. Cole closed the door behind him and pushed in the lock with his thumb. He turned and twisted the wand that closed the vertical blinds.

"What the hell do you think—" Christopher began as Cole reached the desk and randomly pressed one of the buttons on the phone.

"Oops, they hung up," Cole said coldly.

"Get out! Who the hell do you think you are?" Christopher started to stand.

"We're going to have a little talk. I suggest you sit down.

I have something to say, and there is something I want. When I've said it and have what I want, I'll leave. The only options are, when I leave, you're still sitting in your desk, or I've splattered your brains all over that wall." Cole pointed with the baseball bat at the wall behind Christopher.

"What? Are you crazy! Get out of here!"

Cole took the bat and raised it high over his head and, with every sinew in his being, brought it down on the top of the desk. The glass cover shattered and the bat sank deep into the highly polished walnut top. Christopher again started to stand. Cole took the end of the bat and jabbed him hard in the chest. Christopher fell back in his chair.

"First of all, let's get something straight. I really don't care what happens to me. Do you understand what I'm saying? If I killed you and they fried me in the electric chair, I could care less. The only thing I ever cared about, I lost a long time ago. Now she's dying. Why she married you, I will never understand, never. But it's over. Your abuse, your games, all the bullshit ends today. Now, get in whatever drawer you hide things, and I want the power of attorney you had Ellie sign."

"I don't have it."

Cole swung the bat, and the phone exploded against the wall.

"All right, all right, don't hurt me. It's in the safe. I'll get it."

There was a knock on the door. "Allen, are you okay?"

Cole looked at Christopher and gave him a big fake smile and made the okay sign with his left hand while pointing the bat at him with his right.

"Fine, Shelly. I was moving my desk, and the phone fell," Christopher panted.

"Are you sure?"

"Yeah, yeah, be out in a minute."

"Well, okay."

"You lie so well," Cole said in a disgusted sneer.

Christopher knelt by the small gray safe in the corner, fumbling with the combination. He stopped, spun the dial, and began again.

"You know, you really need to get your affairs lined up in the next few days. The police are going to keep you occupied for quite a while."

"And why's that?"

"Let me be the first to tell you. Your friend Richard Anderson has left town. He won't be coming back. He took the diamonds. A big order. You financed them." Cole spoke in short, hard statements, like a prizefighter landing blows to a body. "Have you got $380,000, Allen?"

"I don't know any Richard Anderson." Christopher's shaky voice betrayed the lie.

"Is that what you'll tell the FBI when they come calling? Thin, Allen, very thin."

"I've done nothing wrong."

"Tree Top Jefferson isn't very happy, either." Cole was like a very big cat playing with a mouse.

"I don't have anything to do with him." Christopher was starting to breath hard.

"You ever been to jail, Allen?"

"Please stop. I can't remember the combination."

"Why? You've done nothing wrong. Except for that little matter of offering Sven Elias diamonds to change the zoning on the south side. Bribing a city official is a felony, you know."

Finally getting the combination, Christopher pulled down the handle and opened the safe door. The three shelves inside were covered with various documents and papers. He lifted a small stack of envelopes and sorted through until he found one with a folded sheet of paper clipped to it. He stood and turned toward Cole, then suddenly spun about to close the safe door.

"Not so quick. Leave that open," Cole growled.

"You said you wanted the power of attorney."

"I do. But I'm kind of a curious guy. Get back in your chair."

As Cole moved toward the safe, he rested the bat on his shoulder and looked at Christopher as if daring him to try something. Christopher, sensing that Cole was just looking for an excuse to hurt him, returned to his chair.

"There's nothing in there of interest to you. It's just papers. Birth certificates, insurance policies for my kids, nothing to do with you."

"Important stuff?"

"Yes."

"Hard to replace?"

"Yes, please, you don't need them. Some are *impossible* to replace. They have nothing to do with Ellie."

"The magic words."

Cole reached in the safe and took out a stack of papers. Without directly taking his attention from Christopher, he began glancing through them.

"Okay, you're right, I don't need this stuff." Cole approached the desk and reached out his hand. "Give me that." He indicated the envelope Christopher held.

"Here! Now will you just go?" Christopher was trembling and his hand shook as he handed Cole the papers. "Please." He began to cry.

Cole took the envelope and removed the sheet of paper clipped to it. Unfolding it, he scanned the language and looked at the document. "How did you get this notarized?"

"The girl up front."

"And Ellie's fingerprint?"

"While she was sleeping," Christopher said softly.

Cole would not look at him. Gone was the swaggering, self-assured cock of the walk. Instead, in front of him sat a defeated, sobbing fraud. Cole refused to let go of his anger. He held it close, it warmed him, yet there was something else. He knew he would never hurt Christopher physically. Somehow just getting the power of attorney was not enough.

"Please, go. You got what you wanted." With the back of his hand, Christopher wiped the snot that was running over his lips and onto his chin.

"What did she ever do to deserve—" Cole stopped in mid-thought.

On the wall next to the safe sat a large paper shredder. Cole reached over and flicked on the red power switch. The machine began to whir and small shreds of paper softly waved in the corners of the rotating blades. Cole folded the paper he came for and slipped it into his hip pocket. He paused just for a moment, then turned and started feeding the stack of papers in his hand into the machine. The rollers crushed and cut the papers in a matter of seconds. He reached in the safe and took another stack.

"Oh, please. Please stop, don't do that. My papers, please."

"My, me, mine, that's all you're about, isn't it?"

"My kids, that's theirs, too, their future, please. Why hurt *them*?"

"Why hurt anyone? Ellie has no future. Let's level the field a bit."

Cole started slipping page after page into the shredder. Deeds, insurance policies, birth certificates, passports, letters, envelopes, old photographs, Social Security cards, an autographed picture of Mickey Mantle and Roger Maris, bank books, stock certificates, licenses—everything in the safe, shelf by shelf, was fed into the hungry jaws of the shredder. Christopher only looked up once, when something metallic in an envelope rasped and clattered as it went through the shredder's teeth. The crisp crinkling sound of paper and the crunching thud of paper clips and staples fell silent to the smooth whir of the shredder's fan. Cole was finished.

"I guess that does it." Cole clicked off the shredder and shifted the bat from one shoulder to the other.

"Why have you done this?" Christopher's body shuddered as he spoke.

"Because I hate you."

Cole started for the door, then turned. On Christopher's desk sat a bronze eagle on a thin marble slab atop a walnut box. The thing that caught Cole's eye was the shiny brass plaque. He approached the desk and Christopher looked up at him. The tears had stopped. He wore a strange expression, a kind of mixture of resigned defeat and yet a look of knowing.

Cole picked up the eagle trophy and Christopher shifted in his seat.

"Top Producer 200," he began reading. "You have learned to soar with the eagles." Cole held the baseball bat in the middle and with a quick snap knocked off the eagles extended wing. "Looks like you're grounded." As

Cole righted the trophy to put it back on the desk, the bottom panel opened, and a plastic bag fell out. "I'll be damned." Cole chuckled.

Christopher, without thinking, grabbed for the bag. Just as quickly, Cole struck him with a swift blow to the wrist. Christopher recoiled in pain.

"These look like about enough to bring Ellie's account current and then some." Cole turned the plastic bag in his hand, then stuffed it into his pocket.

"There are close to $40,000 worth of stones there." Christopher panted, messaging his wrist. "I tell you what, we could split them. You can pay for Ellie's care for a while and I can—"

"My God, is there no bottom to how low you'll go? *I* can pay for Ellie's bill? She's your wife, you bastard! Haven't you heard anything I've said? You're through. You can't bribe me. Hell, you couldn't even bribe that poor, innocent Elias. You have no way out. You're going to jail, and what they'll do to you in there, well, you'll see." Cole smiled at the thought. "I'm satisfied now. Goodbye, Mr. Christopher. Not that you would think of it, but don't worry about Ellie. I'll take care of her; the devil can have you."

With a click of the lock, Cole left the office. The receptionist stood gazing down the hall towards him. As he approached her, Cole brought the end of the bat up in a mock salute.

"Mr. Christopher twisted his wrist rearranging his office. You might want to get him an ice pack. Oh, and don't say anything about the way it turned out. He's a little upset with the results. Have a nice day." Cole was out the front door.

"Hey, where'd ya go with my bat?" Asked one of the buzz-cut softball players still lingering in the parking lot.

"I heard there was a rat in there."

"A rat?"

"Yeah, but he turned out to be a mouse." Cole tossed the bat to the mystified player.

FIFTEEN

"Well, mi amigo de Chicago!" Whisper smiled.

"Buenos dias." Cole nodded his head.

"I never thought I would see you again. Have a seat." Whisper motioned to the empty seat across the booth. "What brings you back—more discussion of current political affairs?"

"Well, sort of," Cole began. "Where's your buddy?"

"Luis? Oh, don't worry, he's always around somewhere."

"You remember the fellow I told you about ? Allen Christopher?"

"The guy bankrolling the diamonds?"

"Yeah, well, I think I've put him out of business."

Whisper pushed his Ray-Bans up onto the top of his head. "You didn't kill him, did you?" He looked deep into Cole's eyes.

"No, nothing like that." Cole pressed hard against the

back of the booth as he stretched out trying to pull the baggie of diamonds from his pocket. "I got these." Cole slid the stones across the table to Whisper.

"Santo de Christo," Whisper said softly, "I have never seen such a thing. What are they worth, a million?"

"Not quite. Christopher said they were worth $40,000 wholesale. So, retail is about $250,000, give or take. "

Whisper gently poked at the stones. He looked up at Cole, grinned, and looked back down at the bag.

"So, you think you could move these?"

"Are you serious?" Whisper's eyes widened at Cole's question.

"Look, Christopher stopped paying for his wife's care in the convalescent hospital about three months ago. I am not a rich man. I have a few thousand in the bank but not enough to cover what they're demanding to keep her there. Could you buy these from me?"

"Man, I don't know. This is way out of my line, you know?"

"Mine, too." Cole smiled.

"You think I could do the car thing?"

"Yeah, but it's going to get really hot around here for a while."

"I hear you. Well, maybe I'll make a trip to L.A. I have lot of family, you know? So, okay, let's do this. Forty, huh?"

"No. I'm not looking for more than I need from this. I just want to pay Ellie's bill."

"What are you saying? You don't want the money?"

"I only want enough to keep Ellie well taken care of until—"

"Eres un buen hombre...."

"I'm sorry?"

"A good man. She is a lucky woman to have you. It's sad she didn't have you all along."

"Yeah," Cole said looking at the table. "I'll call the hospital and ask how much they need. Give me that, and you can have the rest. I'm grateful for your help."

For a very long time, Whisper just sat looking at Cole. Anthony "Whisper" Perez was having a hard time knowing what to do with this Anglo from Chicago. All his life, he had been abused verbally and physically by people who looked and talked just like Cole Sage. This guy was different. He spoke from somewhere deep inside. He spoke to Whisper as an equal, a partner, someone who had thoughts and ideas that mattered. They had discussed politics, crime, social reform. Even when they disagreed, Cole never once made Whisper feel foolish or small. Cole spoke to him with respect and yet wasn't afraid of him. Whisper wasn't used to people coming on his turf who weren't afraid of him. Even if it was just a little, it always showed in their eyes.

From the very beginning, Cole had spoken to Whisper from a position of authority. Not like cops or the guards in the juvenile detention center that Whisper so often frequented as a teen, but as someone who knew who he was and what he wanted. Whisper admired this authority. It was born of knowledge, like the sign he had read in the library in junior high: "Knowledge is Power." Whisper had gone to the library out of boredom that day for something to do, maybe to tag the inside of magazines or draw pictures in the books, like he and his friends always did. But that sign, shiny Mylar letters on a black banner, had spoken to him like no teacher or counselor ever had. "Knowledge is Power"—that was what Whisper had wanted more than anything: power.

Now, so many years and books later, he knew that real power was not what he had. People feared him and maybe even respected his organization, if you could call it that. But the power that mattered, the power on the sign, was not what he had. This must change. Whisper wanted a change. Maybe this sad man from Chicago could show him how to get *his* kind of power. Whisper looked down at his hands as they scratched at the top of the table. He realized he had been staring at nothing. How long had he been doing this, seconds, minutes? He looked back up at Cole.

"You hungry? Javie's made some chili verde today that will knock you over. Want some?"

"That sounds good."

"Javie, traigame un cierto chile verde! And a diet Pepsi." Whisper took a sip of the beer in front of him.

Cole took his cell phone from his belt clip and a small notepad from his shirt pocket.

"I'll have the amount I need in just a moment," he said dialing the cell phone. "This is Mr. Sage. I need the total amount to bring Mrs. Christopher's bill current." After several moments, the billing department of Eastwood Manor came back on the line. "I understand the prepayment, yes. That's everything, no hidden cost, no funny business? I'm sure you don't. Fine, I'll have the money to you in—" He looked up at Whisper.

"Tomorrow."

"Tomorrow. Thank you, see you then." Cole clicked the phone closed, then wrote a number on the pad.

"So, where is this place?" Whisper asked, turning the pad around.

"Off Santa Rita on Calder. Eastwood Manor, not the

greatest but not the worst, either. I hate her being in a place like that, but I don't know where else she could go."

"I'll send someone over with a cashier's check. That okay?"

"How will you—"

"My old man has an account for his rentals. He's always moving money in and out, buying and selling houses. They won't ask, I won't tell. Kind of like the Army." Whisper laughed hoarsely. "Then I give it to him in cash later. Little by little, he puts it back in."

"Here you go." Javie the barman set a bowl down in front of Cole containing large chunks of pork in a thick green sauce. "Tortillas coming up."

"Gracias, me gusta chile verde mucho." Cole smiled as he stumbled through his gringo Spanish. "You're not eating?"

"I ate a little while ago. So, what you think, good, huh?" Whisper said, like a proud father.

"Mmm, wonderful."

"Enjoy."

After a second bowl, a discussion of world and domestic affairs, and the promise of a subscription to *The Sentinel*, Cole was about to take leave of his new friend when Whisper stopped him.

"Can I ask you something?"

"Of course."

"You think a guy like me could ever go to college?"

Without missing a beat, Cole said, "Of course. You're smart, smarter than a lot of the people your age working at the paper. I think you would do very well."

"You're telling me the truth?"

"I would never lie to you."

"I believe that," Whisper said softly.

"So, you want to? The community college here is very good. What do you want to study? History, politics?"

"Could I be a writer? Like you?"

"I would hope you would aim higher." Cole smiled sensing the compliment. "Yes, America needs a voice like yours." Cole's smile had gone and he looked the young man straight in the eyes.

"I don't want to go to school around here. Too many people know me. How 'bout Chicago, do they have a good community college there?"

"Last time I checked, there were about 120 colleges in and around Chicago."

"How do I start?"

"You're serious about this?"

"Yes, sir."

Cole was amazed by this turn in the conversation. Whisper had called him "sir." He fought back a smile, then decided to let it go.

"I tell you what. How 'bout I help you? I mean, I can do some research, find out which ones are best. Which ones have good journalism departments."

"I want something else, too. Sort of your permission." Whisper looked down at the table. Like a shy little kid asking a favor from a big brother, he continued. "I don't know a lot about colleges and stuff, but they have what you call 'scholarships'?"

"Sure, we can apply for financial aid, no problem."

"No, no nothing like that. I got money. This is something special. I seen them in stuff I read. They have the names of companies and people, like on PBS, you know? So, I was thinking the extra money from the diamonds.

What if we called it a scholarship? And named it after your lady Ellie? Could we do that?"

Cole couldn't breathe. He just stared at Whisper, Anthony Perez was reborn . Then, he felt tears rolling down his cheeks. He couldn't move. He didn't want to move. He felt a pride and honor like he had never known. This street hustler who wanted out and to become a writer, wanted to pay tribute to Ellie. It was the best gift he had ever been given. *She will be so proud. No, she can't know.* How would he ever explain where the money came from?

"I think," Cole began, "there could be no finer honor in this life than if that happened." He reached up and brushed the tears from his eyes. "Everything you do, everything you achieve, everything you accomplish in life will be Ellie living on in some way. It is a beautiful thing, my friend. A beautiful thing."

Whisper reached across the table and shook hands with Cole. Then he put his finger to his lips and whispered, "Not a word of this to anyone. When I leave, it will be to escape some heat or the cops or something. I will make up a good story and then disappear. No strings, no one will follow, no one will know where I went or what I'm doing. A clean break, cold turkey. Will it work?"

"We will make it work."

"It's a deal then."

Cole stood at the end of the booth. "I am very proud of you. If you were my own son, I couldn't be prouder." Then he turned and walked toward the door.

"Hey, watch your back. Word on the street is you pissed off Tree Top big time. Be careful, amigo, we've got work to do."

Cole looked in his rear-view mirror more than usual

on the way back to the motel. Everything seemed normal. All the same, he wished Whisper hadn't warned him. Cole tended to worry. Now he would hear every footstep, tick, creak, and bump in the night—and a motel makes lots of those. As he drove, he thought of Ellie. He hadn't seen her in a day and a half. He needed to get to Eastwood, but things were finally coming together. Maybe later, after he made some calls. A light gray pickup cut in front of him, and he had to slam on his brakes to avoid hitting it. The violent jerk of the car shattered his thoughts and put his focus back on the road.

When Cole got to his room there was a note on the door. "Brennan. Please call."

Great, he thought. "*When are you coming back? I got a paper to run here. How much longer you gonna be?*" Cole could hear it now. He stuck the note in his pocket and unlocked the door.

As he entered the room, he caught an ever so slight whiff of an unfamiliar smell. Was it cologne, air freshener? Whatever it was, he hadn't smelled it before. Cole took the phone book from the drawer in the desk and opened to United States Government. It was then that something caught his eye.

Cole had a habit of keeping his clothes pushed to the left side of the closet. A jacket, three shirts, and a pair of slacks were all pushed slightly to the center. Someone had moved them. The bed was still unmade. He stood and walked to his suitcase that was sitting on a folding rack near the closet. The suitcase was closed. He knew he had left it open because he had accidentally grabbed an extra sock. He had tossed the sock back into the suitcase as he had gone to brush his teeth.

He returned to the phone and rang the front desk. "This is Mr. Sage in 218."

"I'm so sorry your room has not been made up, sir. Our maid had to go home sick. You see, her daughter is a maid, too, and had to drive her. It should be done this afternoon. I am very, very sorry." The soft Indian accent of the manager only added to Cole's concern.

"Has *anyone* been in my room?"

"Oh no, sir. I am the only one here and I have been in the office, except of course to bring you your message. Did you find it?"

"Yes, thank you."

"The maid should be back by four o'clock. Again, my apologies."

"No problem." Cole hung up.

He turned again to the phone book. After identifying himself to three different people and partially telling his story three times, he was transferred one last time.

"Fergusson."

"Can you take a report?"

"Depends."

"Look, you're the third person I've talked to. You people make it hard to turn in the bad guys. My name is Sage. I'm with *The Chicago Sentinel*. If you want to check me out, call Tom Harris, Precinct 51, Chicago. I've uncovered some things I thought you guys might be interested in. I was diggin' around for a friend of mine and uncovered a scheme that involved interstate mail fraud, bribery of an elected official with stolen property, and probably a bunch of other things you'll find if you start poking' around."

"Okay, I'll bite. Who're we talkin' about here?"

"Allen Christopher. He's a realtor. It seems he defrauded a wholesale diamond broker in Washington. He ordered several hundred thousand dollars worth of stones and doesn't have two nickels to pay the bill. Then there's Sven Elias, the County Zoning Commissioner here. Christopher offered him diamonds in exchange for Elias' changing the zoning for a project Christopher was trying to put together with an outfit back east called Malcor Manufacturing."

"Bingo!"

"Excuse me?"

"Bingo, Eureka, whatever. The duck just came down. You said the secret word."

"I don't follow." Cole was a bit surprised by Fergusson's excitement.

"Malcor. It's a front for the mob. Castigleone Family from Detriot. This guy, Christopher, you think he knows they're organized crime?"

Cole couldn't help grinning. "Well, you'd know better about the mob than I would, but from the way he's connected with the small time hoods around here, I wouldn't doubt it." Cole covered his mouth for fear he would laugh, then coughed. "Sorry, think I'm catching a cold. This whole diamond thing seems too well conceived for some small town realtor—who, by the way, sells very little real estate. He's got street punks buying cars with the diamonds, then turning them for cash. Pretty smart, huh?"

"Evidently not smart enough. Let me get some people on this. Is Elias willing to help us?"

"Yep, a real Boy Scout," Cole replied. "He's been contacted twice by Christopher, and the last time, he got real pushy."

"Got any other names?"

"A local smalltime hustler who was swapping the diamonds for cars, goes by Tree Top, last name Jefferson. When I talked to him, he tried to give me the name of an ex-con named Anderson as the top dog. I think this is a cover that Jefferson and Christopher cooked up. Probably not much to it. Anderson is small potatoes and doesn't have the brains or money for a scheme like this. Jefferson's real jumpy and will probably turn on Christopher with a little coaxing. Oh yeah, and a guy named Brazil, John Brazil. He is Christopher's broker at the real estate office. Christopher got money from him and didn't pay it back. He'll be happy to talk. That's kind of how I got involved in all this. An old friend of mine is Christopher's wife. "

"Aha."

"Not what you think. She's dying, called me for help. Christopher was trying to cheat her daughter, his stepdaughter, out of an inheritance. I was trying to see what I could do. Just so you know where I fit in."

"I didn't mean any disrespect. Sounds like you've been a busy boy. We're really low on manpower right now. Man, if I could tie this Christopher guy to the Castigleones—Okay, where can I reach you?"

"Palmwood Motel, Room 218. My cell is 773-677-8120."

"I'll be in touch. And Sage, don't get too nosy. The Castigleones have a nasty habit of finding construction projects to bury people in, get me? And, for God sakes, don't print anything about these Detroit guys for a while. Please, we need to nail this guy. You go to print and they'll scatter like roaches in the light."

"I hear you. I'm about done here, so I won't be in town much longer."

Cole hung up the phone and went into the bathroom. As he raised the toilet seat, he saw the words "Leave or Die" written on the mirror in something white. He looked around the tiny bathroom and saw his deodorant in the sink with the cap off. He knew it couldn't be the mob guys, at least not yet. Christopher would never think of something like this. It had to be Tree Top's muscle.

Cole had been threatened before. He didn't like it, but it came with the job sometimes. Over the years, people angry about something he'd written would call the paper or send unsigned hate mail. Once, he'd gotten a dead rat with a little sign around its neck with his name on it. Tom Harris told him long ago that people who send or call in threats are not likely to follow through. He said the time to start worrying is when they send a letter to the paper after you're dead, claiming responsibility. Harris had a strange sense of humor. All the same, the message on the mirror gave Cole a knot in his stomach that he never got used to.

The next call was a courtesy. It was a kind of journalistic tradition to tip off the local paper to a story you uncover in their town. That is, if it isn't a scoop you intend to use yourself. He punched in the number for *The Daily Record* and asked for the editor. The editor was out at a luncheon and wouldn't be back until about three. The city editor would have to do.

"Hi, my name is Cole Sage. I'm with *The Chicago Sentinel.*"

It didn't take much to get the city editor excited. It took even less for Cole to accept a free lunch. Cole never understood the meaning of "no such thing as a free lunch." He had eaten plenty of them. He always knew going in that it was *quid pro quo*. The thing that made the meal free was

Cole's willingness to give away whatever he had. He didn't see it as giving anything away because if it were truly of value, he would keep it and buy his own lunch. Most of the time it was a way to have a nice meal, meet somebody new, and have an interesting chat. Even if the chat was boring, two out of three wasn't bad.

As far as the meal was concerned, he had an uncle that shared a philosophy which he had never forgotten. Cole's Uncle George was a multimillionaire. He had started out as a door-to-door salesman, an education he said that was far more valuable than any he'd learned in school. "People," he would say, "are all the same, only different." Uncle George had received a PhD in Education from the University of Oklahoma. He later became the head of Ford Motors in Southeast Asia during the Vietnam War, a dean at O.S.U., and Secretary of Education for the State of Oklahoma. This provided him the greatest opportunity to play golf with a *Who's Who* list of state and federal movers and shakers.

While playing golf with the Secretary of Health Education and Welfare, the Secretary bemoaned the fact that Congress was about to pass a bill requiring asbestos to be removed from all public buildings because of its link to cancer. The fact that the cancer developed after a lifetime of working, mining and processing the stuff had little bearing on Congress's decision. It was all going to have to be removed.

Bright and early the next morning, George contacted the Yellow Pages sales offices for every county in five states, placing an advertisement for All State Asbestos Removal. It was like a broken record. "I've never heard of that before. What do you do?" George gave a simple, nondescript answer. When January 1 of the next year rolled around, All State Asbestos Removal was flooded with calls. It was bumpy at first, but he sold the company—orders and all—in June of that year for a cool $16 million.

George devoted the rest of his life, which sadly was only another six months, to fine food and golf. He died of a heart attack on the golf course one day shortly after lunch. George told Cole when he was a boy that "we eat three meals a day, 365 days a year, so make each meal an adventure." On the rare occasion that Cole had a meal with his favorite uncle that wasn't good, George would stand up from the table, pat his rather large stomach and say, "Well, that was an adventure!" Cole had used his uncle's expression ever since.

Lunch with the city editor of the *The Daily Record* was at one o'clock downtown at the Thailand Cafe. Cole arrived a few minutes early and had a cup of tea while he weighed just how much to tell the local paper. He sat in a booth tucked back in a corner facing the door. The Cafe was bright and cheerful. Everywhere he looked, there were splashes of red and gold. Above the front door was a portrait of the King of Thailand in full military uniform with a very dignified scowl on his face. The waitress was a teenager who probably should have been at school. Nearly every table was full of people who looked like they worked at City Hall. Cole realized, as he watched a man about his age loosen his tie, that it had been nearly a week since he had worn one. He also realized that he had forgotten to call Brennan.

Jerry White was a tall man with a dark crew cut heavily waxed in front. He wore a plaid shirt and a woven tie that had gone out of style with disco. His pocket bulged with the micro recorder that was a dead giveaway he was a newspaperman of the post-1980 variety. Cole was taught to take notes and commit to memory. Memory was his greatest gift and worst enemy.

"Jerry!" Cole waved his arm as he called out.

"Hello." The tall man offered his hand to Cole, who took it.

"Have a seat." Cole indicated the chair across the table from him.

"So, all the way from Chicago." White said, sitting. "How are we so honored?" He took out the mini-recorder from his pocket and clicked "Record."

Cole reached across the table and clicked the recorder off.

"Want some tea?" Cole had grown tired of having to tell about Ellie to people who really could care less.

"Yeah, thanks. So what can you tell—"

"Look, here's the thing. I have made a complete report to the FBI. Since we talked, I'm not quite sure how much I should tell you, mostly because I fear for your safety. So, here's a start. An FBI agent named Fergusson will be in town soon to investigate several leads I gave him. They include attempted bribery of a city official. That, you cannot print. Here's what you can, and it's the tip of the iceberg. Put somebody good on this and who knows what may turn up.

"There's a local street punk called Tree Top Jefferson who's been trading diamonds for cars, boats, motorcycles, and who knows what. He then turns around and sells them."

"What's the point of that?" White replied.

"There's a huge markup in bulk diamonds—five, maybe six hundred percent. So, a $1,000 stone wholesale is worth $6,000 retail. They trade three or four stones for a $16,000 to $20,000 car, costs them four grand. They turn around and sell it for $11,000 to $16,000 and pocket the difference. Slick, huh?"

"So what's illegal? I don't get it."

"You have to pay for the stones. Tree Top's guy didn't, hasn't, can't, whatever—thus, the Feds. Interstate mail fraud."

"Yikes."

"It's like pebbles in a pond from there. Call Fergusson. Let him know you've been tipped off to the diamond scam. He seems like a fair guy. He'll probably give you first shot at the story."

"I really appreciate you giving us the scoop. How in the world did you stumble on this diamond thing?"

"When you turn over rocks, you're gonna find bugs, Jerry. Hungry?"

"I could eat a horse."

"I don't think they serve that here," Cole said dryly.

"What?"

"Never mind. You buying?"

"Of course."

Cole smiled and gently waved at the young waitress.

"Ready to order?" she smiled brightly, pad in hand.

"I'd like the fried rice," Jerry began.

"What! No, no, no. You can't come in a fine place like this and order fried rice. Come on, Jerry, get with the spirit of things." Cole winked at the waitress. "Cancel the fried rice. We'll have Tom Yum Goong, not too hot. Pra Ram Long Song and Tom Yum Talay Haeng. Diet Coke for me. How 'bout you, Jer?"

"I don't see any of that stuff on the menu," Jerry said frowning at Cole.

"He'll have a 7-Up."

"How'd you know..." Jerry trailed off.

"Sit back and relax Jerry, this is going to be an adventure."

SIXTEEN

By the time Cole and Jerry White had finished eating lunch and exchanging war stories, it was nearly four o'clock. Cole had supplied tale after tale of the big city reporter and foreign correspondent. Jerry had told of local scandals and a couple of grisly murders. Cole had told of how Brennan had taken a chance on him when he was just starting out and how he always seemed to end up working for Brennan regardless of where he wandered. Jerry explained how he went from editor of the high school paper "right here in town" to cub reporter. The farthest he had ever gotten was San Francisco for the Republican National Convention.

The one thing that anyone eavesdropping would have picked up on was the love these two had for the newspaper business. They were a million miles apart in experience and recognition, but they were part of a brotherhood that spoke the same language, understood the rush of a scoop, and the thrill of seeing your name in print.

Before they parted, Jerry had written down what they had ordered and said he was bringing his wife back for dinner. He thought it would really impress her. Cole left with a promise from Jerry that he'd send clippings of anything from his tip.

As Cole entered the convalescent home, he noticed that for the first time since he'd arrived Eastwood Manor was bustling with wheelchairs and walkers. He stopped at the front desk and told Skillings, the office manager, that she would receive full payment for the next 12 months and all back payments due. She offered Cole a piece of See's candy from a two-pound box behind the counter. He took two of his favorites—California Brittle and molasses chips—from the little brown paper cups. Money wasn't supposed to make you happy, but it seemed to Cole that the billing department had forgotten to tell Skillings. Suddenly, Cole had a new best friend.

He moved quietly through the halls on his way to Ellie's room, making an effort to smile at everyone he passed. Everyone he saw was well over 70. Why was Ellie in this place? He should have used the money from the diamonds to find a better hospital. Maybe there was a place with younger patients, people with some hope of leaving. It was then he remembered that Ellie *wouldn't* be leaving. Call it denial or whatever you want, but he just couldn't face her not getting well.

When he poked his head through the door, she was propped up in bed watching television.

"*Days of Our Lives*, El?"

"Cole, hi. Come sit down. It's almost over."

"It's been going on for 40 years! You really think it's ending today?"

"Hush." Ellie smiled.

Ellie looked better than he had seen her since he arrived. Her hair had been washed and combed. She no longer had the shoulder-length curls he so adored. Her hair was cut short and was heavily streaked with gray. It was becoming and seemed to fit her. Her eyes sparkled as Cole bent to give her a peck on the forehead.

"Stop, the nurses will all gossip." Her smile grew even bigger.

"Let 'em! They're probably bored. Since when do you watch the opium of the masses?"

"That's religion, not TV. Hush."

Even though speech was difficult, the old sparkle of Ellie's personality still shined through. It lifted Cole's spirits to see her obviously feeling better. As he sat, he looked at her for a long moment. A commercial suddenly blasted the room with a scene of a happy housewife spraying something around a room. Ellie clicked off the TV.

"It is good to see you," she said.

"You look terrific. Must be feeling better today."

"I have good days and not so good ones. With you here, it's a *really* good one."

"Flirt! Got some good news for you." Cole scooted his chair around so he faced Ellie. "I met with Allen, and the power of attorney has been shredded."

"Oh, Cole." Tears welled in Ellie's eyes.

"Knock that off, or I'll go tape it back together."

"Thank you. You just don't know how much it means."

"Oh, I think I do." Cole smiled. "I also have some not-so-good news. Are you up for it? I can wait until later if—"

"My laters aren't always predictable. I'm a big girl. What is it?" Ellie seemed to straighten a bit, bracing herself for what was to come.

"Two things, actually." Cole cleared his throat and took a deep breath. "First, I found Erin." He sighed and looked deep into Ellie's eyes for a long moment before continuing, "She won't come back, El. I am so sorry. I failed you." Cole felt his face redden. "She is a beautiful girl. Looks just like her mom. No wonder you're so proud of her. But there's a lot of hurt and misunderstanding there. Reminds me of you—not just looks, but her laugh and some of her mannerisms."

"Does she know I'm sick, Cole?"

"I told her. She cried and then got angry, kind of like I did. I think I softened her up a bit, though. She'll come around. She loves you a lot, said so. She's just mixed up. I am so sorry, Ellie."

"I hurt her." Tears were streaming down Ellie's cheeks. "I was so wrong to side with Allen. How could I have been such a fool?"

"There's one other thing." Cole looked down at his foot as it traced the lines around the gray speckled tile.

"What is it, Cole? Is she in trouble? Please, Cole, tell me."

"She's married, Ellie."

Ellie gasped and threw her hand over her mouth. "Oh, Cole," she muttered, "I wasn't there with her."

"You might as well have it all. You're a grandma. A little girl named Jenny."

Closing her eyes, Ellie turned her head away from Cole and quietly sobbed. Cole stood and gently stroked her arm, allowing her a mournful moment.

"She's just beautiful. I saw a picture. Lots of curly hair, just like you and Erin. Erin said her husband spoils her something awful."

Ellie reached over and took Cole's hand. "I'll die and never see them. Do you think this is how my parents felt when I was out running all over the country? This is pay-back, isn't it?"

"Come on. I don't believe in Karma. She'll come around. I got a good feeling about it."

"How could I be so happy and so sad at the same time?" Ellie gave a half-hearted laugh.

"I don't know, but when you figure it out, explain it to me, won'tcha?" Cole brushed her cheek with his knuckles.

"So, what else?"

"What?"

"You said you had a couple of not-so-good pieces of news. I hope the second one isn't the 'wow' finish." Ellie smiled softly. "Go on, don't play dumb."

"Are you sure? I didn't, I mean, I hate upsetting you."

"It's all right. I cry a lot lately, it won't kill me. As much as I wish it would."

"Hey, no talk like that."

"Go on, Cole," she pressed.

"It's Allen."

"He's divorcing me," she said flatly.

Cole laughed nervously and said, 'No such luck."

"Well, it mustn't be too bad."

"That really depends on your point of view, I guess. Al-len's in big trouble. He'll probably go to jail."

Ellie stared straight ahead and didn't speak. Her hands were in her lap, and she twisted the blanket between her fingers. Cole could see the muscles in her jaw flexing. She turned with a steely glare and said, "I'm sorry to hear that."

"I did some digging around while I was trying to figure out how to get the power of attorney back, and I guess I turned over too many rocks."

"I don't want to know." Ellie's tone had finality to it. It was the closing of a door.

"I don't want you to worry, though; you'll be taken care of. I promise."

"You can't afford to pay—"

"It's already done. Didn't hurt me a bit, honest."

"Oh Cole, I feel like such a fool." Ellie's voice had become shaky again. "I'm so ashamed to have you see all this. Please forgive me for dragging you out here." She began to cry.

Cole lowered the metal rail and sat on the side of the bed. He took Ellie's hand. She continued to weep gently. Cole had no words. He felt ashamed that the man who had made a lifetime of choosing and molding and polishing words had none in this moment. He felt a lump in his throat and gritted his teeth. He knew his time with Ellie was nearly over. Brennan would want him back in Chicago soon. He ached deep in his chest. He thought of quitting the paper, moving back, and spending Ellie's last days together. He knew that was not the answer.

Cole had spent so many years longing to be with Ellie. He had dreamt and fantasized about how their lives would someday come together again. Now here they were—she, an invalid, he, a ship without anchor. As he sat gently stroking her hand, he tried to imagine a life without thoughts of Ellie. He wouldn't forget her, he wasn't worried about that, but she'd always been his hope.

Few things in life are as important as hope. No one knew better than Cole Sage. He had about lost all hope until Ellie's call for help. His great chance to see her again. His opportunity to provide for her all the things he had always longed to. Two tasks, like some hero from a book. Two tasks to prove his faithfulness, his dedication, his love. He had saved Erin's inheritance. Just like the old cowboy movies, the stranger had ridden in and gotten back the mortgage to the ranch. Only Cole wouldn't get the girl in the end. The end would get the girl.

As they sat quietly side by side, his mind drifted back to the first time he'd lost her. It was a Christmas long ago. Ellie had decided she needed more space. Cole had begun thinking about the future after college, and it included being married to Ellie. She, on the other hand, was beginning to get ideas about travel and "finding herself." He had bought her a book of poems. It was leather bound and had gold letters embossed on the front and spine. It was a collection of Victorian poetry. Soft, sentimental, mushy—just the kind she liked, or so he thought. He couldn't return it, so in an effort to get her back, he drove over to her house. Her father met him at the door and took the package. Cole had paid a lot of money for the book and had made it even pricier by buying authentic Victorian paper and bows to wrap it in, even paying a woman at a framing gallery to add a calligraphy inscription on the flyleaf.

"Waste of time, Cole." Her father told him.

"She's never been a waste of time to me, sir." Cole had said softly.

"Well , you might as well know, she's seeing someone else."

"Merry Christmas, sir, and please tell Ellie 'hello' for me."

Ellie's dad looked hard at the package, shook his head,

and closed the door. Cole walked to the car in a fog. He was in a complete daze, numb, and his hands were trembling. Before he reached the end of the street, he pulled over and vomited out the open car door. He didn't hear a word his professor had said that night in Rhetoric class. Arriving home, his heart skipped a beat when his mother said that Ellie had come by and dropped off a present. She pointed to the hall table, and there was the present he had taken her. He didn't know how to get along without her then and now that she was back in his life, the fear of life without her was just as strong. The difference was that this time there would be no second and third chance.

Getting Erin to come see her mother couldn't be as hopeless as he felt. He knew that a child of Ellie's couldn't be as heartless and selfish as Erin seemed on the surface. He'd connected with her. He could feel her kindness. She had put up a wall that would take some time to tear down, but she would come around. She had to. Ellie seemed so strong today when he first arrived. She was having a reprieve from the pain, and her voice for the most part was normal. Cole prayed that his news wouldn't give her a setback. If they could only have a little more time like today, before he had to leave.

Cole stayed until a nurse came and said it was time for Ellie's bath. Ellie had told stories of Erin as a little girl. They reminisced about their times together. They had laughed and, for just a little while, forgot about the disease that was slowly killing her. Cole told her stories of his times overseas, in the jungles, the food he had eaten, his love of the ocean. He had even confessed about the island girl he'd thought he was in love with.

When the time came to leave, he left her and didn't

look back. Their bond was so strong that even with all the years between them, it had not broken. And for a brief time that evening, they'd been 20 years old again.

SEVENTEEN

Cole drove back to the motel with a big smile on his face. He hit the speed bump at the entrance to the parking lot and realized he'd been on cruise control. Thoughts of Ellie and the memories they had relived were like a tonic. Cole felt a deep healing inside, like the dark cloud that had been in front of the sun was blown aside gently by a spring breeze. His soul was brightened. He began whistling as he locked the car door and started toward the stairs to his room.

As he passed the alcove next to the stairs, he sensed a movement, a shadow, but it was too late to process. As he lifted his right foot to plant it on the bottom stair, he was dropped to his knees by a blow to the back of his head. His hands hit the stair. He pushed up. A pair of arms slid through his and spun him around. With his arms behind his back, he was nearly helpless as he was lifted up to his toes.

Standing in front of him was Tree Top's man with the parrot tattoos. Before Cole could react, the man punched him hard in the stomach. The hours of hitting the body bag in the gym paid off, and Cole heaved out all the air in his lungs.

"Good evening, Mr. Smart Mouth from Chicago," the tattooed man sneered.

Cole gasped for air. He had an aura of sparklers surrounding his vision, and he was afraid he was blacking out.

"What? Nothing clever to say?" The man slapped Cole with the back of his hand on the right side of Cole's face.

His ears rang, but the slap seemed to clear Cole's head a bit, and he raised his eyes to look at the man. He was bigger than Cole remembered and had his head shaved smooth, but the huge parrot tattoos were unmistakable.

"Ooh, look here, Tommy, Chicago looks pissed." Tattoo spoke to the man holding Cole.

Cole listened to the two men banter back and forth and for the first time realized how stupid they must be. Like a couple of really dumb schoolyard bullies who torment their victim, they teased Cole.

"Want some more? Mr. Wise Guy, cat got your tongue?"

"Maybe he likes it," said the voice from behind him.

Cole tried to twist away from the grip on his arms, but he was still dazed. He breathed deeply and tried to calm the pain and the nausea from the blow to his stomach.

"Nice to see you guys, again," Cole gasped.

"See, Tommy, always the smart ass, this one. Hold him tight."

The tattooed man pulled back to deliver another blow. In an instant before he struck, Cole leaned back against the man holding him and kicked both legs out at his attacker. The kick fell short and the tattooed man's blow glanced off his lower calf.

"He likes to kick, Tommy! He's gonna love this, then." Tattoo turned slightly and bounced on the balls of his feet. He did a karate kick shooting his leg out at almost a perfect 90-degree angle. "Okay, here it comes!" He kicked again, this time with the intent of landing a blow to Cole's midsection.

Cole twisted hard to the right and the kick landed just above his hip. Still bouncing, Tattoo spun around and kicked Cole in the ribs. Dancing like a boxer, he hit Cole square in the face. Cole's head flew back, and he felt it hit Tommy's face. Tommy grunted and spit. Cole tried to stomp the insole of the man holding him, but the man pulled back, just missing Cole's heel. Cole's eye ached; it was beginning to swell shut.

"This is getting to be fun!" Tommy cried in a manic laugh.

"Okay, roundhouse! Chokehold, Tommy, hold him still! I don't want to kick you!" Tattoo bounced and laughed.

As he spun around, a big natural leather, steel-toed work boot at the end of a pair of khaki chinos kicked Tattoo in the groin. Tattoo collapsed to all fours. Again, the boot kicked him, this time in the ribs, lifting him off the ground. Tattoo rolled and tried to get up. He made it to his knees when a large brown hand clamped onto his Adam's apple.

It was Luis. He stood behind Tattoo and had him by

the throat. Luis had turned to face Cole and Tommy. Tattoo was looking up at his captor, clawing at his hands and making a gagging, coughing, airless sound.

"Let him go," Luis said to Tommy.

"No, you first."

"Me first? Are you crazy, this ain't no game, asshole, I'm going to kill this piece of shit if you don't let my friend go."

"You ain't killin' nobody. If anybody gets killed, it will be Chicago here. Then you." Tommy brought his forearm tighter against Cole's throat. He had Cole's left wrist and was pulling it up between his shoulders. "Tree Top don't like Beaners to start with, and he'll turn over every taco truck in town lookin' for you."

Luis eased up his grip slightly on Tattoo's throat. While Tommy had been talking, Luis had slipped his right hand into his pants pocket and taken out a box cutter. Tattoo's eyes bulged, and his face was turning from blue back to a reddish hue.

Tommy was calm and forceful. "You let him go and nobody gets hurt. We were just supposed to rough this guy up and scare him out of town. Let him go, and we'll let it go. You don't want to be startin' any kind of war."

Without saying a word, Luis slid the cover back on the box cutter and put the point of the razorblade in the center of Tattoo's forehead.

"What the hell are you doing?" Tommy growled.

From Cole's vantage point, Luis looked like a priest blessing a parishioner from behind with holy water. Then a small trickle of blood ran down Tattoo's forehead and into the corner of his eye. Luis continued to pull the box cutter back. Pressing hard, inch-by-inch, the blade sliced all the way to Tattoo's skull. Tattoo could only feel the pressure on his scalp. Blood continued to run into his eye. Tommy was confused and couldn't understand what Luis was doing. Cole was watching, but his eye had swollen completely shut, and he could taste blood in his mouth.

"What're you doing?" Tommy screamed.

"Let Mr. Sage go."

Tommy began shifting his weight from one foot to the other. He was breathing hard. Luis, perfectly calm, never stopped pulling the blade toward him. When he reached the nape of Tattoo's neck, he brought the box cutter up and turned it slowly so Tommy could see it.

"You're going to pay for this."

"Let Mr. Sage go." Luis said calmly.

Luis pressed the blade to Tattoo's forehead an inch to the right of the first cut and began drawing it back across his scalp.

"Okay, okay!" Tommy shoved Cole forward.

Luis took the box cutter and with flashing speed drew the blade in deep across Tattoo's forehead. Blood gushed from the wound and into his eyes. Luis released Tattoo's throat and kicked him hard in the middle of the back with the flat of his boot. The force slammed Tattoo to the pavement.

"You need to leave," Luis said. "If we see you near here or anywhere near Mr. Sage again, I will cut off your head."

Tommy, trying to get Tattoo to his feet, didn't respond. Tattoo was coughing and trying to wipe the blood from his eyes.

"You tell Tree that he is in deep enough shit already, and he don't want what we can bring down on him. You hear?" Luis handed Cole a red bandana from his back pocket.

"Tree will kill you, man."

Luis flipped open his cell phone and punched three numbers. "I need an ambulance. Palmwood Motel on McAllister. Man's bad hurt, hurry." He flipped the phone closed and put his hand on Cole's shoulder. "You okay, man?"

Cole took a deep breath, groaned, and said, "Thank you."

"An ambulance is on the way. It would probably be a good idea if I wasn't around when they get here. You be okay by yourself?"

"I'll be fine. I think I need to sit down a minute." As he spoke, Cole's knees buckled.

A car door slammed, and Tommy ran around the back and opened the driver's side door. He turned and raised his middle finger to Luis, then jumped in the car and started the engine. Luis took a 9mm automatic from his waistband and pointed it at the car. The car burned rubber, and sped across the parking lot, hitting the speed bump hard and exiting without slowing down. The sound of Tommy's screeching tires was nearly drowned out by the sound of brakes slamming cars to a stop in the street.

"I don't think that guy likes me," Luis said, helping Cole to the stairs and sticking the gun back into his waistband.

In the distance, a siren cut through the night air. Cole sat on the second step of the stairs and put his head down between his legs.

"I'll see you around, amigo."

Cole sat up and offered his hand to Luis. "You better get out of here. Be safe."

Luis shook his hand, then turned and disappeared back into the dark alcove. Cole spit on the sidewalk. His head was spinning. He could only see out of one eye, and he got a sharp pain every time he breathed in. A few minutes later, an ambulance pulled into the Palmwood parking lot. The driver used his high beams and a searchlight mounted in front of the door to scan the lot. The blinding light came to rest on Cole.

"Good evening, sir. What seems to have happened?" A fresh-faced, young blonde man with a red goatee approached Cole.

"I fell down the stairs."

"Well, let's take a look."

On the way to the hospital, Cole tried to think what he was going to do, but he kept blacking out. His head throbbed and everything was cloudy.

"Try not to go to sleep, Mr. Sage. You have a pretty good concussion, and I'd sure like the doc to take a look at you before you catch a few Zs."

EIGHTEEN

"Good morning, Mr. Sage. How are we feeling?"

Cole winced as he tried to open his eyes. His right eye felt swollen. A small, bright-eyed Asian woman was standing at the foot of the bed.

"The doctor removed a pretty nasty clot in your eye, and you have a few stitches on your eyelid. Let's see, what else, one broken and one cracked rib, a badly bruised sternum, a concussion, and six stitches in the back of your head." She smiled at Cole and said, "You feel like visitors? There is a policeman who has been waiting for you to wake up. Another guy, too. You say no, I get rid of them." There was no doubt from her tone that this little woman could get rid of whomever she wished.

"No, it's okay. I have a feeling I'm going to feel bad for awhile."

"You sure will, but as soon as the doctor sees you, you gotta go. We need the bed. Good news is, you won't die."

"You are a real ray of sunshine."

"That's me!" she said flicking her nametag with her index finger. "Sunny!"

"Bring on the cops, Sunny," Cole said raising his head. "Ouch," he groaned.

Cole tried to shift his weight in the bed. A sharp pain shot through his side, and he felt a heavy bandage wrapped around his midsection. The pain pills he had been given gently fogged his thoughts. His mouth was dry and his tongue felt thick. His speech sounded slurred. Cole reached for the cup of water on the bed stand. He took a sip, shut his eyes and held the cool, moist cup against his swollen eye.

"Mr. Sage?"

Cole opened his eye to see a tall thin man in a blue uniform standing where Sunny had been moments before. "Yes." Cole's voice seemed to echo in his head.

"I'm Officer Winton. I need to ask you a few questions about last night."

"I fell down the stairs."

"Well, that doesn't account for all the blood on the sidewalk," Winton said flatly. "I have reports from several witnesses that you were attacked and a fight ensued."

"The windows at the Palmwood are awful dirty, Officer."

The officer decided to change tactics. "Do you know a Tommy Thorson?"

"Nope."

"He is the registered owner of a black Acura that was seen leaving the Palmwood Motel at a high rate of speed.

He is identified by witnesses as one of two men seen attacking you. What do you say about that?"

"I dropped a piece of candy and when I bent over to pick it up, I lost my balance and fell down the stairs."

"Had you been drinking?"

"Coffee," Cole replied. "Hershey's Kiss."

"What?"

"Thought you were going to ask me what kind of candy."

"Sir, we're trying to catch the people who did this to you."

"At Hershey's?"

"Here's my card. If you should decide to be more forthcoming, give me a call."

"I'll do that." Cole closed his eyes.

"Stairs, my ass." A wide-faced man with bushy graying eyebrows and black horn-rimmed glasses had taken the chart off the end of the bed and was reading it. He pulled on his nose like he was trying to make it longer, and then shook it. He put the chart back on the hook.

"Finding anything interesting?" Cole asked.

"Says here you have a bad case of lying to the police."

"That so. Is it curable?"

"At your age, probably not. I'm Fergusson." He casually flipped open his ID wallet and stuck it back in his inside breast pocket.

"What brings you here?"

"I called your motel, and they said you had moved here."

"Bed's not as soft, but I think it might be cleaner."

"I called your buddy, Harris, in Chicago. Good guy. I told him I'd keep an eye on you. But I wasn't expecting this."

"Me either." Cole smiled.

"So, who used you for the punching bag?"

"Tree Top Jefferson's guys. You call him?" Cole asked.

"Not yet. Got a warrant for his residence. The Treasury folks and IRS are looking at his taxes. Department of Motor Vehicles has been tipped off to his car dealings, but that's a state problem."

"Somebody called him. That's what they were upset about."

"You want to tell me how all that blood got splattered about?"

"You really need to know?"

"No, not really, but from the looks of you and seeing how there were two of them, I don't think it had anything to do with the punishment *you* inflicted on them. That one guy was sliced like an apple."

"You see him?"

"When I was looking for you, I talked to the doctor in ER that stitched him up. Refused to be admitted. Left as soon as the doctor finished. Couple hundred stitches.

"Here's something for ya: The doctor said the cuts across his scalp severed several sets of nerves. He was sliced down into the bone and then some. Unless he has surgery to repair the damage, and real soon, he'll be left with one side of his head and face numb and the other with a permanent tingle. Get this: The numb side might lose him the ability to grow hair. Weird, huh?"

"Can he still wiggle his ears?"

"Funny."

"So, what's next?"

"When I leave here, I'm going to have a chat with your friend Mr. Christopher. Done some checking on him. He's been investigated twice by the Real Estate Licensing

Board. He's received two letters of sanction in his file and a formal warning that the next time his name comes up, his license will be revoked.

"It was alleged that Mr. Christopher was putting a $5,000 personal representation fee in all his transactions with non-English speaking clients. Since it was added at escrow, his brokers never saw it, and the buyers thought it was part of the closing costs. Usually, it was first-time Spanish speakers who were excited to be buying a house. Their translator, if they had one, either wasn't able to translate Christopher's doubletalk or didn't want to look stupid, so they went along with it. What got him off the hook was that the translators either couldn't be found or claimed they'd explained it to the buyers."

"Un vato malo."

"Meaning—?"

"A bad man."

"Ah. Harris says to give him a call when you're able. I really appreciate your help on this. You didn't have to do it. Most people wouldn't want to get involved."

"I don't."

"Yeah, yeah, I know, Harris said you're a real do gooder. Anyway, thanks. If I can ever return the favor—"

"You *can* do me one favor. If the name Whisper, Whisper Perez, comes up, he's clean. Well, not clean-clean, but he doesn't have anything to do with all this. He's kind of a pet project of mine. He's trying to straighten up, and I don't want anything to distract his efforts, you know?"

"Fair trade."

"No, I mean it. He's not involved in this. He just helped me turn over a few rocks. That's how you're going to get Christopher. So—"

"You got it."

"Thanks."

"Well, you take care. When they say you can leave?"

"Soon as the doctor checks me out."

"Maybe I'll see you in Chicago sometime." With that, Fergusson was out the door.

When Fergusson knocked on the door jamb of Allen Christopher's office, Christopher was going through his desk drawers. Papers were stacked in disheveled piles on the floor. He was obviously intent on finding something and didn't look up until Fergusson spoke.

"Allen Christopher?"

"Yeah," Christopher said, sounding annoyed with the interruption.

"I'm Special Agent James Fergusson, FBI."

Christopher sat straight up in his chair. He fumbled with some papers on his desk like he wanted them to disappear somehow. As he straightened the stack, Fergusson noticed a strange long dent in the top of the desk.

"What can I do for you?" Christopher said, trying to sound casual.

"You've made quite a mess here. Looking for something special?"

"What? Oh, this? Just sorting through things," he said nervously.

"Do you know a man named Jefferson, goes by Tree Top?"

"No, who's he?" Christopher spoke a little too quickly.

Fergusson took a pile of papers off the chair facing Christopher's desk and sat down. "How about the Malcor Corporation?"

"No. Well, not exactly. I have heard of them."

"This can be a lot easier if you just tell the truth." Removing a micro recorder from his jacket pocket, Fergusson said, "Mind if I tape this? I want to make sure I get everything right."

"Yes. Record it. I want this very clear."

"This is Special Agent James Fergusson interviewing Allen— I'm sorry, what's your middle name?"

"James. Allen James Christopher."

"Now, I ask you some questions, and you tell me the answers. Real easy, so enough with the lies. You're not very good at it. Now, tell me about Tree Top Jefferson."

"He is, well, I, there is an associate of mine named Richard Anderson. He and Tree Top were doing business together."

"What kind of business?"

"Oh, I don't, I'm not, they—" Christopher began shuffling papers again.

"He said you bought diamonds, and he bought cars with them. Your boss, a Mr.—" Fergusson flipped through a notebook, "—Brazil, he's told me that you had the stones shipped here. Now, cut the crap."

"It was that bastard, Sage, wasn't it? He's the one! He told you everything didn't he?" Christopher was now standing and yelling at Fergusson.

"Mr. Christopher, this won't help you at all."

Fergusson closed his notebook and shoved it into his jacket pocket. "When I come back, it will be with a federal warrant to arrest you. Now, you can make it difficult or you can come clean."

"It was Anderson. He's the one. He introduced me to Tree Top. He ordered the diamonds. I just did him a favor by signing for the packages. He, he—" Christopher stuttered.

"We checked out Richard Anderson. He's a small-time conman who served a total of 18 years at various facilities. The people at Zeff Wholesale Jewelry said they once had a customer named Anderson, but he always paid cash and bought silver that he sold in carts at various malls around the state, not diamonds. On the other hand, Mr. Christopher, they have your signature on numerous invoices and cashier's checks drawn on your bank. More importantly, there's an outstanding invoice for $380,000 dollars that's 90 days old. They're not very happy about that. Do you have $380,000 to pay that invoice, Mr. Christopher?"

"I don't have that kind of money."

"But you had enough to buy a new car. Euro Motors says you paid cash. Where does a realtor get cash like that?"

"You got this all wrong." Christopher's face was a deep red.

"Here's what I know. You are in tight with Malcor."

"Finally, some facts." Christopher seemed to relax.

"Again, Mr. Christopher, are you familiar with Malcor Corporation?"

"Yes."

"In what way?"

"They're my clients. I'm helping them put together an industrial project on the southeast part of town."

"Would you say your relations with them are friendly?"

"Friendly? Yes, I would say so. I hope to be part of Malcor soon."

"Do you know Sven Elias?"

Christopher stood up. "Get out!"

"Now, Mr. Christopher," Fergusson said patronizingly, "you don't want me to leave, do you?"

"Get out!"

Fergusson stood and walked to the door. "Agent Wallace, will you please come in?"

A handsome black man with dark glasses appeared in the doorway.

"Christopher Allen, you have the right to remain silent." Fergusson began.

"What! You can't arrest me. I haven't done anything!"

"Anything you say can and will be used against you in a court of law."

"I don't need any lawyer! You got nothing. Hearsay and circumstantial evidence."

"You have the right to consult an attorney before speaking to the police and to have an attorney present during questioning now or in the future. Do you understand?"

"What do you want to know?"

"If you cannot afford an attorney, one will be appointed for you before any questioning if you wish. Do you understand?" Fergusson pressed on, ignoring Christopher.

"Okay, okay, I'll talk!"

"If you decide to answer questions now without an attorney present you will still have the right to stop answering at any time until you talk to an attorney. Do you understand?"

"I don't want to go to jail!" Christopher pleaded.

"Knowing and understanding your rights as I have explained them to you, are you willing to answer my questions without an attorney present?" The mini recorder still sat on the desk.

"Yes, yes. What is it you think I've done?"

"You will be charged with mail fraud, conspiracy to commit grand theft, and the attempted bribery of an elected official on behalf of the Castigleone crime family.

It's over, Christopher. Now if you are willing to work with us, we might be able help you."

Christopher sat down. Everything Cole Sage said would happen, had happened. He was guilty. He knew it, they knew it. Richard Anderson had set him up. The money had blinded him to it. The noose around his neck was real. There was nowhere to run, nowhere to hide. He was going to prison. All of his posturing was for nothing. He knew it, they knew it.

"Okay, look, I don't want to go to prison."

"That's up to a jury."

"I thought you said we could make a deal?"

"No, I said I might be able to help. What is it you want to tell me?"

"I did it."

"You did what?"

"I worked with Tree to buy and sell cars with diamonds."

"That's not a crime and not what I'm here for."

"I was going to pay for the stones with the proceeds. It just didn't work out."

"Do you have any stones left?" Fergusson asked.

"I did, but Sage stole them from me."

"Look, Christopher. There's a warrant for two of Jefferson's guys for attempted murder and another for Jefferson for ordering the attack. Cole Sage is an award-winning newspaperman, highly regarded by the Chicago police. Now, whatever you have against him doesn't matter beans to me, but save the 'Cole Sage did this, that and the other thing,' 'cause nobody's buying it."

"What attack?"

"On Cole Sage. He's in the hospital right now, beat to hell."

"I had nothing to do with that!"

"You said Jefferson was your man. I have a feeling Jefferson's orders came from you."

"I know nothing about beating up Sage. My only connection to Jefferson had to do with the cars, nothing else. He's on his own otherwise, I swear."

"So you burned Zeff for the diamonds, right?"

"I guess."

"You mean yes?"

"Yes."

"Did you offer Sven Elias diamonds to change the zoning on the property you were trying to buy for Malcor?"

Christopher looked down at his feet. "Yes."

"Mr. Wallace, will you please prepare Mr. Christopher for transport?"

"Yes, sir. Mr. Christopher, please stand and put your hands behind your head."

Without a word, Christopher stood and did as the man said. Wallace turned him around and quickly patted him down. He removed a pair of handcuffs from his belt and restrained Christopher. Fergusson knew his federal case was not very strong. A good defense attorney could probably whittle down some of the charges, but with the confession, Christopher would do time. More important was his link to the mob. Putting them on the West Coast, involved with criminal activities, would give him some leverage, and that's what really mattered.

The raid on Tree Top Jefferson's crib was far more productive than Fergusson had imagined. Although there were no federal violations per se, the local police had a field day. Built into the house were several false walls and safe rooms. It took two police cargo vans to haul away the loot they found stashed behind the walls: Neatly shelved, tagged, and complete with inventory sheets on clipboards hanging from the walls, was a fortune in stolen goods.

Along with the dozens of DVD players, car stereos, laptop computers, and a myriad of other electronic devices, there were several hundred cell phones. Many new in boxes, others in plastic Ziploc bags. In each of the bags was a photocopy of instructions on how to reprogram the phone and the name of several people who could, for a price, hook up the purchaser with an untraceable account to activate the phone.

The real score was in Tree's bedroom. The top of the dressers was a veritable contraband pharmacy. Bowls of crack and powder cocaine, apothecary jars of marijuana, and a crystal candy dish of Ecstasy. In one of the drawers was a large Ziploc bag later identified as methamphetamine.

In his closet, along with enough shoes to make Imelda Marcos blush, were four assault rifles and three sawed-off shotguns. On one shelf at the end of the closet were stacked several heavy-duty aluminum travel cases. Each case was full of handguns. Glocks in various calibers, nickel-plated Colt 45 automatics, 9mm Smith & Wesson automatics, a variety of fancy engraved ivory-and-pearl-handled pistols, and enough ammunition to launch a small war. On the floor behind a rack of shoes was an Army green wooden box about six feet long. Inside the box were two surface-to-air missiles and a grenade launcher—a federal arms felony violation.

During the search of the bedroom, the phone next to the bed rang.

"Jefferson residence, Special Agent Fergusson speaking."

"Yeah, yo' funny. Where's Tree?"

"Haven't seen him. But if you get a hold of him, will you let him know I'd like to speak with him?"

"Who is this, again?"

"Fergusson, FBI," he said, but all the Special Agent heard was laughter and a dial tone.

Fergusson sat down on the side of the bed and made a couple of notes. As he pressed down on the mattress to stand to his feet, a small ebony box slid out from under the green velvet brocade pillow on the bed and hit his hand. Inside the box was a piece of red velvet folded over and tucked in at the sides. Fergusson turned back the cloth to find several hundred diamonds. Jefferson had been skimming off the supply. This tied him directly to Christopher. Even without the diamonds, there were enough felonies represented in this raid to send him away for a long, long time. He would let the local cops take care of the dirty work. The federal violations were minimal. Fergusson chuckled to himself. The guy from Chicago had certainly made a lot of cops look good around here.

This would be the end of Tree Top Jefferson's career as the city's flashiest street hustler. By the time he'd get out of jail, the streets would be filled with hydrogen-burning hovercraft.

Cole checked out of the hospital around three o'clock and into the Holiday Inn. He figured after the lumps he'd taken, the upgrade to a softer bed and nicer surroundings would be worth the expense, and aid in his recovery. The television had a remote, and there was a refrigerator in the room with lots of ice. He had kept the icepack from the hospital and had it on his eye while he tried to watch a Cubs game on TV. His eyeball ached and his ribs were sore, but the call from Agent Fergusson around nine o'clock made it almost worthwhile. Christopher had folded like a house of cards, and Tree Top had been caught holding the bag. The Cubbies were up by two, God was in His heaven, and all was right with the world. Around midnight, Cole drifted to sleep with the help of Tylenol with codeine.

NINETEEN

Cole awoke with a sharp pain in his side as he tried to roll over. His head and neck were throbbing from being propped up on pillows for so long. He reached for his wristwatch on the nightstand. It was 9:15, and the light through the curtain's gap told him he had survived the night. *What day is it, though*? he thought. *Must be Sunday*. Another jolt of pain shot through Cole's middle as he sat up and put his feet on the floor. He made his way to the bathroom and didn't much like what he saw in the mirror. Thankfully, his eye was in far better shape than he expected. It was badly bruised, but the butterfly bandage covered the stitches and most of the swelling had gone down. He was in need of a shave, and his hair needed shampooing. Overall, he looked pretty much like he had been stomped by a herd of buffalo.

After a shave, shower, and a long hot soak in the tub,

some of the stiffness receded and his mobility improved. He dressed and went to breakfast, stopping at the gift shop in the lobby on the way to buy an overpriced pair of cheap sunglasses. He was able to avoid the stares of the Sunday brunch crowd and idle chitchat of a waitress by going through the buffet and sitting in a dark corner. If anyone noticed him at all, they probably thought he had a hangover.

Cole ate mostly scrambled eggs and blueberry muffins. He got his $12.95's worth by drinking three cups of Cafe Mocha from the coffee bar. His jaw ached, and his bottom lip had a raw gash on the inside, so soft and warm was the order of the day. As he drank his last cup of coffee, he glanced through the paper. No mention of Allen Christopher or Tree Top Jefferson yet, but on the bottom of the front page of the local section there was a teaser for a feature story coming Wednesday on the new Zoning Commissioner entitled "Getting it Right."

By the time Cole got to his car, he was feeling pretty good. On the drive to Eastwood Manor, he rolled down the windows and turned the radio up. "Good Day Sunshine" blasted from the speakers, and Cole did his best Paul McCartney impersonation as he sailed through traffic on the way to see Ellie. It felt good to be alive! Even a little battered, he was grateful to be in one piece. When "Sunshine of Your Love" came on a few minutes later, Cole proved he knew every one of Clapton's guitar licks as he mimicked the Stratocaster, *wah-wah* pedal and all.

Cole was excited to see Ellie. He had decided as he'd lay on the gurney in the ER that he would tell her straight out how much he loved her, how much he had missed her all through the years, and how much he regretted ever letting her get away. There would be no skirting the issue anymore. He wouldn't hold back. He'd ask her forgiveness. Their parting long ago was mostly his fault, and he knew it. There was no doubt that this was the right thing to do. He could go home knowing he had said all the things he had dreamed of saying for a long, long time.

"Baby, now that I've found you, I won't let you go, baby even though, You don't need me, now, You don't need me." Cole was singing along with The Foundations at the top of his lungs, singing like he hadn't in years. As he drove, the hits just kept on comin' and Cole just kept singin' and smilin'.

The Eastwood Manor parking lot was full. It was a beautiful Sunday afternoon, and the visitors had turned out in droves. *Good for them*, he thought. *They need to visit the folks in here.* Cole finally found a spot on the far side of the main building. As he walked to the entrance, he smiled and greeted several people making their way to their cars. A middle-aged couple approached the front door with a big bouquet of colorful flowers. Cole opened the door for them and made a theatrical bow and sweep of his hand inviting them to go in first. *This place doesn't look that bad*, he thought as he made his way toward Ellie's room.

Her door was open, and Cole heard voices coming from inside. He was surprised to see two nurses putting things from the closet into a bag.

"Hi, how are we doing today?" he began.

"Fine," the older of the two nurses replied.

Cole did not like the way they looked at each other.

"Have they moved Mrs. Christopher?"

The nurses once again looked at each other before the younger of the two answered, "No, she, uh, she got sick. I'm not sure where they put her."

"Sick? What kind of sick?" Cole demanded.

"Maybe you should talk to Mrs. Elliott. She's the manager on duty. She's at the front—"

Cole was running down the hall before the nurse finished her sentence.

"Where's Mrs. Elliott?" Cole called out to the woman at the front desk as he approached.

"What's wrong, sir." The woman stood to her feet.

"Mrs. Christopher, Ellie Christopher in 224, where is she? Where have they taken her?"

"Just a moment. Let me see. It will be okay, sir, please don't be upset. I'll find out." She saw Cole's panic and picked up the microphone. "Mrs. Elliott, Code 15. Mrs. Elliott, Code 15, front desk please."

A thin, graying woman came jogging up the hall toward Cole. She moved with a graceful gait with no self-consciousness in her movements.

"How may I help?"

"Mrs. Christopher. Where has she been moved?"

"Are you family?"

"Yes," Cole said without thinking.

"Mrs. Christopher has been moved to the county hospital. She has been diagnosed with pneumonia. We thought it best if she—"

Cole was already running to his car. He started the engine and sped, tires squealing, from the parking lot. He turned off the radio with an angry snap. The county hospital was 15 minutes away. Cole ran three stoplights in a row and was about to fly through a fourth but spotted a city bus and stopped. He had no thoughts. He only wanted to get to the hospital. His focus was speed and avoiding hitting anything that would stop or slow his getting there.

The rental car nearly left the pavement as Cole turned into the hospital parking lot and hit a speed bump. He parked and ran the 50 or so yards to the entrance. Pulling the automatic door open with a hard yank, he walked quickly to the reception desk. A woman in her 70s in a red-and-white striped bibbed jumper watched with apprehension as Cole approached.

"Ellen Christopher. What room?"

"Let me see." The woman ran her fingers down a typed list under a rippled sheet of plastic. "That was Christopher?"

"Yes, yes, what room?"

"That would be, ahh, yes, here it is, 318B. Now remember, B indicates the right side of the room." She spoke quickly but ended up speaking to Cole's back.

A blue curtain was drawn around the right side of Room 318. A shadow of a person standing with their back toward Cole could be seen through the curtain. Cole had stood for a long moment trying to decide what to do when the curtain pulled back and a small black woman stepped away from the bed.

"Hello," the woman said softly.

"Hello."

"Are you here to see Ellen?"

"Yes, what has happened?"

"Are you her husband?"

"No. He won't be coming," Cole said coldly.

"I can't discuss her case with—"

"Look, I'm all she's got right now. What's her condition?" Cole said in a pleading voice.

The woman looked deep into Cole's eyes, then down at the floor. "I'm Dr. Ewing, Ellen's physician. She has pneumonia. I'm afraid it is a complication that she really can't afford right now. We have her on strong antibiotics, but that requires taking her off her ALS meds."

"How bad is she?"

"I'm not going to lie to you. It is very bad."

"Is she awake? I really need to— I mean I have to let her know...."

"Please don't distress her. She's very weak, and I don't want her upset."

"I need to tell her how much I love her." Cole's throat felt as if he had been swallowing sand.

"I see." The doctor looked up at Cole. "Well, that never hurt anyone, did it?" She walked past him and out into the hall.

Cole approached the side of the bed, and Ellie turned and looked up at him. "Hi, big guy. You look like hell," she said weakly.

"So do you." Cole smiled and gently nudged her arm.

"Thanks." Ellie's lips smiled, but her eyes looked far way.

"I am so sorry I wasn't there, El," Cole offered.

"They've killed me, Cole," Ellie said weakly.

"What do you mean? Who?"

"At Eastwood. They put me in the bath." Ellen coughed, finding it hard to breathe. "They left me in there. The nurse went off duty, didn't tell the girl coming on duty. I was in the bath nearly three hours. I got a chill from the water getting cold."

"You're going to be all right, sweetie, don't worry." Cole gently stroked Ellie's hair back onto her forehead.

"You haven't called me 'sweetie' in a long time." Ellie smiled and seemed to focus.

"Ellie, there is something you need to know. Something I have wanted to say for a long, long time." Cole began.

"How we doin'?" a short, slightly overweight Filipino nurse chirped in a singsong voice. "Time to check your oxygen."

The nurse looked at the dials at the head of the bed and made an adjustment. She gently moved the small tubes feeding oxygen through Ellie's nose and adjusted the elastic straps around her head. Taking an electric thermometer from a clip on her waistband, she popped on a new tip, and placed it in Ellie's mouth.

"Your wife is looking better today."

Ellie smiled, lips tight around the thermometer. There seemed to be a twinkle in her eyes.

"She always looks good to me," Cole said softly.

"How you feeling, Hon?" the nurse asked, removing the thermometer.

"I've been better," Ellie said with a weak smile.

"Always with the jokes, this one. I want you to keep still and rest. You got a nasty bug, and you got to be strong to fight it off." With that, the nurse bustled out of the room as quickly as she had entered.

"I would get more rest if they would just leave me alone for awhile." Ellie said thickly, "I wonder if—" Her words were cut short by a cough. Her coughing continued, and she gasped as she inhaled. Ellie rolled to her side and her knees pulled up nearly to her chest as the harsh rasp worsened.

Cole stroked her back as her thin body convulsed with the cough. Ellie gasped like a drowning person. Cole fumbled for the control that had been laid on the bed. He pushed the button to call the nurse. He was starting to panic. Several seconds passed, and her cough was worsening.

Cole went to the hall. He looked in both directions and saw no nurses in sight. "NURSE!" he screamed at the top of his voice.

The small Filipino woman appeared from a room down the hall. She saw Cole and broke into a run.

"What is it?" she called.

"She can't breathe. She's coughing. It won't stop."

The nurse immediately hit the red button by the door as she entered Ellie's room. A bleating alarm rang in the hall, and Cole could see a rotating blue light bouncing off the walls.

"Try to relax, Mrs. Christopher, look at me now." The nurse was rubbing Ellie's back with deep rapid movements.

Suddenly the room was full of nurses, and Doctor Ewing ran into the room.

"Who lowered this bed? She needs to be elevated! Get her upstairs, Stat! OR 3 is free. We've got to drain her lungs if she's going to make it. Get her on her stomach. Go, go, go!" Doctor Ewing was out of the room and running toward the elevator.

Cole stood just outside the doorway, trying not to get in the way. The two male nurses were pulling the bed from the room. The oxygen tubes snapped from Ellie's head and dangled, hissing, from the wall. As she passed Cole, her body was lifting from the bed with each convulsive cough, and all he could see were the whites of her eyes. Cole's back was to the cool green wall of the hallway. He put his hands on the top of his head and closed his eyes.

"God, don't let her die. Please, Jesus, just a little longer, oh, God, please, just a little longer." Cole was rocking back and forth, hitting his shoulders against the wall. "Not now, not yet, not like this, please, oh, please, not like this."

"Come, please. She's going to be okay. Come. Sit." Cole felt the little Filipino nurse's hand take his and guide him into Ellie's room to a chair. "You rest here. Keep praying. God listens."

"How long will this take?"

"I'm not sure. They are very good at their job. Doctor Ewing is the best, you'll see." The little woman smiled down at Cole.

"She was doing so well. I can't believe this," Cole said aloud but to himself.

"You gonna be okay?"

"Yeah, I'm fine. I just was a little...you know, overcome, I guess."

"It's okay to pray, nothing to be ashamed of."

"She's all I've got, ya know. It's not time. I've got some things to say yet."

"You got God, too." The nurse reached up, unclasped a thin gold chain from her neck, and handed it to Cole.

He looked at the medal she had placed in his hand.

"Saint John of God, he's the patron saint of nurses and the sick. You pray, he'll hear you. My father gave it to me when I became a nurse. It works, you see."

Cole stood and offered his hand in thanks to the nurse. "I'm Cole Sage. Ellie isn't my wife, but she should have been. Thank you. I think I'll go get a cup of coffee or something."

"Good idea. You'll feel better."

Cole left the room and, as he made his way down the hall, he slipped the chain and medal into his pocket. He didn't believe in saints but it made him feel better to know the little nurse did.

The cafeteria was crowded and noisy. Cole got his coffee to go and went out through the side door. The aches and pain he'd thought had gone were back. His neck ached, and his eye felt more swollen. He remembered the pills on the seat of the car the doctor had given him. He didn't like pills much but, this once, they might be what he needed.

Cole slipped into the car, opened the white pharmacy bag, took two of the small pink pills and washed them down with the bitter coffee. He put the key in the ignition and turned on the radio. He thought of Ellie contorting and fighting for air. Once again, he breathed a prayer and sipped his coffee. His eye felt scratchy and out of focus. He finished his coffee, leaned his head back against the headrest and closed his eyes.

Many years before, he had seen Ellie fight for air. It was a hot July day, and Cole had borrowed an inflatable kayak from a friend. They thought it would be fun to take it down the river. Ellie packed a picnic lunch. Cole got some paddles, a portable radio, suntan lotion, and some towels, and they were off. Cole's parents had lived not too far from the river in those days. The plan was to raft down the river five or six miles from the Crows Ferry Bridge and get out at the small park on the bank about 200 yards from his parents' house. It was going to be an afternoon of rafting and swimming, then a barbeque with his parents.

A friend dropped them at the bridge and they had set sail with waves goodbye and laughter. The day was glorious and the river smooth. Cole and Ellie had laughed and talked, swam, and even had time for a few kisses along the way. They dined on cold fried chicken, deviled eggs, and some strange pink stuff Ellie's mother had made. They had let a net dangle in the water behind the kayak filled with cans of Coke. The day was perfect.

They were less than two miles from the park when they rounded the bend at the little town of Sheridan. Ellie was telling a story about something that had happened at work, and Cole was half listening, half drifting when something caught his eye. Fifty yards ahead, several large Spiky Elms had fallen across the river at a narrow bend. At first, he thought they could just maneuver around them, but as he sat up and took a closer look, he realized the trees were completely blocking their passage.

The 50 yards closed quickly, and the current became swifter. Cole told Ellie to hang on while he tried to paddle them to the shore. He realized as he began to paddle that the strong current was swirling just ahead of them. The Elms had created a whirlpool of sorts, and they were in it before Cole could get up enough speed to pull out of it. From their limbs and trunks protruded needle-sharp thorns that grew as long as three inches.

Before they could react, the rubber kayak slammed into the trees. The thorns made a thousand holes in the rubber sides and deflated it almost instantly. The current was pulling the kayak, now a heavy mass of rubberized canvas, under the trees. The contents of their little boat were in the water. Cole hit the side of the first tree and fell headfirst back into the water.

Cole knew he was in trouble. He was a strong swimmer and had spent many summers in the backyard pool. This, however, was different from racing or playing roughhouse games with the neighbors in six feet of calm water. The current was pulling him down. He opened his eyes and saw light above him. The ice chest was drifting by and he thought for a moment of Dorothy when she was up in the tornado in the *Wizard of Oz* and all the things that had passed by her window.

Cole could not see Ellie. He remembered how his father had often spoken of his Navy training during World War II. *Relax*, he would say, *let the water do what it will, then as it eases, you take control.* Cole relaxed, pointed his feet toward the bottom, and let the current drag him down. In a matter of seconds, he felt his feet hit firm sand. With all his strength, he pushed off and, with his arms stroking and pulling as hard as he could, he shot toward the surface.

Gasping and sucking in air, Cole burst from the water. He grabbed the trunk of the Spiky Elm and felt the sharp prick of the thorns in his palms. At that moment, Ellie's head bobbed up from the water. She faced Cole and screamed for help, then went under. Without thinking, Cole dove after her.

His thoughts were not for his safety, but Ellie's. He couldn't let her drown. For the briefest of moments, he'd seen her parents, and him having to tell them she had died. *This will not happen*, he'd thought. Grabbing Ellie's arm, he'd pulled her towards him. Pulling her closer, he wrapped his arm around her waist and grabbed the top of her denim shorts. With strength he didn't know he possessed, he pulled her over him and out of the water. Arms flailing, she grabbed the tree.

Cole stroked and kicked back to the surface and again grabbed the spiky trunk. He caught an area where the thorns had either been worn away or broken off. Ellie was lying motionless across the trunk. Her hair was covering her face. Cole saw her ribs and chest expanding and could hear the sound of gagging and gasping coming from her.

Cole broke off a piece of rotting limb from the tree. He used it to knock off thorns from the trunk. Once cleared, he pulled himself up on the trunk and knocked more thorns off with the side of his tennis shoe, careful not to puncture the soles. Just as he reached Ellie, she slipped off into the water. A second before she would've gone under, Cole caught her wrists and pulled her out of the water like a crane would lift a heavy load, and stood her on the huge trunk.

Ellie wretched violently and threw up. She had obviously swallowed a lot of the river water. She spit, gasped, and wretched some more. Cole wasn't sure if she would catch her breath. She bent over, palms against her knees, and heaved great breaths of air. Finally, she'd stood straight.

"You saved my life," she gasped, pushing her hair out of her face.

Cole looked around. The whirlpool the trees created had caused brush and trash to pile up behind the trees where they stood. In that moment, he realized that if Ellie had gone under the second time, she would have been swept under the brush and would never have resurfaced. His knees buckled. He suddenly felt lightheaded.

"Cole, you saved my life!" Ellie threw her arms around Cole's neck.

Cole shook all over. Ellie held him tight and started to laugh.

"You. Saved. My. Life, Cole Sage! You're my hero for real!" Ellie stopped laughing and tossed back her hair. "You are quite a guy." Her fingers were laced behind his head and she leaned back at arm's length and looked deeply into Cole's eyes. "I will never forget what you have done. As long as I live, I will owe to you whatever good becomes of me." For a long moment, they just looked in each other's eyes. Then, as if the seriousness was too much for her, Ellie said, "I'd kiss you, but it would taste like puke." Then she bent down, pushed against Cole's chest with the top of her head and began to laugh once more.

Overcome by the moment, Cole threw his head back and laughed until they both nearly fell in the river again. It took almost an hour to get out of the deep ravine the river had cut through the foothills. The walls were very steep, and the dirt was dry and dusty. When they finally made it up to the highway, they both looked like gingerbread men. All that was visible were their eyes and smiles. They were alive and even deeper in love.

From far away, Cole heard a knocking sound. No, it was close up. *What is that?* he thought.

"Hey, you okay?"

Cole opened his eyes. A man with black horn-rimmed glasses, multiple piercings, and rotten teeth was looking though the car window at him. It was nearly dark outside, and he was very groggy. Where was he? He rolled down the window and stared at the man who stood peering in, dressed in a powder blue shirt with a badge on it.

"What's going on?" Cole said trying to clear his head.

"That's what I want to know. This ain't no campground."

Cole looked at his watch, it was 4:45. He realized he had fallen asleep. Cole straightened in the seat.

"I must have dozed off."

"You drunk?"

"No, no, I took some pain pills and they must've knocked me out," Cole said.

"I can't have people sleeping in my parking lot." The man, who Cole now realized was a security guard, took his job very seriously.

"I'm sorry. I'll be out of here real soon."

"Good," the guard said flatly, then strutted off, feeling he had done his best to secure the premises.

Cole rubbed his face and reached for the bottle of pills beside him on the seat. "What is this crap?" he said aloud. "Percodan. Take *one* every four to six hours for pain and muscle tension. May cause drowsiness. Great."

Cole got out of the car, rubbed his face again and stretched as he headed for the front door of the hospital. He was ashamed at falling asleep, and hoped Ellie did not know he had gone. *Maybe she has been asleep, too,* he thought.

As the doors of the elevator opened on the third floor, Cole could hear a man's voice singing. A loud, clear baritone came from the hallway towards Room 318.

"Farther along we'll know all about it,
Farther along we'll understand why,
Cheer up my sister, live in the sunshine,
We'll understand it all, by and by.

"Thank you, Lord. Thank you for your unceasing love. Thank you for being with us in our times of sickness and times of health. Thank you for touching these frail bodies with your Almighty hand." The voice boomed like thunder from on high. "Precious Lord, we come to You tonight and ask You to touch our beloved sister, touch her with Your mighty power, touch her, raise her up. We don't know Your plan, Lord, but if it be Your will, reach down from glory and take this burden from her and restore her strength so that she might find a closer walk with Thee." The prayer gave way to more singing.

"When we see Jesus coming in glory,
When he comes down from his home in the sky,
Then we shall meet him in that bright mansion,
We'll understand it all by and by."

Cole made his way down the hall. As he passed the nurses' station, he saw two nurses standing in the corner holding hands, eyes closed and heads bowed. He stopped as he reached the open doorway to Ellie's room. The Reverend Edwin T. Bates stood next to Ellie's bed, one large strong hand on her forehead, the other reaching heavenward. His lips were moving, but Cole could not hear a word. This was the real heart of the old preacher. The bluster was gone and the man of faith was talking to his God.

"Amen," the old man whispered.

"How is she?" Cole said breaking the silence.

"Hello there, Mr. Sage."

"Reverend. Thank you for coming," Cole said, waiting for an answer.

"Let's talk in the hall so as not to disturb our patient."

If Ellie had slept through Bates' prayer and singing, she was not going to wake with hushed talking, Cole thought, but he slipped through the door into the hall just the same. The preacher looked tired and weighed down with his thoughts as he put his hand on Cole's shoulder.

"I'm afraid the news isn't good, son. The doctor was just leaving when I got here. She told me that they drained both lungs and doubled her antibiotics trying to fight off the pneumonia. The problem is the coughing convulsions have weakened her terribly. The other disease she suffers from—"

"ALS," Cole injected.

"Yes, ALS, it seems that stopping her medication has weakened her immune system and the disease has taken advantage of this to progress pretty quickly. I'm afraid she is failing fast. I'm so sorry."

Somehow the truth coming from Bates made it easier for Cole to accept. Cole had seen and faced death many times in his life, but all that pain, shock, and grief had not prepared him for what was to come. There were no tears, just a deep hollow feeling in his soul.

"You really believe she will be in a better place? I mean, with all the fire and brimstone and ministerial theatrics aside, you truly believe, don't you?"

"As I believe in the air I breathe. Without that promise, I really can't see much point to this life. Frankly, I just can't understand the pain and sorrow and suffering I see around me. It wears me down some days to where I don't want to get out of bed. It is not my plan, it's God's, He knows what's best, whether we do or not. Like the song says, 'We'll understand it all by and by.' That's my hope. Without hope, there is nothing."

"I'm not sure what I believe, Reverend," Cole said softly as he turned and went back into Ellie's room.

"Just remember, God knows your heart, son. He's always ready to listen." The old preacher turned toward the elevators. "I'll check back tomorrow."

Cole pulled the chair up next to Ellie's bed. Her breath was soft and shallow. A tube to drain her lungs ran under her gown to a plastic bag hanging on the bedrail on the far side of the bed. Two IV drips were in her left hand, which was taped to a short stiff piece of cloth-covered plastic. Oxygen tubes were again held under her nose by elastic straps behind her head.

"I love you, Ellie," Cole said, leaning toward the pale woman in the bed. "I have been a fool for so long." He gently took her hand in his.

Cole gently stroked the top of her hand with his thumb, and Ellie ever so softly squeezed his hand. Cole smiled, knowing she had heard him, and scooted the chair closer to the bed.

Over the next couple of hours, the nurses bustled in and out frequently, taking Ellie's temperature, checking her IVs, and monitoring her breathing. At about 6:30, a young man brought in a cart with several monitors and attached a series of wires and pads to Ellie's chest, connected to a small device that slipped over her finger on the hand with the IVs.

At seven o'clock, Ellie turned her head toward Cole, opened her eyes, and gave a faint smile. Then her eyes slowly closed again and she sighed. Cole rested his head on the cool steel bedrail and brought up sweet memories of his time with Ellie when they were together. Oddly, Cole had a peace about this time, about Ellie and her certain passing. *She will just stay asleep,* he thought. And that was fine. It did hurt him that they wouldn't have a chance to say goodbye, but she wasn't in any pain that he could see, and that was good.

When a nurse came in and asked Cole to step out of the room for a few moments, he took the opportunity to use the restroom and find a coffee machine. The coffee was hot and strong. As he passed by, several nurses gave him sweet, melancholy smiles as if to say, "We know, we're sorry," and it made Cole feel not quite so alone.

The sun had gone down, and the lights in the room were soft and gave off a golden glow. Down the hall at the nurse's station, a radio was turned on and was a welcome alternative to the silence. On one of Cole's strolls to stretch his legs, he had noticed the third floor had very few beds filled. The nurses busied themselves with paperwork or chatted quietly at the desk.

Cole had just returned from a walk when Ellie turned and opened her eyes. "Cole?"

"Yes, Ellie, I'm here."

"Can I have a sip of water?"

"Of course." He poured a couple of inches of cool water from the plastic pitcher into a small cup and brought it to Ellie's lips.

"Thank you." Ellie cleared her throat and said, "How long have I been asleep?"

"Since about four o'clock, I guess."

"I am so tired. What happened? What *is* all this?" She indicated the wires and tubes with a slow wave of her hand across the bed.

"You gave us quite a scare. They had to drain your lungs; that's what that tube is. It should help."

"This is a lousy way to go, Cole."

"Let's not talk about that. I need to tell you something. Are you strong enough to listen?"

"I want to listen, please. I'll be asleep a long time." Ellie smiled.

"I love you, Ellie. More than anything in the world. I was such a fool. How could I have ever let you go? I have thought of you every day of my life, wished for you, longed for you. I was a coward, and I am so sorry." Cole felt like a man who was suffocating and could suddenly breathe.

"Are you getting mushy on me?" Weak as she was, Ellie

needed to be the girl he had loved. "I love you, too, Cole Sage. I have held you in my heart all these years. We would have been good together. I was a fool, too. It was my hurt pride. I could have reached out. I made some very bad choices, and letting you go was the worst. Forgive me?"

Cole brought her hand to his lips and kissed it. Ellie closed her eyes.

"Are you asleep?" Cole said softly.

"No, just taking it all in." She wiggled her hand in his. "Do it again."

Cole held her hand to his cheek and then kissed it for a long moment.

"You still got the stuff to melt a girl's heart, big guy." Ellie's breathing came in quick shallow breaths.

"Flatterer." Cole could feel Ellie weakening.

"Time to check that temp." A nurse came sweeping into the room, and Cole didn't look up.

"Oh, my baby." Ellie pointed at the doorway with Cole still holding her hand.

"Hi, mama, can I come in?" Erin said softly.

"My angel, yes!" Ellie tried to lift herself in the bed but was too weak.

"Aren't you the popular one this evening!" the nurse said breezing back out of the room.

Cole stood as Erin ran to her mother's bed. Ellie's free arm was stretched out to embrace her daughter. Both women were crying, and Cole slipped from the room.

"Oh, Mama, I am so sorry," Erin sobbed.

Ellie stroked Erin's hair as the young woman wept into her mother's shoulder.

The thrill of Erin's unexpected appearance was a strong tonic to Ellie, and she spoke with a clear strong voice. "I was wrong, Erin, please forgive me. I was so wrong, I hurt you so."

"No, I was stupid. Will *you* forgive *me*?"

"There is nothing to forgive. I am so happy you're here. Let's forget the past. I want to hear about your life." Ellie brushed the tears gently from Erin's cheek. "Look at me. I want to see you."

Ellie's face lit with a radiant smile as Erin stood holding her mother's hand.

"I have missed you."

"You, too, Mama."

"Cole was right. You are a beautiful young woman." Ellie realized that Cole was no longer in the room. "Cole!" Ellie's voice strained hoarsely.

"Right here." Cole had been standing just outside the door.

"I thought you had gone," Ellie said, panting. The adrenaline was starting to recede.

"Hello, Mr. Sage," Erin said shyly.

"Glad you could make it," Cole said as the girl turned and hugged him.

"Thank you." She whispered in his ear.

"This is so important to her," Cole said softly.

For 10 minutes, Erin showed Ellie pictures and told stories of her life. Then she told her about husband Ben, his work, and their life together. And, last, she smiled and informed Ellie she was a grandmother and told her about Jenny.

Ellie was beaming, but her voice betrayed her. Little by little, her strength was slipping away. Cole sat quietly watching Ellie and Erin from across the room. He had not failed her. Her last days would be spent knowing that he had come and fulfilled her last request. Knowing that Erin was here would make the pain of what was to come a little easier.

"You have become everything I always prayed you would be. I do love you so." Ellie squeezed Erin's hand. "Cole, please come closer. My voice seems to be giving up on me."

Cole crossed the room and stood beside Erin. He sensed her weakening would signal the end. Her voice had become shaky and her breathing now seemed difficult. *It's all right, now. She has seen Erin*, he thought. He would be strong.

"I need to tell you something. I hope you will both forgive me. I have wanted to say this for a long time but never knew how or when. Say you'll forgive me." Ellie's voice had become almost a whisper.

"Anything," Cole said.

"Of course, Mama, what is it?" Erin's concern showed on her face as well as in her voice.

"Erin, sweetie, I have lied to you. About your father, I mean. He didn't die in Mexico. He never lived." Ellie closed her eyes and seemed to be pulling her last moments of strength together. "Cole, I have been unfair to you, too," Ellie's breathing was so soft Cole thought she had slipped away.

"El?" Cole said flatly.

"Mama, please..."

Ellie opened her eyes and seemed to be pulling in as much air as her exhausted body would allow. "I have kept a secret deep in my heart," she gasped. "Erin, this is your father. Cole, I'm sorry I didn't tell you."

Cole stood staring at the dial on the oxygen gauge

above the bed. He couldn't breathe, he couldn't move. His ears were ringing. His head felt like it was disconnected from his body. *What had she just said?*

Erin's voice shattered the spell. "I don't understand."

Ellie spoke with her eyes closed but she had taken Cole's hand as she began. "Before you went to Southeast Asia. When we fought, I was going to tell you I was pregnant. I had been trying for days. But you left and I was so hurt and angry. My parents, my parents...." Her voice trailed off for a moment. "I ran, I ran to New Mexico. I made up the story of a husband in the oil fields. From the newspaper, I got the idea from the newspaper." Ellie's voice came in powerless puffs.

"I don't know what to say." Erin said, her hand over her mouth.

"Say you'll forgive me, please, and love him. He is so good and kind. He loves you already, I could see it when he talked of you. Say something, Cole, please."

"I only love you more. Thank you." Cole looked at Erin for the first time, but she was staring at her mother.

"Did Allen know, is that why he hated me?"

"No one has ever known. I swore to myself I would tell Cole first."

"It would have been so easy if I had known," Erin said more to herself than anyone else.

Ellie opened her eyes, her lids were heavy, and it was difficult for her to focus.

"I have the two people I love most in the same room. I could just die I'm so happy." Ellie closed her eyes and a smile came across her lips.

Cole laughed and kissed her hand. "Naughty girl." He bent and kissed her on the lips for a long moment. "I love you so."

"I love you too, big guy," Ellie said so softly only Cole heard her.

Erin and Cole sat on each side of the bed in silence. At 11:33, Ellie slipped into eternity.

TWENTY

Cole called Mick Brennan on Monday morning and told him of Ellie's passing. The next call was a little more difficult. The Reverend E.T. Bates was supposed to know all the right things to say. His years of standing beside hospital beds and caskets should have given the experience to have a repertoire revised, honed, and practiced thousands of times. Yet, it seemed as though the old preacher couldn't find the words he wanted to comfort Cole.

"I didn't know her, Cole," Bates said with unusual softness in his volume, "but she touched me. I have seen many, many people facing death. She had such a peace, such dignity. I hope when my time comes, I can face it with as much concern for others as she showed. She loved you very much. We talked for a very short time, she was so weak, but she spoke of you and her daughter. She was so afraid you would be tormented by not getting the girl home. You know, Cole, we can lead the way but the prodigal has to make the choice to return."

"She came back," Cole said, "last night."

"Thank you, Jesus," the old man said reverently. "I prayed she would."

"Would you do the service?"

"I would be honored."

"I'll have the funeral parlor call you with the details. Let's keep it simple. She didn't like a lot of falderal. I know you'll have the right words, maybe a song. She didn't want a chapel service, just something by the graveside. She loved the outdoors, you know?"

"I'm praying for you, brother." This was a benediction. The conversation was over, the volume was back up.

Cole and Erin had spoken only briefly regarding the funeral. She had given her blessing to whatever he decided. Cole had asked her if there was anything special she wanted done. There wasn't. With great difficulty, he had asked her to get something for Ellie to wear. Erin said she already had.

"Are you going to call Allen and the kids?" Erin had asked hesitantly.

"To hell with them," was Cole's only response, subject closed.

Cole felt very awkward, and Erin was all business. The call only lasted a minute or two. When he hung up, he felt very alone. He walked to the curtains and drew them closed. He hadn't dressed and wouldn't. He lay back on the unmade bed and pulled the covers up tight around him. The room was dark and cool. Cole Sage was totally and completely alone. The future loomed like an ancient tapestry before him and, as he thought of his life without the possibility of Ellie, he drifted into sleep.

After waking early, showering, and forcing down a paper cup of bitter instant motel room coffee, Cole left the hotel and went for a long drive into the foothills. Near a grove of live oak trees, he stopped and ate a sandwich and apple he'd gotten at a little grocery along the way. He realized it was the first food he had eaten in two days. Cole climbed over a sagging barbed wire fence and walked to the top of a hill. The grass was dry and the wind gusted.

At the top of the hill, he lay back in the grass and watched the huge billowy clouds roll by. *This was Ellie's kind of day.* He thought of a day just like this when they lay in a meadow full of daisies and talked of what their life was going to be like. They laughed and dreamed about a life together, growing old, having had brilliant careers and a houseful of kids. They talked of trips to Europe and a big ecologically sound fireplace crackling in a roomful of books and big pillows. Cole knew that's the way it would have been.

Call it closure, call it resolution, call it atonement, but Cole was at peace. Ellie was gone. He had asked forgiveness, declared his love; he had gotten the gift of a daughter. He knew if they'd had the time, they would have been good together. Just as he had dreamed looking out of a thousand airplane windows, he did not regret his loneliness; it had prepared him for the sweetness of their coming together again. Ellie had prepared him for a life without her, this time separation with a loving goodbye. This time there was no guilt, nor despair. The loss of Ellie was as she had told him; the beginning of a life of beautiful memories and love remembered. He knew he was going to be all right and, at this moment, his heart felt as big as the clouds overhead.

Cole left the hill with a sense that the new life Ellie had promised would become a reality. The drive back to town was free of dread. The grapefruit-sized knot he had lived with since Ellie's phone call was gone. He didn't know when it had disappeared, but it seemed he was breathing freer, deeper. He thought of Erin. He hoped they would keep in touch. He hoped for a relationship with her, but he was realistic, too. Why would she suddenly want a stranger in her life just because they were linked biologically? He wouldn't push it. If it happened, it would be wonderful; if it didn't, he already understood.

Erin had spent the morning making calls. The first was to her husband, Ben. He had often wondered if his wife would ever reach out to her mother, and was quietly pleased when Erin said she was going to see Ellie. It saddened him that he had never met her. Although estranged, Erin often spoke with deep fondness of her mother. He had heard her many times while putting Jenny to bed sing little songs or tell stories that she said, "My mama told me when I was your age...." Ben had hoped and prayed that the trip would put things right between Erin and her mother. Although he would never tell her, it had always deeply troubled him that she had felt such bitterness towards the woman.

Ben's family was very close, and his relationship with his own mother was something he treasured. His father had passed away when he was in his first year of med school. Ben would've taken a leave of absence, but his mother and sister wouldn't hear of it. Their argument was that his father would never have accepted putting off the goal. In the end, he knew they were right and could hear his father's voice directing him to push on. Without family support and cheerleading on the sidelines, he was sure he never would've made it through medical school.

Erin told Ben she'd be back Thursday night after the funeral. She turned down his offer to join her. She thought it would be best if he just stayed with Jenny. Ben volunteered to tell her supervisor of Ellie's death and arrange time off for Erin. Mrs. Bishop would take care of Jenny during the day as usual, and Ben would trade shifts with Joe Jaramillo so he would be home every night that Erin was gone.

Erin found it hard to express how much she appreciated Ben's support. It wasn't what he said, it was who he was. His strength and caring for her was more than she thought she could have expected from anyone again. It was the same inner strength her mother had possessed before she'd surrendered to Allen Christopher's dominance. Erin told Ben she loved him, sent kisses to Jenny, and said goodbye. She did not say a word about Cole.

Later in the afternoon, Erin drove around town for a while and bought a dress and new shoes for the services the next day. She checked into the Holiday Inn, ate a salad from Wendy's in her room, and cried herself to sleep. Cole went to a florist when he got back to town and ordered flowers for Ellie. He had a burrito from a taco truck and stopped to watch a group of college age kids playing soccer in the park. He later fell asleep in his motel room with the television on.

Cole and Erin found themselves with nothing much to do. Erin called an old friend from school and went to lunch with her. In the afternoon, she felt a strange urge to see the house where she grew up. As she pulled up across the street, she thought something wasn't quite right. The curtains looked different, and several large juniper bushes that had been under the front windows were gone. In their place was a beautiful bed of flowers. New white shutters were decorating all the front windows, and the front door had been painted a deep green. She was shocked when a tall, slender black woman came out of the house and loaded three kids into the minivan parked in the drive. The woman gave her a broad smile and a friendly wave as she pulled out. Allen had sold. *Just as well,* Erin thought.

Cole had gone to a used bookstore and tried in vain to get interested in looking at the mystery section. The store smelled old and musty, the woman behind the counter chatted on the phone. Her voice was grating, and he found the classical music irritating. He was in and out within five minutes. The new multiplex cinema on McAllister was his last hope. He paid the matinee price for a ticket to see a mindless blood-and-guts fest about a tattooed drifter who finds himself protecting a beautiful blonde, whose husband had been killed by renegade Indians, and her little boy. It was just what he needed; in fact, he stayed and watched it twice. Nobody noticed.

Around six, Cole returned to the Holiday Inn and was unlocking his door when someone called his name. Turning, he saw Erin unlocking the door next to his.

"Hello, neighbor," Erin said with a smile.

"Hello yourself."

They stood looking at each other for the longest time. Neither of them wanted to move. It felt good, comforting even.

Finally Cole said,"Have you had dinner?"

"No. You?"

"Nope."

"Would you like to?" Erin said shyly.

"Very much."

"Okay, let's."

"What are you in the mood for?"

"Mashed potatoes and gravy." Erin smiled. "Comfort food, you know?"

"I know just the place."

Fifteen minutes later, they walked into Gustav's Hof Brau. The windows were steamed over, and a TV in the corner silently played a baseball game. At the far end of the room was a cafeteria-style counter. Behind the counter stood an ageless Chinese man, who could have been 40 or 80, in a white shirt and apron. On his head was a white paper diner hat and in his hand was a carving knife.

"That's Lou, he's owned this place for a hundred years. Your mom and I used to call this place 'German Mao.' He's got just what you need." Cole turned his attention toward the man. "Hi, Lou, how about mashed potatoes and gravy for the lady. I'll have a barbecued pork sandwich on a roll and a side of dressing and gravy."

"Just like when you a kid. You never change order? This your daughter? She look just like mom. Make me feel old, you know," Lou beamed. He loved showing off his memory.

"It's good to see you again. It's been a long time."

"I read your stuff. Pretty good most of the time."

"Thanks," Cole said with a touch of irony in his voice.

"She very pretty girl. How's your mom? I haven't seen her in four or five years."

Erin looked at Cole and smiled warmly, "I think she's doing fine."

"You tell her hello for me. She a very pretty lady, nice, too."

"So, how's your wife?" Cole interjected.

"She died. Five years now."

"I'm so sorry," Cole said.

"It's okay, part of life, you know? I still got five kids and 13 grandkids. Without my Fay, I would have nothing. It's good, part of life. I miss her, though." Lou put two steaming plates on their trays. "Here you go."

Cole paid and they went to a booth. There was an elderly man sipping tea sitting at a corner table; otherwise, the restaurant was empty. Cole removed their plates, took the empty trays, and slid them across to the table in the next aisle.

"Looks good," Erin said not lifting her eyes from her plate.

"The Comfort Food Palace." Cole smiled.

"So, what happened to your face?"

"Ran into some bad guys," Cole said with embarrassment, having forgotten about his bruises.

The two sat eating in silence for several minutes. Cole's mind raced for something to say that wouldn't sound stupid. He was thankful that each time he looked up she was looking down. When he looked down at his plate, he could feel Erin's eyes on him. Being a newspaperman had put Cole across a lot of tables with a lot of people who either didn't want to talk or were afraid to. This was a case of neither. The table was silent but not strained. Cole felt he needed to say something because he wanted to talk to Erin, he just didn't know where to start.

"So, what do we do with each other now?" Erin said, not looking up.

"I don't know," Cole began. "What would you like us to do?"

"I don't know how to say what I am feeling exactly. I want to—" Erin stirred her mashed potatoes with the tip of her fork.

"Let's pretend I'm not here. You talk to yourself out loud and I'll listen. How 'bout that?"

Erin looked up at him for the first time and smiled. "I'll try that. You see, well, in the last 48 hours, I've replayed the tape of my life in my head. I'm not sure if it is the eyes of an adult that is making some things clearer or that I just want to see them a certain way. You know what I mean? You are a kind of mythological figure in my life story. This hero that my mother told stories of, someone who, to me, was untouchable, who was like a character from the books we read at bedtime. As I grew older, the Cole stories were like *Aesop's Fables*, the little Cole antidotes for the latest adolescent problems."

Cole knew his face was flushing, and it was made worse by his realizing it would soon turn beet red.

"My mother, I can see now, never stopped loving you. Allen was a way of making sure I had a home. The fact it turned out to be something like out of Dickens is another matter." Erin smiled. "What I am trying to say is, finding out you are my father is like one of my mother's fairytale Cole stories. I know it's true, but it is just, I don't know, too perfect, and not real somehow, and I am having a hard time believing it."

"She didn't make it up, Erin," Cole said rubbing his hand across his mouth.

"I'm not saying that," Erin replied quickly.

"We loved each other very much. I was stupid; I let pride and some kind of macho bullshit get in the way of the only thing that ever mattered to me. I'm to blame for any pain and any hurt that you have been through. Saying 'I'm sorry' sounds so trite. I've tried time and again in these last couple of days to think of what to say to you, try to explain, and it all comes out sounding like a lame excuse, which I guess in the end, it is. But this you have to believe: Whether we ever see each other again after tomorrow or not, if I could have died instead of your mother, I would have, in a heartbeat. If I could've given you two a chance to spend time together again, for Ellie to see her granddaughter, to meet your husband, I would have done anything, *anything* to have made that happen."

Erin looked down again at her plate. Cole looked at the top of her head, her beautiful curly brown hair, and tried to imagine her as a little girl. Something he could have seen, could have been part of, but unknowingly threw away.

"I guess I wasn't as hungry as I thought."

"Me either." Cole reached for a napkin and wrapped the remaining half of his sandwich. He shrugged and sheepishly said, "Starving kids and all that."

The drive back to the Holiday Inn was quiet. Cole played the radio and nervously hummed along. Erin looked out the window. They exchanged quick goodnights and went into their rooms. As his door clicked shut, Cole remembered he needed to ask Erin about the details and procedures for in the morning, returned to her room and knocked.

"Who is it?"

"Uh, me," Cole said at a loss for a comfortable answer, "Cole."

Her door opened a few inches. "What's up?"

"I guess we have a limo tomorrow, from the funeral chapel, I mean. Would you like to ride there together?"

"That would be nice."

"About 10:30?"

"Okay."

"See you in the morning."

The door closed softly, and Cole returned once again to his room. It had been made up and smelled slightly of cleaning products. He picked up the newspaper that lay at the foot of the bed. In the right corner below the fold was a picture of Ellie and a headline that read, *Local Humanitarian and Volunteer Passes.* This had Mick Brennan all over it. Cole smiled as he read of Ellie's impact on local charities and selfless volunteer work on behalf of numerous causes. The article ended with an appeal to give generously to one of her favorite charities. *Perfect,* Cole thought, *she would have loved it.*

At 10:35, Erin knocked on Cole's door. He was struggling to get his tie the right length. Cole had a habit of always making a bed when he got out of it so his room looked far tidier than Erin's. After another attempt, he got his tie to reach his belt line.

Erin was in a long-sleeved dark blue dress with large white buttons down the front and a simple white lace collar. She wore a pair of low-heeled navy blue-and-white spectator pumps. Her hair was pulled back in a tight bun, and a pair of large dark sunglasses adorned her face. Cole had a surge of pride suddenly; she was truly a lovely young woman.

As they turned into the cemetery, they could see cars parked everywhere and people walking toward a green canvas canopy not far from the east wall. Several hundred people were already gathered near the wall—people Ellie had touched with her life. Here to celebrate her, to honor her, to show their love. The sight of all these people reinforced what Cole had always believed, that the love that shone so brightly from Ellie, for life and those around her, didn't go unrewarded.

"Look at all the people!" Erin said in astonishment.

"We aren't the only ones who loved her," Cole said with a wistful smile.

The limo pulled up and stopped across from the canopy.

"Look at all the daisies!" Erin exclaimed.

"I wanted it to look like a field. I didn't know how many it would take so I ordered one hundred dozen," Cole tried to explain. "Is it too much?"

"It's so lovely. She would have loved it," Erin said softly.

The door opened and Cole slid out. After several seconds, Cole looked back into the limo. Erin sat with her hands tightly pressing against her mouth. She was weeping and gently rocking back and forth. Cole reached out his hand and she took it. He gently pulled her from the car and they walked side by side to the chairs facing the daisy-covered casket.

Atop the coffin was a picture of Ellie. It was at least two by three feet and in a simple walnut frame to match the coffin. From the picture, a beautiful 19-year-old Ellie seemed ready to step out of the frame. Cole took a deep breath as he saw the billowing yellow dress and brilliant summer smile. He remembered the day he took it.

"Where did that come from?" Cole said, as if to himself.

"That's the picture I always carry in my wallet. I had it done yesterday. Is it okay?"

"It's more than okay. It's perfect."

As Cole and Erin took their seats, people began to draw in closer. E.T. Bates was seated at the end of the front row. Next to him sat a small woman with a dark scarf tied tightly around her head. Bates reached over and patted her arm. The woman rose and went to the head of the casket.

She cleared her throat and spoke softly at first and then with more confidence. "I have cancer. I never met Miss Ellie, but we're going to meet very soon in heaven. I haven't got long on this earth, but I know my Jesus is waiting for me on the other side. My time with Him has been the sweetest of my life, and my wish as I face eternity is that I'll see you there, too." The woman closed her eyes and in the clear voice of an angel began to sing:

"When peace, like a river, attendeth my way,
When sorrows like sea billows roll;
Whatever my lot, Thou has taught me to say,
It is well, it is well, with my soul.
And Lord, haste the day when my faith shall be sight,
The clouds be rolled back as a scroll;
The trump shall resound, and the Lord shall descend,
Even so, it is well with my soul.
It is well, with my soul,
It is well, with my soul,
It is well, it is well, with my soul."

As she sang, Cole studied the picture of Ellie. She was standing in the doorway of a shop on the wooden walkway in Columbia State Park, holding onto a brass door handle and leaning out at a 45-degree angle. Her other arm was raised, and her skirt was flowing around her knees. Her face was tanned and her hair held back by a yellow silk scarf. Her eyes were bright and her smile radiated a joy that just made you feel good to your soul. This old photo captured the essence of the woman he had loved for so long and so deeply.

As the song ended, Reverend Bates stood and asked the crowd to bow their heads with him in prayer. His awesome voice called upon the Almighty to bless each one present and to open wide the gates of heaven for His beloved child to come home. Bates painted a picture of a heaven that Cole thought was just made for Ellie. As the prayer went on, the old Evangelist called upon each person to search their heart and make sure they were ready to meet the Good Shepard on the other side.

Cole had not bowed, nor had he shut his eyes, they were fixed on the picture of Ellie. In the instant that the "Amen" was said, Cole saw himself.

On the edge of the picture to the left of the door was his reflection in the glass. There, at 20 years old, stood the tall, handsome Cole so deeply in love with Ellie. In his hand was the old Hassleblad 500 camera he had lost so many years ago in a Cambodian river running from Communist guerrillas. The young man in the picture was somewhat distorted by the reflection in the old glass, but the smile on his face was not to be mistaken. Here, captured forever, was a picture of the love they shared. Somehow, this image made the loss deeper than ever. How had he ever let her get away?

"Do you see it?" Erin's voice broke into Cole's thoughts, "It's you."

Cole turned to see Erin was pointing at the photo. Her mouth was slightly opened and a look of amazement was on her face.

"I have had that picture in my wallet since I was in the

fifth grade. Mama put it in there," Erin whispered. "That's you, isn't it?"

Cole hadn't noticed but Bates had stopped speaking. The woman with the headscarf was singing again. Bates was now standing, his hands grasping his Bible, his head bowed. The service must be almost over. Cole had been totally lost in his thoughts and had hardly heard any of Bates' sermon.

"Yes, that's me," Cole leaned and whispered to Erin.

"I can't believe I never saw it before. It's so clear, so obvious."

As the woman in the scarf sang the last phrases of the Lord's Prayer, "For thine is the kingdom and the power and the glory forever, Amen," Cole stood. He didn't know why, but he had to stand. The glory of this small woman's voice surely reached the gates of heaven. Cole could feel tears streaming down his face. He closed his eyes and let the majesty of this frail woman's song embrace his heart.

Cole knew in that moment that there was a God and that Ellie was now with Him. He looked out across the crowd gathered to honor Ellie and knew her life had meant something. He swallowed hard to try to lose the lump in his throat. Ellie had touched him most of all. All the years she had been with him in his thoughts and dreams, she had pushed him on. His own selfishness and self-pity had held him back, but no more. His life would now honor her memory by doing what she was always so proud of. He would write and fight for what he believed in. He would once again search out the things that needed to be exposed and put the healing light of the press on them. This was Ellie's memory put to a use that she would have chosen. If they had been together, she would have inspired him, pushed him, and cheered him on. That's how it would now be; he knew it, and he believed it.

The Reverend Bates crossed the short distance to face Erin. Cole could not hear what he said, but Erin put her arms around the big man's chest and rested her head on his broad shoulder. She looked like a little girl in his arms.

"I hope my words—" Bates broke off and looked at the ground, "I hope she would have liked what I said."

"I think the two of you could've become great friends," Cole said with a small smile.

People began to file past and lay flowers, notes, and cards on the casket. Cole recognized very few of them as they went. Some spoke and called him by name. Many greeted Erin and they shared hugs and a word or two. But the majority was unknown to both Cole and Erin. They filed by, giving a nod of the head or a smile. It took nearly an hour for those who wanted to pay their respects to do so. *Ellie would have been so humbled at the outpouring of love for her*, Cole thought.

Shortly before she left, Cole had thanked the little woman in the scarf. Her name was Lillian. She told him she had come to The Revival Center just before she was diagnosed. Cole took a daisy from the casket and slipped it through her jacket lapel. They shook hands and she slipped away.

Near the end of the mourners, standing off to the side, stood Ann Christopher. She was dressed in a pair of black jeans and a dark burgundy sweater. She was leaning forward trying to see around a couple in front of her. She had her middle finger in her mouth and was chewing at the nail. Cole leaned in the same direction and acknowledged her presence with a nod. She turned and half-trotted back toward the cars. *Ellie had touched even Ann.* Cole smiled. Erin didn't see her.

Two men approached the canopy from the backside. They were dressed in sweat-stained green khaki work clothes, and one carried a shovel. E.T. Bates went to the men.

"I want all these flowers put on top when you're done and arranged to look real pretty."

"Yes, sir, pastor, we can do it right. You don't worry about it a bit," the taller of the two replied.

"God bless you, son. I knew I could count on you. See you in church?"

"Yes, sir. This Sunday."

"And the kids?"

"Oh yes, sir! My wife, too."

"I'll count on it."

One old man who identified himself as Peter Duncan, a neighbor of Ellie's until she was a teenager, was the last to approach the casket.

"I can tell who you are," the old man said to Erin. "You look just like Ellie when she was a girl."

"Thank you," Erin said smiling.

"You her husband?"

"No," said Cole.

"This is my dad," Erin said to the old man. Then, putting her arm in Cole's, she said, "I think it's time to go."

Cole bent and softly kissed the top of Erin's head.

Cole Sage Will Return in ...

Cellar Full of Cole

ABOUT THE AUTHOR

Micheal Maxwell was taught the beauty and majesty of the English language by Bob Dylan, Robertson Davies, Charles Dickens and Leonard Cohen.

Mr. Maxwell has traveled the globe, dined with politicians, rock stars and beggars. He has rubbed shoulders with priests and murderers, surgeons and drug dealers, each one giving him a part of themselves that will live again in the pages of his books.

The Cole Sage series brings to life a new kind of hero. Short on vices, long on compassion and dedication to a strong sense of making things right. As a journalist he writes with conviction and purpose. As a friend he is not afraid to bend the law a bit to help and protect those he loves.

Micheal Maxwell writes from a life of love, music, film, and literature. He lives in California with his lovely wife Janet.